Husbands and Other Sharp Objects

ALSO BY MARILYN SIMON ROTHSTEIN

Lift and Separate

Husbands and Other Sharp Objects

MARILYN SIMON ROTHSTEIN

LAKE UNION
PUBLISHING

Text copyright © 2018 by Marilyn Simon Rothstein
All rights reserved.

Published by Lake Union Publishing, Seattle

www.apub.com

Amazon, the Amazon logo, and Lake Union Publishing are trademarks of Amazon.com, Inc., or its affiliates.

ISBN-13: 9781477823828
ISBN-10: 1477823824

Cover design by PEPE *nymi*

Printed in the United States of America

For my daughters,
Sharyn Rothstein
and
Marisa Rothstein

Chapter 1

Whenever anything was in need of repair, I called a man. We had a lot of men. Plumber Man. Electric Man. Air-Conditioning Man. We also had guys. Gutter Guy. Plow Guy. Tree Guy. Chimney Guy. Guys tended to be younger than men. Harvey used to say that a checkbook was the only thing in his toolbox. That wasn't really true. Harvey didn't have a toolbox. One less thing for him to take when he left.

I was standing in the family room, finishing a blueberry muffin and watching CNN breaking news about a woman who shot herself in the foot. Suddenly, the large-screen television and all the recessed lighting blew. I went into the kitchen and turned on the paddle fan above the English pine table. Nothing happened. I recalled something about a fuse box, but I had no idea where it was. I went to my bag for my phone. I called Electric Man. I had to go to the airport to pick up my friend Candy, so I left the door unlocked and headed out as planned.

Of course, it was snowing. It was late March in Connecticut, but I could drive to the airport in August and it would be snowing. Worse, I had to do this trip again on Friday to meet my daughter Amanda, who was flying in from Seattle. Why couldn't everyone in the world just fly in on the same day?

The nearest airport was Bradley International. It was "international" because there was one flight a day to Toronto. When I arrived, parking was a mess. Worst of all, there were patches of black ice. Anxiously, I crept up and down the short-term lot, desperate for a space. My kids were grown, out of the house and on their own, but I still drove a Volvo station wagon with a roof rack. My friend Dana always said that a Volvo is the world's safest car—but that's only because the most risk-averse people drive it.

At last, I came upon a space. But as I turned in, another car swerved in front of me, into *my* spot. I quickly slammed the brakes. Lurching forward and then slumping back in my seat, I heard the heart-stopping sound of metal smashing metal. It was just what I didn't need, an accident. When I opened my eyes and caught my breath, I realized my airbag hadn't deployed. So things weren't as bad as they could have been. I was rattled, but I was okay.

I looked out my front window and saw a silver Lexus. Already the driver was walking toward me in the snow, so I guessed he was fine. As I stepped out of my car, I read the sexist word bubble floating high above his head. All I could think was *Yes, I'm a woman driver. And you are an asshole.*

"Are you okay?" I said as the cold hit my face.

He pointed to his Lexus. "What the hell happened?"

"I was trying to park," I said.

"I was already in the spot," he said.

And I was on the moon.

"Are you okay?" I asked again.

I had a tendency to communicate like a concerned mother. At the end of *Gone with the Wind*, I would have begged Rhett Butler to take a sweater.

"Fine," he said. "But now I'm going to be late." He took out his cell and began texting.

Just then, a woman wearing fake-fur earmuffs came along. She glanced at us, shook her head disapprovingly, unlocked a van near the Lexus, started it, and backed out.

He looked up from his phone. "There's a spot. And it's the best kind. It's empty."

My face reddened, but I laughed. He was a good-looking guy with dark-brown hair and brown eyes. Maybe midthirties? Under his coat, he wore a charcoal suit, a French-blue shirt, and a well-knotted tie. He seemed very broad shouldered, but that could have just been the coat.

I hurried to my Volvo and checked to see if there was any damage. Just a dent. I pulled into the spot left by the van. Then I grabbed my scarf from the car and wrapped it around my neck. I held my winter hat, because I look awful in hats. I have this crazy theory that if I carry my hat, my head will be warmer.

When I returned, the man said, "If you don't want to report this to your insurance company, I'll get a price for repairs, and you can pay it out of pocket."

I was surprised. Circumventing the insurance company? Harvey would love this guy.

I nodded to indicate that this would be fine.

"So let's exchange information, and I'll contact you when I have a price."

I typed my name into his iPhone. I'm slow at texting, using one finger at a time. This is generational. If I'd had an Apple from the time I had begged my parents to buy me a Barbie, maybe Mr. Impatient wouldn't have had to tap his foot.

When I returned his phone, he checked my information. He had an odd expression, like maybe he thought I had plugged in a phony name or something. He should have known better. Women who drive Volvos do not give aliases.

Suddenly, he smiled. Then he actually laughed. He had a honk of a laugh.

"Marcy Hammer? Are you married to Harvey?"

How did he know Harvey the Home-Wrecker?

When I said yes, he grinned as though he had just won the sweepstakes.

Did I know this guy?

"I'm Jake Berger. I represent your husband."

I looked at him blankly. My husband was the Bra King. He owned Bountiful Bosom, and his lawyer was Steve, my cousin Leona's husband.

"International business," he said, as though he could hear my thought process.

"Oh," I said. I wondered if he knew that Harvey and I were living apart. I was in the house. Harvey was at an inn. And his rate was long term.

I considered, as I always did when I met someone Harvey knew, whether the person had been in the wash with my dirty laundry. The laundry being that my husband had had a baby with another woman.

I don't know you. You don't know me. But tell me, can you see from the look in my hazel eyes that my husband has a new baby mama? Do you also know that she is in her twenties and is Argentine, and he sent her back to Buenos Aires with the funds to open a business?

"So you're Harvey's lawyer," I said, smiling. "Then why not just bill the repairs to Harvey?" *And it's okay with me if you double your hourly rate as well.*

"Don't worry about a thing," he said.

"Perfect."

We shook hands, and I turned to leave.

"Wait. Are you here for Amanda too?" Jake asked.

"Excuse me?" Now what did he want?

"I'm here to pick up your daughter."

I was taken aback. It was Monday. Amanda had told me she was flying in from Seattle on Friday. Admittedly, my mind was going fast—I could misplace reading glasses perched on my nose. The day before, I had looked for a tube of Colgate while I was holding it. However, I still knew a Monday from a Friday. Besides, when did Harvey start dispatching lawyers to pick up his children?

"Well, I'm sorry. Harvey sent you on the wrong day. She's flying in on Friday."

Jake shook his head.

Okay, I thought, *maybe she changed her plans.* In which case, I wished she had called to tell me. Whatever. I was excited that I was going to see her sooner than expected. With a few extra days, we would have time to go into Manhattan together, and I'd heard there was a limited-time-only Monet show at the Metropolitan Museum of Art.

"So let's go meet her," Jake said, stretching his arm out toward the terminal.

"I came to the airport to pick up a friend, but if you prefer, I can take Amanda home as well, and you can go back to work. Get those billable hours!" I said, punching the air with my fist.

"That's okay," he said, meaning "not in this lifetime."

I suddenly realized something was up. This guy wasn't just doing a favor for Harvey. He was way too cheerful for that. I looked at my watch. My friend Candy wasn't arriving for quite a while. It was a good thing I liked to get to the airport early, so I had time to have an accident and see my daughter.

Jake walked quickly, and I was panting to keep up. I would have just let him go ahead, but there was no way I was going to miss Amanda.

He stopped for a moment. "Am I going too fast?" he asked pleasantly.

Not for a racehorse. "Slower would be better."

He smiled. "I see the resemblance," he said as he studied my face.

"Actually, Amanda looks like Harvey's side of the family. Only thing is, she is not bald." Harvey didn't have a hair on his head, but he had recently topped himself with a toupee. Honestly, he looked better bald.

"I mean the resemblance between you and Elisabeth. You're about the same height and have the same color hair. She has hazel eyes too, right?"

"You've met Elisabeth?" I was taken aback. Exactly how did he know my Elisabeth? Elisabeth was a doctor. She had nothing to do with Harvey's business.

"Amanda introduced us."

What the . . .

He continued. "Elisabeth only stayed for one drink, because she had to rush back to the hospital."

So he had met my eldest daughter. Had he also met my son?

"Do you know Ben too?"

"No. I hear he lives in the city, in Chelsea. The first year of law school is tough. Big drop-out rate."

"Ben isn't dropping out."

"Of course not. I wasn't saying he was. I meant in general."

He picked up the pace.

"Do you think you could slow down?" I asked between huffs. In addition to keeping up with Secretariat, I was deep into figuring out what the deal was with this guy and Amanda. How involved were they if he had already met Elisabeth, and why had no one mentioned this to me? *It's so true,* I thought. *The mother is always the last to know.*

"Are you dating Amanda?" I asked, blunt as a two-by-four.

"There's Mans," Jake said as he waved across the arrival area to my daughter. Mans? Man's what? Man's hands? No one ever called Amanda anything but Amanda.

I looked at Jake's face. Times Square was not that bright on New Year's Eve.

6

"Mom, what a surprise," Amanda said when she saw me. I knew that wide-eyed look on her gorgeous face. I'd seen it when she was a freshman in high school. I had stopped at home to drop off groceries in the midst of a school day. She was on my living room couch with a popular boy nicknamed Mother's Hell. The two had matching outfits in that neither one was wearing a shirt.

Amanda hugged me. It felt wonderful to give her a squeeze. But I couldn't stop myself from saying the motherly thing. "I thought you told me you were coming in on Friday morning."

She smiled at Jake and turned to me. "I was. That was the plan. But at the very last moment, I decided to fly to Connecticut early to spend time with Jake."

I had no idea that Amanda had been seeing anyone since leaving her last boyfriend, Arnold the Famous Producer, pining for her in Los Angeles while she moved to Seattle. He had taken a stand. He said she should stay in Los Angeles, and they should get married. She moved anyway. That's the gumption I wished I had. Why wasn't gumption taught in every school? Gumption was more important than geography, because even if you can read the map, you're not going anywhere without gumption. That's what the world needs—Gumption 101.

"How long have you been seeing each other?" I asked, trying to sound nonchalant. As though I could fool her.

"Not long," Amanda said.

"Not long" meant an eternity, because if it were really not long, she would have given a precise amount of time. I had been left out of the loop, and as a mother, I didn't like any loop I was left out of.

"Wonderful," I said, patting her. Once your children are a certain age, it is best to be agreeable. They're going to do what they want anyway. Anything but agreeable comes off as combative.

For example, if a girlfriend remarked to Amanda that her skirt was too short, she'd check the first mirror she passed. If I mentioned it . . .

Me: Do you think maybe your skirt is a bit short?

Amanda: Mom, it's fine.

Me: Okay, it's not short, but your crotch needs a waxing.

Amanda: Mom, only old people say "crotch."

Me: I'm just saying what your friends will be thinking when they see you in that skirt.

Amanda: Fine. Then don't go to lunch with me. Don't go anywhere with me.

Amanda took Jake's hand. "Dad told Jake to look me up when he was in Seattle on business. His firm has a large office there. We got to know each other," she said, gazing into his eyes.

So Jake was her man of the moment. When Amanda gravitated to a person or a locale or an activity, it was immediate, pronto, and she was the world's biggest fan, head over heels. On the other hand, when someone rubbed her the wrong way, she disappeared like a rabbit in a magic act.

Amanda cuddled up to Jake. She was short and slender. He was tall. He kissed her on the forehead. I thought that was sweet. He kissed her nose, then each of her cheeks. He pulled her close, rubbed her back, and petted her long, loose auburn hair. If they were any closer, I'd be a grandmother in nine months. *Please, please don't make love in front of me in the midst of a jammed airport.*

I looked away, toward the escalator.

"So Mom, why are you here?"

"I thought you were coming four days from now, and I didn't want to be late."

She rolled her eyes. She was the Great Eye Roller.

"I'm here to pick up Candy. She flew from Milan to Philadelphia, then home to Connecticut."

"You must be glad she's back," Amanda said. "How long was she away?"

"Three weeks."

"Would you like us to wait with you?" Jake asked. *That's ten points for the boyfriend. Apparently, he is extremely polite when he isn't driving.*

Amanda shook her head. "I want to get going. By the way, Jake, how did you meet Mom?"

"We bumped into each other in the parking lot," I said.

"You had an accident *again*?" Amanda said.

"Oh, so I'm not your first victim, Mrs. Hammer?" he joked.

"I've had two accidents in two years, and the last one didn't even count. A tree hit me."

"Mom, you have to be more careful."

I *was* careful, but Romeo here had pulled into my spot.

"I'll see you on Friday," Amanda said unceremoniously. She gave me a kiss, then zipped her puffy black coat. She reached for the handle of her rolling suitcase, but Jake said, "Mans, I've got that."

"So Jake, would you like to join us for dinner on Friday?" I asked. *And can you stop calling her Mans?*

"Are Elisabeth and Ben coming?" Amanda asked, looking hopeful.

"No. They're both so busy."

"I'm sorry, I'm tied up too," Jake said. "I haven't had a chance to tell Amanda, but I just got word that I need to be in Wisconsin for business."

She looked at him as if to say "You're kidding—I get here and you're leaving?"

He gave Amanda an apologetic squeeze, then a soulful look.

"It's a drag to be out of town when Amanda is here, but as long as I'm in Wisconsin, I have to stop by to see my parents."

So he was handsome and successful, and he visited his parents. The guy was a winner and a far better choice than Arnold the Famous Producer, whom I had met just once, because Amanda always liked to keep her life under wraps. And that was easy enough when you lived three thousand miles from your mother.

We said our good-byes. Despite the accident and our rough beginning, I liked this Jake. Unfortunately, he worked for my soon-to-be ex-husband.

The walls were closing in.

∽

Preoccupied with the kids, I almost forgot that I had come to the airport to pick up Candy. Children, no matter their age, and it might even be worse when they're older, have a way of occupying your mind until you need a "No Vacancy" sign. A crowd descended the steep escalator from arrivals. I scanned for Candy, who, short and slight, could easily be blocked from view.

There she was, appearing not one iota like a woman who had been aloft for hours, but rather like a Hollywood star in a commercial for the pleasures of flying. She was dressed in a winter-white suit and long silk scarf. I was sure she wore an Hermès scarf even while in her house in her underwear. She was, after all, the kind of woman who sprayed perfume into the air and then walked through it.

For many reasons, I always thought Candy was a better person than me. She had garnered national awards for her children's books, including *Walter in the Water*, which was about a walrus but really about her father. If I had written a book about my father, it would have been called *Do What I Tell You or Die*. She was elegant, sophisticated, and soft-spoken.

Candy gave a surprised look and a salute from the top of the escalator. I gave one back from below, but mine was akin to someone waving at a Yankees game.

"You're here?" she said. "I told you I would take a cab."

"I couldn't wait to see you." Candy had become my rock. I hugged her gingerly. She was not a hugger.

"I'm thrilled to be home. I can't wait to sleep in my own bed. And I missed my mail."

"Your mail or your male? You know, m-a-l-e?" I said.

"There were so many times I wished you were with me. We would have had an unbelievable adventure in Florence. Talk about art. The *food* was art."

That, I didn't doubt. But I was sure she ate very little of it.

"Harvey went to Italy a lot on business, but I never went with him."

"Please, Marcy, Italy is no place to go with a husband. The men are incredible."

"I bet you can't wait to see Leonardo."

Leonardo was Candy's personal trainer and lover. Her casual relationship with Leonardo had helped her through the breakup of her marriage to a physician known around the hospital as Dr. Bang.

"I did miss Leonardo," she said. "But it's not that difficult to make do in Italy."

"Tell me, tell me."

"Let's just say the pasta was delicious."

"Describe the pasta."

"Long," she said, raising an eyebrow.

We walked to baggage claim, smiling at each other, and waited. One suitcase at a time dropped onto the carousel. We craned our necks for Candy's luggage.

"How have you been?" Candy said.

"Good, but eating too much if I want to stay in shape."

"It's important to watch that," she said, and I wondered if that meant she thought I had gained some weight. It's not like she would ever say it.

"You're right," I said, nodding seriously. "No more strawberry shortcake in bed. You're home, and the good times are over."

"How are your kids?"

"Elisabeth and Ben are great. Ben has a new boyfriend named Jordan. You just missed Amanda. I'm fine, but I had a minor mishap in the parking lot with the guy who was here to pick her up."

"Marcy, you have to be more careful."

I was beginning to think "you have to be more careful" was my middle name. Who was more careful than me? I'd been careful for over thirty years. Married to the same man, living in the same town, in the same house. I had bought the same brands of detergent, deodorant, and toilet paper since I had first left my parents' home.

In fact, prior to the last few months, my biggest risk was driving to Walgreens without a seat belt.

"Wait a minute. What makes you think I caused the accident?" I said.

"Um, I've seen you drive? Tell me about Amanda's guy."

"Turns out he's Harvey's lawyer."

"She's seeing her father's lawyer?"

"Yes, and there are countries where that is considered incestuous."

Candy pointed to her rolling suitcase. We hustled to the carousel to pull it off the track.

I grabbed her second bag. "All done?" I said.

"No. There's a third."

We waited for what seemed like a few months until Candy's largest suitcase appeared. Of course it matched the first two. I wouldn't need multiple suitcases unless I was leaving America for good, which I wouldn't do, because I'd miss my family too much.

I hoisted the final piece of luggage. "Geez, what's in this? A safe made of steel?"

Outside, it had stopped snowing. We trudged to the lot and found my car.

"I'll drive," she said.

"You don't want me to drive?"

"Marcy, a blind man wouldn't want you to drive."

I was happy to hand her the keys.

"Leonardo is coming over tomorrow," she offered as she started the car and looked over her shoulder to back up.

"What's the story with him?"

"It's all good for now," she said.

"For now?"

"He may decide to move on. I may decide to move on."

"Very cavalier," I said.

"Well"—she shifted into drive and headed toward the exit—"I guess there are other alternatives. I'm fifty-six. We could start a family. First, a boy; then in a few years, if we're very lucky and I consult a world-class specialist, I could have three girls at once."

"And you could name them after me!" I patted my heart.

"Yes, Marcy, Marcy, and Marcy. By the way, in Milan, I met a *real* Leonardo."

I was happy she had had such a good time.

Candy turned out of the lot and onto the slippery road. "Did you decide whether you are going to move?"

The car slid forward on a patch of ice. Candy took her foot off the gas.

"I'm still thinking," I said. "The market is slow now, so I have time to decide. I ran into my Realtor at the library. She was checking out the maximum number of books."

"Before I left for Italy, I told you to stop thinking and start doing. You don't even like your house. Didn't Harvey have to talk you into it all those years ago?"

"I can't shake the memories. When we moved to Connecticut, Elisabeth was a baby. I brought the other two kids home from the hospital to that house. When Harvey and I arrived with Amanda, my mom was in the driveway, waiting."

"I miss your mom," Candy said.

Not long before, Candy and I had become fast friends at Saint Mordecai Hospital. I had been visiting my mom. She had been there for her father. We had held each other up. When they both passed on, we held each other up some more.

"I wish I had known your mom longer," Candy said. "Most of all, I wish I had met you sooner. Can you imagine if we had been friends all through high school? Or if we had been roommates in college?"

"You will know me for a very long time," I said.

Hopefully, I thought, *for a lifetime.*

Chapter 2

When I came home after dropping off Candy, I was thrilled to see my house lights ablaze, not just because the electrician had come, but because Jon London's Subaru was in the driveway.

In the kitchen, Jon, tall and sturdy, with longish blond hair, blue eyes, a strong nose, and an eternally scruffy face, was cooking at the grandiose stove that Harvey had imported from some European country where people really care about stoves. He was wearing a red-and-black checked flannel shirt, jeans, and his signature thick red wool socks. He was holding a carton of eggs.

My habit was to buy whatever eggs I found on sale, but Jon had introduced me to organic cage-free eggs. His favorite brand was Cluck in the Muck, so that's what I bought. I felt virtuous when I thought that the hens that laid my dinner eggs were not poisoned with the pollutants and ingredients that I myself consumed in highly processed foods on a regular basis. Also, I liked that the chickens roamed free.

Jon kissed me hello.

"Eggs?" he asked.

"Yes," I answered, joyously. As far as I was concerned, a great-looking guy kissing me hello and saying "Eggs?" was the fulfillment of a lifelong dream. What's more, I adored the way Jon made eggs, the manner in which his sculpted wrist appeared to crack with the shells, how he stirred his lovely yolks in a chef's bowl with a whisk, how he heated the copper pan and melted a bit of his organic butter from Maine so I could sniff the scent while listening to the sizzle as he poured the lustrous eggs. And, finally, how Jon reached for a little bit of salt and freshly ground pepper. Watching Jon make eggs was a sex act.

But there was a lot more to Jon. I had met him eons ago when we had both started volunteering at the Guild for Good. In college, I had majored in art history and enjoyed being with creative people. He was involved with the Guild, because in addition to being an English professor, he was an accomplished painter who was well recognized for his work. He had two paintings, coastal scenes of Maine, in the Portland Museum of Art. Now Jon was on the board of the Guild, and I had recently been hired as executive director.

My new position, paid with benefits, was the only decent thing that had happened to me in the previous year. In addition to my husband's announcement that he wasn't certain he wanted to be married anymore and, even more impolite, that he was having a child with a girl young enough to have another baby in about twenty years, my mother had passed away. In a matter of weeks, Mom had fallen off a stool and broken both legs, found out she had cancer, and died in a rehabilitation facility. My mother was such an overachiever.

During this time, Jon had commiserated with me in the office. Commiseration had led to coffee, which had led to organic eggs. I never again planned to eat an egg that cost less than seven dollars a dozen.

"The electrician was here a while ago, but I told him you didn't need him, that I had already changed the fuse."

"How did you know where to find the fuse box?"

"I looked in the basement."

16

"Oh," I said in wonder. Jon was just so talented. "Guess who else was at the airport?" I was anxious to tell him about Amanda.

"Harvey?"

"Wrong Hammer."

Jon liked his eggs soft, so he emptied half the eggs onto a plate. He left the other half frying on a very low fire for me.

"Amanda. With Harvey's lawyer."

"Harvey's lawyer? Did you tell him to triple his rates?"

I laughed. "Darn it. I only said to double them."

"Thinking small, Marcy."

"What about this, then? I banged into his silver Lexus and recommended that he bill Harvey for all the repairs."

He put down his plate. "You had an accident?"

"A scrape." I really didn't want him to make a big deal about it.

"You have to be more careful."

Okay, so that was the third time in a day someone had told me to be more careful.

"I *was* careful."

A moment passed; then Jon switched the subject.

"Will I meet Amanda this week? I would really like to meet her— and Elisabeth and Ben."

I wasn't ready for such an occasion.

"I don't know," I said. "Amanda might be too busy."

"Too busy to meet me? No one is that busy," he said with full-throttle sarcasm.

"Jon, maybe it's too soon for you to meet my kids."

"Well, I've been listening to all of these stories, and I would like to meet them. No pressure. I understand they've been through a lot, and you've been through a lot, but without knowing them, I feel like I'm missing out on a part of you."

Lightly, he shook Tabasco on his eggs. I don't know why, but there is something alluring about a man who likes to spice things up. Harvey used ketchup on his sunny-side-up eggs. Often, he ordered them one up and one down, driving the waitress in our breakfast place, Kerry's, crazy.

I kissed him.

"Is that 'Yes, Jon, you will meet my tribe'?" he said.

I had just separated from Harvey. Jon was the only man I had dated since—except for a blind date in a Chinese restaurant. It was so awful that I swore I would never eat a spring roll again. I was such a newbie that I had never been on a dating site. If I had, I would have chosen a Jewish one. Maybe Lox on Bagel or Matzoh Finds Ball. I would have posted an Instamatic photo taken back in the 1990s, when my skin had tone.

"Don't you think they want to meet me?" Jon asked, interrupting my thoughts.

No. I don't think they want to meet you. I think they would be elated if I had a group of women friends, divorcées and widows who enjoyed Wednesday matinees in the city, women who split the prix fixe pretheater lunch bill ten ways with a pocket calculator. We just weren't to the point where my children thought their mother needed a man—unless of course I wanted to go back to Harvey. I hoped the meet-the-kids conversation would wrap up soon.

"Eggs?" Jon said again, this time handing me mine on my Mickey Mouse plate. I loved that plate. I'd bought it for Ben at Disney World when he was five and kept it all these years. I had lots of stuff like that. I also prized the talking-moose cookie jar we had procured when my Amanda was four and screamed in the general store until Harvey bought it. Those were the things that mattered to me. Everything else, who cared?

"I thought you told me Amanda was flying in on Friday," Jon said. "And why would Harvey send his lawyer?"

"Amanda is seeing the lawyer. She came in early to spend time with him."

"What did you think?"

"Once we got past the scrape—again, a very, very minor one—in the parking lot, I liked him. I don't understand what the big secret is, except that Amanda likes to keep her personal life to herself. She's always concerned that people will criticize her or interfere with her plans."

"What people?"

"I guess mostly me."

"You? You couldn't care less about what your children do," he said, sarcastically.

I wanted to get off the subject. "Do your trick," I said.

"My trick? I have lots of tricks," he said, flirting.

"The one where I say the name of a novel and you recite the first line from memory."

"Shoot."

I started easy. *"David Copperfield."*

He was amused. "I see you are pitching softballs."

"So let's hear it."

"'Whether I shall turn out to be the hero of my own life . . .'"

"The Great Gatsby."

"'In my younger and more vulnerable years, my father gave me some advice that I've been turning over in my mind ever since.'"

"Harvey quoted a book once. His checkbook. He recited the amount I had paid for a day at a spa."

"Oh, I forgot," Jon said. "Do you want toast? I didn't make any, but I could."

I really wanted toast, specifically sourdough, but I said no, recalling my conversation with Candy at the airport. What's more, I had read online that if I eliminated all white foods, I could drop a pound or two quite easily. *Is bread still considered white once toasted?*

"You always have toast," Jon said.

"I think Candy thought I could lose a few. You know how she is—her name is Candy, but she'd rather expire than touch a piece of it."

"That's ridiculous. You're perfect."

I cracked a smile. I seized two thick slices of pumpernickel from the breadbox, because pumpernickel is definitely not a white food.

"Have a third piece and pile on the butter," Jon said. "You could gain a few pounds and still look great."

Hmm. Maybe I should introduce him to my children after all.

Chapter 3

I am Jewish. My friend Dana is Narcissist. Every Wednesday at noon I have lunch with Dana at Francesca's Café. The restaurant is painted magenta and white. The floors are weathered gray. We had our regular table—a booth with a picture window overlooking snowbound woods. Above the booth, an enormous white lampshade hung from the ceiling on a slender white cord.

That morning, I had dressed for work in a hunter-green V-neck sweater that set off my strawberry-blond hair. I was like Christmas—I looked good in green and red. I added corduroy pants, knee-high leather boots, and a wide silver belt. Dana liked thick belts, and she had bought the one I was wearing for me. It was my birthday present. I don't really know how I became this unmentionable age—because the last time I checked, I was thirty-four.

Once lunch was served, my phone rang. It was my Realtor, Judy Redstone. Back when our kids were in high school, I had been president of the PTO, and Judy had served as treasurer. I was president for six years. It was so long that other parents had called me "president for life." Judy had since gone into real estate. Her picture and her company name were flashed before the movie in the local theater. That thing with having your photograph all over town, that's why I could never be a Realtor.

When I picked up the phone, Dana winced, but I said it was important when I saw it was my Realtor calling.

"Have you decided about the house?" Judy asked.

The house I had been admiring was a serene color, a buttercup yellow. It had three good-size bedrooms, two and a half baths, a great kitchen large enough for a table and chairs, a living room with an archway connecting to the dining room, and best of all, a front porch. I loved that porch. I imagined myself in a rocking chair with a glass of lemonade, lots of ice, and a book. Sometimes, I imagined three chairs lined up and all my children sitting there, waiting for me. What could be better than that? Talk about living the dream. To top it all off, the house was on a winding country road just two miles from Candy's place.

"Did someone else make an offer?" I asked Judy, afraid to hear the answer.

"No, no. Just checking in."

Whew, I thought. I wasn't sure if I should buy it, but I certainly didn't want anyone else to come along.

"Still thinking," I said to Judy.

"Well, I know you're in a situation. But a lot of women don't stay in their homes after a divorce."

I hadn't told her I wasn't divorced yet. I wondered what percent of women moved *before* the divorce. I would have to look it up online. I didn't think it was common.

"I'll call if I hear of another offer."

When I hung up, I decided to ask Dana for her opinion. Dana was the perfect person to ask, because she was always direct, a pot of strong black coffee, always with grind, devoid of filter. Dana smoothed her long blond hair, flipping it over her silk blouse, which was the hue of vanilla custard. Anyone could see her cleavage, but I guess that was the point.

"I guess you heard most of it," I said to Dana. "What do you think? Yellow house or no yellow house?"

Dana held up one hand like a stop sign. I assumed she was about to advise, "Halt. It's too soon to move. Don't buy. Don't rent. Don't do anything."

Instead, she fixated on her pinkie and said, "I need a manicure."

"Dana, I'm asking you a question. Focus."

She took a nibble of her kale.

"Marcy, I think you should stay where you are. The grass is not always greener. In fact, sometimes it's brown."

This advice was from a woman who was on her third marriage. Though, the third time really did seem to be the charm. She adored Calvin.

"My mother told me to move," I said.

"When she was alive?"

"No, I imagined her saying it the first time I stood outside the yellow house."

I could feel myself choking up at thoughts of my mom. But it wasn't just about my mom. I had lingered on the porch, looking at the sky, telling my late mother that I was okay, convincing myself that I was solid enough to move on, to transfer from my colonial on steroids to the kind of place I thought was really me. I had felt that doing so would signify moving on. Dana's advice was breathtaking.

"Candy said I should move," I pointed out like a petulant child.

"What is this? A poll?" Dana said.

Candy was my newest friend, my personal crisis center. She was 911. As for Dana, we had been best friends since before infants were in car seats, before real men changed diapers, before people worshipped their own kids. When I first encountered Dana, the only way to call home was to take a coin from your penny loafer.

We had met in a bodega on Ninth Street in Greenwich Village, both wearing bell-bottoms, tight T-shirts, and brown sandals. She looked like the blond Cher. I looked like an NYU girl in jeans. That day, Dana had been choosing a flavor of yogurt. It wasn't difficult. In the late 1970s, the only edible yogurt was Dannon with fruit on the bottom—Greek yogurt was mostly found in Greece. I had a cache of Dannon in my wire basket, mostly strawberry, some coffee. Dana had pointed to the mountain of yogurt in my basket and asked if I had a boyfriend. I said that if I had a boyfriend, I wouldn't be into yogurt at all. I'd be eating cookies. She had laughed. Then she bumped my shoulder. I bumped her back, and we have been bumping shoulders ever since. Such a simple sign of kinship. It was a cinch to start a friendship back then. You could make a friend waiting for a red light to turn green. At my current age, initiating a friendship practically took FBI clearance.

I explained my problem. "You know I have trouble making decisions. And, now that Harvey and I are kaput, I have to make all the decisions on my own. For example, the other day I decided I am only using the largest garbage bags. You know, the green ones. Harvey used white kitchen-size bags, but I like lawn bags."

"You're one person. You're filling a lawn-size garbage bag?"

"I have a very large carbon footprint," I said.

"What else are you doing? Let's hear about your changes."

"Harvey always took the Volvo in for repair, but after the airport incident, I went to Atherton Auto Works on my own."

"Big deal," she said, unimpressed.

I would not allow her to belittle my accomplishment. "What do you mean, 'big deal'? It is a big deal. Those mechanics poke each other and size up your legs before you open your mouth."

She joked, "So what? You have good legs."

"That's not the point."

"Wear pants," she said.

"Thanks, Dana. I'm going to present your advice at a conference."

"I've been to that garage. The owner wears a white oxford shirt. He smiles, offers you a coffee, a fat muffin, and a ride home so you don't have to wait for the car. The waiting room has a TV, a playpen, and more magazines than Condé Nast."

"I can't believe you're knocking my achievements."

She chuckled. "I'll tell you about an achievement. Monica got a scholarship to go to Paris to study fashion this summer."

I was happy for Dana's daughter. But I knew one thing—if I asked Dana about Monica's trip to Paris, I'd be in a nursing home before I heard what to do about the house.

"The house, Dana. What about the house?"

"Okay. So here's what I think. If you're planning to move out of your current place, you better tell Harvey. And I mean, up front. Before you do anything. Because whether it's out of big-time guilt or because he loves you, he still hasn't filed for divorce, and he has been a regular Boy Scout about paying the bills. You don't want to piss him off right now. You lost your mother and your husband. You don't want to lose your best friend."

"Dana, you are my best friend."

"I was thinking about your other best friend—American Express."

I sighed. "I don't know what Harvey is up to—about money or anything else. Everything he has done made me think he would file for divorce. But I'll tell you now, I am *not* filing. He owns this mess. He started it. He has to finish it. My kids will never be able to blame me for the demise of the marriage. Not happening. I spent my entire life trying to set a good example. It's not going to be ruined by him. And no matter what, I am taking the high road."

My throat felt dry, as though I had made a major speech in the driest heat. I poured some water.

"Want me to come over, sit next to you, and knock your shoulder?" Dana said.

"No. I am fine."

"Then taste this salad," she said, lifting a fork laden with kale and baby lettuce. I hate the term "baby lettuce." Worse is "Boston baby lettuce." It's not bad enough you're eating the baby. You have to know where it comes from.

Obligingly, I tasted the salad. I didn't like the dressing.

Dana hailed the waitress. Here's a sentence I never heard before 2005: "More balsamic vinaigrette, please."

"You should try my soup," I said. "It's great."

"I only like the cheese," she said.

"Dana, it's onion soup. The cheese is the whole point."

She took the spoon from my hand and scraped it around the rim of my bowl, taking the cheese. Worst of all, she took the burned cheese, which was my favorite part.

Now I looked for the waitress. She was helping another table. When she turned, I waved her over. "We would like one more soup, please. Heavy on the Swiss."

"It's Gruyère," the waitress said.

"Heavy on that too," I said, but I could see she didn't know I was joking. After she left, I said to Dana, "Ask me how Jon is."

"I don't have to ask. I could see from your smile when you just said his name. Jon!" She swooned as I tried not to grin.

"Thank you for asking. He's fine."

"Okay, what's up?"

"He wants to meet my kids."

"Too soon. I would wait. Spare myself the aggravation."

"Well, when do you think I should introduce them?"

"About four years after you marry him," she said, picking at her salad. "I have news, big news." Her eyes lit up. "I'm opening a satellite office. In Boston," she said, proudly.

"That's fantastic!"

Dana had been looking for a way to expand her advertising agency. I was almost excited enough to jump out of my seat.

"Do you have clients there already?"

"My lips are sealed," she said as she placed a finger over her mouth.

"Wow. What an accomplishment!" I raised my water glass. We clinked. "How often do you plan to commute?"

"Right now, twice a week. But if everything works out, Calvin and I will relocate," she said.

I put down my water and threw up my hands. "I can't decide whether to move down the road, and you're *relocating?*"

"I said Boston. I didn't say Anchorage."

I wondered what the rules of best friendship were, exactly. I was pleased about her success. But I didn't want her resettling hours away. I decided I wouldn't speak of myself first. I wouldn't mention that if she moved, we wouldn't be able to lunch at Francesca's every Wednesday or stop by and hang out together at a moment's notice. Also, I wouldn't see her family as often. Her son lived in Boston and when the girls came home from college, they would go to Boston. But Dana could see what I was thinking. It was on my face.

"I will miss you, Marcy, more than anyone or anything else, but it's an ideal time for us to relocate. Calvin is retired. So he's up for it. And Boston is a larger market. There's just no comparing. Anyway, it's not happening for a while. I have to get things going."

Dana is moving. That was all I could think about as I walked to retrieve my car. Her Boston venture would be a huge success in no time at all. Then, poof, she'd be gone—gone from my lovely dot of a town, Atherton, Connecticut.

◌

After lunch, I returned to work. My job at the Guild for Good, where I worked with artists who were interested in doing good, was perfect. But there was a problem—I didn't know enough about social media. I definitely needed an assistant. Maybe a college kid who thought making a telephone call was a lifetime commitment. I had called Price College, looking for someone.

Since I had been promoted, the Guild offices had relocated down the hall. There was an outer area, completely decked out with the work of our members—paintings on walls, ceramic on shelves, sculptures sitting on posts—just like at a museum. There were two royal-purple armchairs, an oak reception desk, a copier, an inset coffee area, and a brand-new red sofa. The end tables had art magazines. There were three offices, one for me and two with conference tables for the volunteers who came by to help out.

I sat at my glass-and-chrome sawhorse desk, which I thought was young and cool, looking at the best picture ever of my three kids. It was taken at Harvey's last birthday bash. I loved the way my kids all looked so related.

I heard the front door open and close. I looked out to the reception area, and there was a girl.

She was slim—and like me, about average height. She had thick black hair. I noticed an earring in her nose, a chain of minute beads extending from the bottom of one nostril to the other. She had two studs in her lip. Her face had more jewelry than Tiffany's.

She was in a short romper the color of bubblegum. Her ankle-high hiking boots were untied. As she approached my office, she dragged a tweed winter coat behind her, mopping the floor. I hadn't seen a bigger mess since my basement was flooded.

The girl was college age, and I knew immediately she had shown up for the job interview without an appointment. I thought back to the Age of Aquarius, when I went on interviews at New York advertising agencies—in a boxy Bobbie Brooks navy suit and a white blouse with a bow in front. Navy tights. Navy shoes. Navy bag.

Stay open-minded, Marcy. This is no longer the Pepsi generation.

"Come in," I offered as I approached the wreck of the *Hesperus*, extending my hand. "I'm Marcy Hammer."

"Cheyenne. I go to Price. My counselor told me you had a job?"

She followed me to my desk, pulling up a chair and putting her coat and her camouflage knapsack in her lap, covering her romper.

"Let me hang that up for you," I offered.

She said she was fine.

Because of her name, I asked whether her parents were from someplace out west.

"No. Brooklyn."

Makes perfect sense, I thought.

"They were on a road trip, stopped in Cheyenne, and had me."

I figured she was fortunate they hadn't stopped in Podunk or Iowa City.

"You know your website sucks," she said out of nowhere.

Yikes. Don't hold back, Cheyenne. Come right out with it.

"Really bad, but don't worry, I can make it better," she said.

"That's good to know," I said, thinking she was the only person I knew who was as direct as Dana.

"And you need a social media platform."

I said, "Hmm," and nodded. Of course, she was right about that.

"I mean, to find out anything about you, I had to read up on your daughter."

"Elisabeth?" I said.

"The doctor. Did you know she was seeing a married man?"

What is this girl, a CIA agent? "You found that out online?"

Why, I wondered, would anyone put anything so personal on the Internet? It was nobody's business at all. I decided I should mention this to Elisabeth. Then I remembered she was not in junior high school but was thirty-one years old, and I needed to put that whole married man incident behind us. Still.

"She broke up with him December something," Cheyenne said. "It's her important date."

I asked Cheyenne if she wanted a bottle of water. She nodded, and I went to fetch her one.

"Can I see your laptop?" she said when I returned. She twisted the cap off the Poland Spring.

I turned my computer toward her. "Can you teach me how to use Facebook?" I asked.

"How do you reach people now?"

"E-mail. Sometimes I even phone."

"That must annoy them," she said, concentrating on the screen.

"I use a pay phone," I said, joking.

"I've never used a pay phone," she said, typing away.

Her casual attitude made me feel chatty. "When I was your age, I kept a quarter in my pocket."

"Just in case you were in trouble?"

"Yes," I said, sipping coffee.

"But you would have to be in trouble near a phone," she concluded.

"Back in the day, life was extremely inconvenient. If you wanted to meet a friend, you had to agree on a time and place in advance."

"But what if you were running late?" she asked as she looked at the screen.

I thought back. What *did* we do? I shook my head and shrugged.

"What else?" she asked.

I couldn't believe Cheyenne was interested. This was exactly the type of "in my day" conversation that would result in my two daughters fleeing the earth for a planet devoid of oxygen.

I tried to think of something that would boggle her mind. "No microwaves."

"But what if you wanted to eat immediately?" she joked.

"You're hired," I spouted.

She looked up from the computer. Her eyes widened. "I'm hired? Just like that?"

"Just like that."

"When do I start?"

"Today, if you can. Right now."

Cheyenne pulled my picture off the Guild website she had just criticized. She rattled off a few questions. I gave her the answers. In no time, I was on Facebook.

"Who do you want to friend first?" she asked.

"Dana Davenport," I said.

The screen flashed with a message from Dana. "Dinosaurs are no longer extinct. My best friend, Marcy, is now on Facebook."

"How many friends do you have?" I asked her.

She went to her page. She had 540.

"You know that many people?"

"I don't know them. I'm 'friends' with them."

"Of course," I said, as though I thought this made sense.

"So, in addition to promoting Guild for Good, you may want to post some personal stuff. In that case, post only good news—unless, of course, you have to put your pet to sleep, or you are diagnosed with a really atrocious disease."

"I would put that on Facebook?" I shook my head, baffled. "Tell you what. You're in charge of posting."

❧

The next day, the Guild was closed due to a storm. Jon came over to my house, because he loved to go out in the snow. Everything about him was cold when he walked in the door—his parka, his jeans, his face, and his hands. Yet I rushed right up to him, and somehow warmth enveloped me. I made him a cup of hot cocoa. We squirted whipped cream into one another's mouths. He started a fire in the fireplace.

For a while, we simply sat on the sofa in the family room, each one of us with a novel. The whole thing reminded me of Ali MacGraw and Ryan O'Neal reading together in *Love Story*. That movie was a conundrum. I always thought that if I grew long straight hair and wore tights, a pleated skirt, and a beret, I might attract a handsome Ivy Leaguer. On the other hand, I worried that, like Ali, I might die too soon to enjoy it for long.

"Do you think I should move?" I said.

"Never. Stay right here on this couch in front of this fire with me forever."

I grinned. "I meant should I move to another house." I had asked him once before what he thought, and he had been noncommittal.

"I don't think I should weigh in."

"Why not? Everyone else has. Dana practically said I should start a polling company before the next presidential campaign. But most important, your opinion really matters to me."

"Am I more important than 85 percent of people polled?" Jon asked. Then he said, "I'm good with being wherever you are. Let's leave it at that."

I might have had my own little *Love Story* going.

∽

Later, Jon and I looked out the front window to find the roads had been cleared. We sat down in the kitchen, discussing what to have for a snack. Amanda rang on the house phone. That was surprising. People I knew hardly ever called on the landline anymore, which was good because I liked to keep that phone open for insurance types who mispronounced my name and financial advisors hawking upside-down mortgages.

"Sorry for any confusion at the airport," Amanda said.

It was Thursday. I hadn't expected to hear from her until Friday.

"So tell me," I said, fiddling with the phone cord, "are you having a good time?"

"Yes," she said, full of cheer.

"Good for you."

"I know. Isn't Jake great? He was called into work for a few hours, so maybe I will stop by today."

"Terrific!" I was second fiddle, but at least I was in the orchestra.

"Is your boyfriend around, Mom?"

I hadn't ever thought of Jon as a boyfriend. I hadn't thought about what to call him. I was sure he had a word to describe us.

"He's here," I said.

I smiled at Jon. He smirked, up-to-the-minute on the gist of the conversation.

"You know what?" Amanda said. "I just peeked out, and there's so much snow. Snow the first week of April, so New England. I think I'll stay in," she said, and added her good-bye.

When I hung up, I realized that I was relieved she didn't want to meet Jon. I wasn't ready for it.

"So she doesn't want to come over, because I'm here," Jon said, resigned.

"I'm sorry. But I have to say I don't think it would be enjoyable."

"Why? Isn't Amanda delightful? Doesn't she take after her mother?"

"Actually, she's more like her father. By the way, she referred to you as my boyfriend."

"I am your boyfriend."

"You *are*?" I said, touching his face on my way to the fridge. "In high school, I wanted a boyfriend so badly."

"You didn't have a boyfriend in high school?" he said. His voice had a tone of disbelief, which made me feel good about myself.

"I went on one date," I said, taking ice cream from the freezer. The half gallon had three flavors. Jon liked strawberry. I preferred vanilla. We shared the chocolate. If that wasn't the makings of a great relationship, what was?

"His name was Arturo, but I had to tell my parents his name was Arthur so they wouldn't know he wasn't Jewish."

"What was he?" he said, enjoying the story.

"He was Italian and Catholic. I grew up in a diverse area of Queens. Everyone in my neighborhood was either an Orthodox Jew, a Conservative Jew, or an Italian."

"So, what happened?"

I spooned out the ice cream and walked over with his bowl and the can of whipped cream. I squirted some on his nose.

"We went to a diner and to the movies, but all I could think about was how I had lied and put one over on my parents. I was guilt-ridden and had a rotten time. When we returned to my house, he tried to kiss me on the stoop. My mother blinked the porch light on and off, on and off."

He went over to the switch and turned the six-bulb light over the kitchen table on and off.

"Just like that."

"Wow. That's chutzpah."

"When it came to me, she had no barriers. I don't even think there was an embryonic sac. I hear her all the time. Right now, she's saying, 'That's how you talk about your own mother?' Anyway, when the light started blinking, I went into the house. My father was reading the newspaper in the living room in his Archie Bunker chair. He called me in. He rolled the *New York Daily News* into something you would hit someone with. He held it in his right hand and said, 'Don't ever date a non-Jew again.'"

"That's amazing," Jon said.

"Downright chilling," I said. "Except once I had a kid of my own, I got it. My parents wanted what they thought was best for me. Besides, back then, people were so xenophobic. My friend Caterina was Italian American, and her parents wouldn't let her see a boy whose parents were from a different region of Italy."

"Well, I'm Jewish, and I would have asked you out in high school."

"You lived in Portland, Maine," I said, enjoying the vanilla ice cream.

"I would have come to Queens. You could have taken me to see the Mets."

I thought about how wonderful that would have been to go with Jon to see the Mets, to run into everyone from high school, to introduce him as though I had boyfriends all the time.

He stood. "I have to get going. I have a ton of student essays to read by tomorrow."

"So which great novel are these essays about?"

"Philip Roth, *American Pastoral.*"

"I love that book. It proves my most time-tested theory."

"What's that?" he asked.

"Your children will do you in."

"Not fair. There are lots of novels in which the parents do the children in."

"Yes, but in literature, the children usually rise above that. Speaking of books," I said, "how about a first sentence?"

"Name your book."

"*Moby-Dick.*"

"A whale of a good choice," he kidded. "Now let me see."

"Oh, come on. Even I know that one. 'Call me Ishmael.'"

"Aha, but there's an epigraph preceding those three words. 'The pale Usher—threadbare in coat, heart, body, and brain, I see him now.'"

"Is there anything you don't know?" I asked, staring at him in wonder.

I went to the closet for his ski jacket. A Connecticut Lottery ticket fell from the pocket to the floor. He was standing right next to me, so we both bent over to pick it up. We looked at each other and smiled, as though doing the same thing at the same time was a good omen about our relationship.

"Trying to win the lottery?" I said.

"I've already won," he said, pulling me close.

Then to my delight, he threw out a first sentence.

"It was then I knew that she was the one."

"What's that from?"

"Nothing. I just made it up."

He kissed me good-bye. I wanted him to stay. What if I had met him when I was young?

Chapter 4

On Friday, Amanda showed up at the house. She was dressed in all black—pants, long-sleeve shirt, and boots. She wore black sunglasses.

"I've never seen you in a total blackout," I said.

"I'm making a statement. I no longer wear colors. I wear black, cream, or white."

"Why?"

"I wanted something signature. You should try it. It makes you feel very gallant and decisive."

"I might just do that. Black, cream, or white for me."

"Can't you pick your own colors?" she said as she pulled out a chair at the kitchen table.

"Not really. You took all the good ones. I can't make my signature color chartreuse. I live in Connecticut."

"You could do green and navy," she said. "I'd love a drink, by the way. Do you have Wild Turkey?"

"Wild Turkey for you, Grey Goose for me. I adore the animal kingdom." As I went to the liquor cabinet, I said, "So, tell me about Jake."

"He was going to Seattle for a deposition, and Dad gave him my number."

"I got all that at the airport."

Amanda reminded me of that World War II sign, "Loose Lips Sink Ships."

"Does Jake get to Seattle much?" I asked.

"He came west twice, but I've visited him in Connecticut maybe four times."

She was in Connecticut without calling me? I didn't say a word. The hardest part of being a mother is keeping your mouth shut.

"I would have called, but we were . . . you know. Just to be fair, I didn't call Dad either."

Now I felt better.

"I have some incredible news," she said. "I've been offered a new position."

"Nordstrom is promoting you?"

"No. I'm going to a start-up. Retail Rebellion. I'll be vice president."

"I don't know of it," I said, trying not to act disappointed. She was leaving a major retailer to take a job at a company I had never heard of. My mother's voice came to me: *Tell her to stay at Nordstrom—they're so nice there. Once, I returned a pair of shoes I had worn for two years.*

"Like I said, it's a start-up. We'll be selling similar lines but at just 10 percent above wholesale. That's the retail rebellion. And, of course, it's all online."

"It sounds like taking a chance," I said tentatively. I was into brick and mortar. Strolling through real stores—department, specialty, and my favorite, grocery—was therapeutic for me.

"Mom, do you see why I don't tell you things? Nothing ventured, nothing gained," she said, exuding confidence.

I wasn't convinced, but I wasn't in the retail business. I was just married to it.

"Right now, retail establishments, especially large department stores, are floundering."

"But Nordstrom is solid."

"Guess where the office will be when we start everything?" Clearly, she had decided to move forward in the conversation.

"I hope you're not moving to Hong Kong."

Her eyes lit up. "Connecticut."

I jumped out of my seat. "Oh, that's fabulous! I love your new job. Don't even think twice about taking it."

"Excellent opportunity!" my mother cheered from heaven.

"When do you start?" I asked.

"Not until we have space. When I tell my boss that I'm leaving, she'll ask where I'm going, and when she hears to a fashion start-up, my bonsai plant will be in a carton outside my office door."

I no longer cared if it was a Retail Rebellion or a Wholesale War. "Do you want to stay with me until you find an apartment? I would love the company."

"I'll be living with Jake."

That was fast, I thought. *It's nice to meet you. Let's live together.* I tried not to raise an eyebrow, but it's a natural reflex of being a mother.

"Another reason this opportunity is perfect," Amanda said.

She had lived with other men, including Arnold the Famous Producer. And some other nut named Cody, who sniffed her sweaters when she was gone. I have no idea how she found that out.

"In fact," she continued excitedly, "we're going to have dinner with Jake's parents the Friday night after next. They're flying in from Wisconsin."

"Who is 'we're'?"

"Jake, me, his parents, Dad, and you."

"That sounds great. Let me check my calendar." I reached for my phone to look. "I'm sorry. I'm going to the theater that Friday night," I replied, without considering the import of the invitation—that if Jake's parents were flying in to meet us, things were serious. "Can't do it."

"I knew you were going to cause a problem," Amanda said as her face dropped. "What's the story? You don't want to be with Dad?"

Here we go, I thought. "Not at all. I just have tickets."

She rolled her eyes. She frowned. She pouted.

I imagined her pretending to pull her hair out, which was what she did as a kid when she'd had enough of me. Brat.

"Tickets to *Hamilton*," I stressed. "Candy and I bought them months ago. Can't we make it another night?"

She waved her arms like wings. "They're flying in. Don't start a revolution, Mom. It's *Hamilton*. Candy can find someone else in the world who's willing to see *Hamilton*."

"Of course. But I want to go. I don't know when we'll be able to get tickets again."

"What's more important? A dead Founding Father or me?"

"I just don't understand why it has to be that day."

"You're the only one who can't make it."

Yes, and I am sure I was the only one who wasn't asked about the date in advance.

"This is very important to me," she said.

"Amanda, let me think about it."

"You have no idea what a big deal this is. His mother doesn't like to fly. If we alter the date and cancel the plane tickets, she may never come."

"Hasn't she been to Connecticut to visit him?"

"No. Never."

I stood and poured more vodka with orange juice. I noticed the date on the juice cap. Best if consumed by three weeks ago.

"Are you listening?" Amanda said in the same voice I would have used when my children were in grade school. Maybe I was better off when she was sneaking into town to see her boyfriend and not telling me she was around.

That night, I took the theater ticket from my desk and reviewed it. Seat C8. I was third row, center. I hated to give up my seat, but maybe this Amanda thing was some big deal. If it was, I didn't want to miss it. Furthermore, my separation from that rat bastard Harvey—although it was totally his fault—had done a lot of damage to my family already.

True, our three kids were grown-ups, people with their own lives, but I knew the situation was difficult for them. It was hardest for Amanda, who idolized her father. Worse, she had always believed I was an impediment to anything smart she wanted to do—including getting into cars with college boys when she was sixteen. The divorce volcano had erupted, and I didn't want to be the obvious cause of repercussions.

Like any mother in the history of motherhood, I was into martyrdom. I thought about other mothers who'd sacrificed for their children. Recently, I read in the paper about a young mom in California who got a flat tire. With her twins in the back seat, she stopped the car near the edge of a cliff. The car began to roll forward. Her brakes wouldn't work. She pumped frantically, then raced out of the car and dashed to the front grill to push it back, to save her children.

The moral of the story was if I could surrender the last slice of life-changing banana cake from Sweet Heaven Bakery because my son, Ben, was two and a half and whining, "Me want it," I could give up a ticket to *Hamilton*.

The following day, I promised to meet Amanda at the health club. I could use some exercise. I drove to the front door of the gym, looking for a spot. Nothing. Cars were jammed together. I couldn't believe it. I had to park in another lot. I'd be exhausted before I showed my gym pass.

Finally, I found Amanda and claimed the treadmill next to hers.

"I had to park at Trader Joe's," I said.

"Mom, Trader Joe's is next door."

"How much exercise do I need in one morning?"

I walked three miles per hour, zero incline, as Amanda ran a mountain. She was perspiring so much, the front of her sleeveless T-shirt was soaked. Admiring her determination, I decided to intensify my speed to four miles an hour. I would've upped the incline as well, but I was too young to die.

She turned her head to look at me. "Way to go, Mom."

I could feel myself beaming through my sweat.

"That was great," I said, huffing as we stepped off and headed to the lockers.

"Is that the fastest you ever went?" she asked.

"I think it was."

"So, did you decide between the American Revolution and me?"

I took a breath. "I'll be at the dinner."

"You could sound happier about it," she said.

Kids—sacrifice wasn't enough. You had to be happy about your sacrifice. *Yes. I will tear down the twelve-foot electrified fence with my bare hands so you can have a better life in America. But that's not all. When the shocks course through me, and my body looks like a twisted rag, I will smile.*

I decided to tell her how I felt. Ever since the separation, I had made a pact with myself to speak more forthrightly to my family and friends. It was hard for me to do.

"I'm not happy with this situation," I said.

This was a big statement for me. When the words "I'm not happy" came out of my mouth, I was proud. *Good for you, Marcy,* I thought. *Good for you. Progress.*

"You need to ask before you plan something like a dinner party and assume I am available."

"Since when?" she said.

"That's enough, Amanda. The next time tickets are available to *Hamilton*, I'll be the oldest living woman in America—stone deaf and blind and unable to control my bladder for two hours."

"I'll make it up to you," she said as we entered the locker room.

"How's that?"

"I'll get two tickets to *Hamilton*—one for you and one for me."

"See you in the next century," I said.

Amanda laughed. Of course she laughed. She had bulldozed me, a talent she had inherited from her father.

"Where will the dinner be?" I asked.

"Mad Maestro. Dad loves Mad Maestro."

We sat on the benches to remove our sneakers, T-shirts, and shorts. "Amanda, I have some news of my own," I said. "I'm thinking of moving out of the house."

"You can't move out of the house. It's our house," she said adamantly as she unhooked her sports bra.

"It is, but I am the only one living there," I said, thinking how she returned home about four times a year for three days at a time. And how with this visit, she was staying at Jake's.

"True, but I like coming home to that house. It gives me comfort."

She was my tough kid, and I'd never thought of her as a child who needed much comfort. But okay.

"Elisabeth and Ben will be very down on this. Elisabeth was annoyed when you asked her to clean out her room."

"Well, I just wanted you to know that I'm thinking about it."

"But where will you go?"

"To a smaller place."

"Is that to punish yourself?"

"Amanda, you have to understand that things have changed."

"Exactly. So we shouldn't change any more things," she said, walking off in a towel to the shower.

⎯⎯⎯⎯⎯⎯⎯⎯

Several days later, after Amanda had returned to Seattle, I followed Dana's advice. She had been correct at lunch. If my heart was set on moving to the yellow house, I needed to talk to Harvey first. I thought it best to do this in person, so I called and asked pleasantly whether we could meet.

"When?" he asked. I could feel over the phone that he was smiling in the face of what he thought would be an immense opportunity.

"Now?" I said.

"Where are you?"

"In Atherton. Near Starbucks."

"Great. I was headed out for bras."

Harvey was the Bra King. He had a chain of lingerie stores as well as a wholesale business based in Connecticut that took him around the world. His business, which was started by his great-grandmother, was called Bountiful Bosom. Recently, in an effort to sound contemporary, Harvey had shortened the name to Bountiful. This was something I had been suggesting for years, but Harvey only made the change when it was recommended by an advertising agency. A lot of our relationship had worked that way. If I said the sky was blue, he would call in a consultant.

Amanda was a lot like Harvey. The two of us could be standing in front of a restaurant, examining the menu posted on a window. I could say, "This is a great restaurant. I've had delicious meals here." She wouldn't go in before she looked up the place on Chowhound. The opinion of a hundred strangers without taste buds was more reliable than a five-star review from her mother.

"I can stop in town. No problem," Harvey said.

He was so agreeable. It was startling. Before our separation, he wouldn't have left his office to meet me in the middle of the day if I were pinned under a school bus. *"Should we call your husband?"* the ambulance driver would ask. *"Not unless your wife needs a few minimizers,"* I would answer as I bled to death.

Harvey is a workaholic—and a late-blooming moron. But I'm past all that. I refuse to think about him anymore. I've moved on, as they say. On occasion, I do think of that line "Love means never having to say you're sorry." Not in my house. In my house, love means never having to say, "I'm having a baby with another woman."

"Thanks, Harvey," I said.

"I am glad to hear from you," he said.

He had been trying to get back together with me. My kids were all for it. But I just couldn't do it—there was too much baby under the bridge. I was revved enough without caffeine, so I simply took a seat by a window. Another table abutted mine. I didn't want anyone to sit close to us, listening in, so I pushed the table and chairs further away.

I remembered when Harvey and I had found our house, and how much he had wanted it way back then. He had wanted it so much that he put a deposit on it after I told him I did not want it and that I wasn't leaving Manhattan, that Connecticut was just a nice place for trees.

Ten minutes after I sat down in Starbucks, someone tapped my shoulder.

I looked up. It was Harvey. "Get off my shoulder," I almost blurted. But I didn't say it, because I wanted to maintain the peace. He was holding a box.

"I brought you something," he said.

He really was trying to get back in my good graces. The week before, he had sent my favorite cake from Sweet Heaven Bakery.

I untied the ribbon and opened the gift. There were three cream-colored lace bras and matching underpants, very similar in color to the ones he had given me decades ago when he was apologizing for waiting weeks to call me after we had met at my cousin Leona's engagement party.

"What do they remind you of?" He showed his pride, like a man who finally remembered an anniversary and bought carnations.

"You know that I know," I said, unwilling to relive old times with him. I folded the tissue papers back over the lingerie. He was disappointed.

"What's going on, Marcy?" he said.

I decided to pepper him with talk about our kids before throwing my H-as-in-house bomb.

"Ben called," I said, smiling at the thought of our youngest child.

"What's up?"

"He's working very hard. He says a lot of people don't make it through the first year of law school."

"What, was he going to be a waiter until he was too old to carry a tray? Law school was the obvious decision."

"Our son, the attorney," I said, hopeful Ben would start to enjoy studying law. But I didn't want to ruin the mood of the moment by discussing the fact that Ben already thought law school was as tedious as ditch digging and that it gave him no time for anything else, including his new boyfriend, Jordan.

"Our son, the Supreme Court justice," Harvey exclaimed.

No one could ever accuse Harvey of thinking small.

I looked around at the pounds of coffee on the wall dividing the room; at the signage for this and that; at the woman in a white shirt and green apron behind the counter; at a man with his laptop, iPad, and phone in front of him at once. It all felt just as familiar as Harvey.

"Did you see Amanda?" I asked.

"She stopped in at Bountiful. We went for lunch. I gave her a carton of brassieres to bring to her friends in Seattle. In fact, Elisabeth came to lunch too. We were celebrating."

Great. Now my family celebrated without me. What were they celebrating? It wasn't anyone's birthday.

"I have amazing news," he said.

Amazing news to Harvey was something related to his business—like his sports bra was going to be the official undergarment of the US Olympic women's archery team. Once, that would have made me proud, but now I just wanted one of the team members to pick up a bow and shoot him with an arrow.

"We're expanding. We're starting production on men's underwear and briefs, then boxers."

"That's huge," I said. "Bountiful Briefs. I like the promise of that, Harvey."

His grin reached from Starbucks to the Panera Bread on the next corner.

"I have some news too," I said.

"Wait a moment. I want to get coffee. You?"

"I'm fine," I said.

Harvey went to the line, then returned with a Frappuccino. He was a diabetic, and he was about to drink a six-hundred-calorie frozen drink with whipped cream on top.

"Watching your blood sugar, I see."

"You won't take me back. All I have left is food."

Boohoo, I thought. Impatient, I waited for him to sit down.

"There's a house I want to rent," I said.

I felt "rent" was less inflammatory than "buy." "Buy" was permanent. "Rent" was "I'm thinking about it."

"Rent? Why would you rent a house?"

"To live in?"

"I repeat, why would you rent a house? We have a house." With the end of the straw, he spooned some whipped cream into his mouth. "Want a taste?"

I shook my head.

I thought it would be in my own best interest not to remind him that he had left the house "we" had, a house I came to find out was actually in my name. A little something Harvey had done in case anyone ever sued him personally. If we were held up at gunpoint in a dark alley and the thief told me to hand over my necklace and rings or die, all Harvey would think about was how glad he was we were insured.

"Harvey, why do you care what I do? You're living in the Presidential Suite at Five Swallows."

He leaned forward. "Marcy, it's simple. If you leave our house, I'll move back in."

"What?" I was stunned. I thought I would move. Sell the house. Take anything I wanted from it.

"You can't live in the house," I said, my voice rising. I looked around. Two middle-aged women in turtlenecks, tweed shirts, and corduroy pants were staring at us. *Go order some more clothes from L.L.Bean and mind your own business,* I thought. They must have had telepathy, because they turned away from me and back to their conversation.

"Why can't I live there?" he said with a laugh I could have done without.

"Harvey, you don't even know where the washing machine is."

"I'll hire a search party. I love that house and everything in it," he said. "My garbage can from Paris is there."

Harvey had traveled a lot for Bountiful, and he had always brought home some treasure. Like the garbage pail in the shape of the Eiffel Tower and the hand-carved end table from Switzerland shaped like a wheel of Swiss cheese.

No problem. Take your tower and your cheesy end table and move into a condominium like all men in your situation do. Haven't you ever seen one of those movies where the blond bimbos in bikinis lounge in the courtyard around a bean-shaped pool—and everyone has cheap towels?

But I knew Harvey hated condominiums. Fine. He could buy a house we hadn't raised our children in, a house devoid of great memories. He was not going to keep our memories.

"You can't move back into the house," I said again, drumming my square-tip fingernails on the table.

"Why not?"

"It's my house. You put it in my name."

Customers on their way out of Starbucks were glancing at me. People in Connecticut do not stare. They glance— and I was speaking loudly and way too aggressively for the Constitution State. I definitely had my New York City voice on. The difference was several octaves and the pronunciation of the word "coffee."

"What did you think would happen to the house?" he said as he stationed his cup on the table. He must have been very upset, because it appeared he wasn't going to suck down his Frappuccino. Usually, he finished everything.

"We'd sell it," I said.

"Sell it? It's our home." *He is so damn nuts,* I thought, *he shouldn't be allowed within ten feet of a child with an allergy.*

"Our? *Our?* There is no 'our.' You made sure of that."

Temper yourself, Marcy. Inciting him never accomplished anything.

He got louder. He realized it, and he lowered his voice to a whisper. "I'm telling you now, Marcy, that I am perfectly happy with you living in the house. Forever." He said the word "forever" like it was longer than forever. Like it was forever and a half. "But if you move out, I am moving in."

Maybe I was being petty. But this scenario had never occurred to me, and I am a person who always wants everything to go just the way I planned it. There are a lot of people like me. We are disappointed most of the time. Many of us are very depressed. Fortunately, I take an antidepressant—quite liberally at that.

Suddenly, Harvey stood up. He swiped the Frappuccino from the table and headed toward the door. For a moment, he looked back.

I held the lingerie box in the air. "You forgot your underwear!"

As I sat alone, Dana happened to walk into Starbucks. I stewed until she got a coffee and joined me for a moment. Before I could say a word, she rattled on about her vacation plans. She was thinking of going to Cape Cod, but there was too much traffic on Route 6. She was considering Paris, but she hated the French.

"Harvey just left."

"I knew I'd smelled a rat."

"So do you want to know what happened when I took your advice and told him I was thinking of moving?"

"You just told him? Here? Now? What did he say?"

"He said if I move out, he's moving in."

"Whoa. I didn't think of that."

"You're not the only one."

"Now, listen. You don't want him moving into the house. Do you have any idea how bizarre that would be? He might move a woman in. Can you imagine his girlfriend living in your house, sleeping on your bed, setting your table with your silverware, inviting your kids for the holidays? It's a total yuck."

I could feel my face turning white, but before I could respond to Dana, she stood up again. "I've got to go, but I have to say that I wouldn't move. I'd sit in that house until Harvey was too old to use the staircase."

Chapter 5

Mad Maestro was a traditional steak house. A twenty-four-ounce dry-aged porterhouse was the most popular entrée. It came rare, medium—or on the installment plan. A side of asparagus or a baked potato was about the same price as a car payment. The restaurant was in downtown Stamford, off jam-packed I-95. It was in the neighborhood where young New Yorkers settled when they had a baby and no longer wanted to live in a walk-in closet on the Upper West Side. As I pulled up to the restaurant, which was on the first floor of an elite office building, it occurred to me that I had never arrived at Mad Maestro alone. I had always been with Harvey.

A valet, about the age of the new dress I was wearing, took my car. Strawberry-blonds, like me, look great in green. I had chosen the crisp shirtdress because I had no idea what Jake's mother was like, and I didn't want to be too fancy. I wore a jade necklace, jade and gold earrings, and silver shoes.

Mad Maestro was as noisy as an echo chamber, a tough place to have a meaningful conversation. Of course, as was my habit, I arrived early. I knew Harvey would be late, as usual, and then excuse himself to chat about business on his phone. I passed the hostess and headed directly to the ladies' room.

The bathroom attendant welcomed me from her chair. She had sunken eyes and a thick, crocheted net restraining her hair. When I finished rinsing my hands, the attendant offered me a paper hand towel and a spritz of perfume.

At the sink next to mine was a little woman with curly gray-blue hair. Her eyeglasses, on a plastic beaded chain around her neck, hung to her bosom. I wondered if her breasts were nearsighted or farsighted. She dawdled with her lipstick and seemed to be killing time. She poked through the wicker convenience basket on the shelf above the sinks. When the attendant went to clean a stall, the woman grabbed several Tampax Pearl tampons. She placed the tampons into her purse, which featured silver studs spelling "Paris" but screamed Target.

She reached for a fistful of peppermint candies. I watched, entertained, as she dropped the loot into her bag. I understood her pilfering the hard candies, but I was puzzled about why a woman my age— maybe older—needed tampons. Did she know many teenage girls? I pretended I hadn't seen a thing and deposited a dollar in an otherwise empty tumbler for tips.

I turned to check the mirror one more time, and I saw the little woman take my George Washington. I didn't say a word. I hated confrontation. If she needed the cash that bad, she could have it. I decided I would tip the attendant again on a return trip to the bathroom before I left Mad Maestro.

I proceeded to the cocktail lounge. It was dark, and all the windows were covered with wooden blinds. There were round, high tables and a long bar. The place was packed. There was no walking through it; there was only squeezing by.

Amanda waved. After I kissed her hello, she introduced me to Jake's parents. I couldn't take my eyes off his mother. She was the tampon thief. Jake didn't look like either parent. I hoped he was adopted. I didn't need Amanda involved with a man who was genetically predisposed to thievery.

Amanda was wearing a white dress and an ingratiating smile. The last time Harvey and I had gotten a smile like that out of her, it was because we'd agreed that she could go to the Atherton High School prom with Mother's Hell.

"Mom, Mrs. Berger couldn't wait to meet you."

Mrs. Burglar, I thought.

"Call us Mug and Bernie," Mrs. Burglar said to me.

Apparently, she didn't remember me from the crime scene.

"Marcy," I said. "It's a pleasure to meet you." *Can I have the tip back?*

"Dad called. He'll be a few minutes late. Let's order drinks," Amanda said.

"Two whiskey sours," Bernie said. I hadn't heard the words "whiskey sour" since I was at a bar mitzvah in 1978.

"Chardonnay," I said.

Jake made his way to the bar. We sat at the high-top table on backless swivel stools. There was an awkward silence, so I said, "How long will you be in Connecticut?"

"Just tonight," Bernie said.

Silence again.

"So, Mug," I asked, "how did you get such a great nickname?"

"When my brother was a baby, he called me Mug. My real name is Maud."

If I had to choose between Mug and Maud, I'd ask people to refer to me as "Hey, you."

Jake returned with the drinks just as Harvey entered. He was heavier than when he'd moved out of our house. Even a bit heavier than when I had seen him in Starbucks a week before. Or was that just wishful thinking? Was there anything better than your husband leaving you and then becoming as big as a house? When he first moved out,

I had a nightmare in which he had taken up exercising and gotten in dating shape. Apparently, the only thing he had taken up was drinking six-hundred-calorie Frappuccinos with whipped cream.

Harvey grabbed Amanda like he hadn't seen her for years. Like she had left our shtetl barefoot, wrapped in a blanket, with one frying pan. He kissed me on the cheek. *Get off my cheek,* I thought. He shook Jake's hand, and Jake introduced him to Bernie and Mug.

"What a pleasure," Harvey said with gusto, shaking Bernie's hand so heartily that Bernie's cap fell off. Jake caught it and adjusted the hat so it sat perfectly on the old man's head. It was easy to see that Jake loved his dad. My heart went to mush whenever I saw a grown man being kind to his parents.

"Just let me make one call," Harvey said.

"Your table is ready, Mr. Hammer," the maître d' said.

"You go ahead," Harvey said, scrolling through his phone.

We followed the maître d' to a table near the back of the dining room. Jake seemed jumpy and, beside his tiny parents, ridiculously tall. I cased the table to make sure I did not sit next to Mrs. Burglar. I liked my jade necklace too much.

The round table had a crimson tablecloth, white dishes, and white napkins. Mrs. Burglar left a seat free next to me for Harvey, and I wondered whether she knew we were separated. In any case, Harvey and I *were* separated, and I felt uncomfortable having a seat saved for him next to me. Wasn't there anything available in the coat check?

Mug scanned the menu and then reached into her vinyl Paris bag for a tissue. As she took out the pink tissue, a sole tampon fell to the floor. Nonchalantly, she placed it back into her bag.

Bernie Burglar, who seemed to be the weak, silent type, said nothing. Squinting at the menu as though he had seen a ghost, he rolled his eyes and sniffed as though his nose was about to run. I was so uncomfortable about bringing Jake's parents to this expensive steak house that when Harvey returned, I nudged him with my knee. *Speak up already,* I thought. *Say you are treating. Say it now, before I have to say it.*

"I'll have a baked potato," Mug told the waiter before he asked for her order.

"Two," her husband said, squeezing his red nostrils. Apparently, he was now allergic to the prices.

Finally, Harvey spoke up. "I'm happy you could join us. In Connecticut, dinner is always on me. Do you like steak? If you're a meat eater, go for the rib eye."

Mug smiled. "Two rib eyes. Medium."

"Do you still want the potatoes?" the waiter asked.

"Yes, of course," she said. "Also, shrimp cocktail would be nice. Are the shrimp colossal?" Then she turned to me. "No one likes a shrimp of a shrimp."

To be polite, I laughed at her big remark about little shrimp.

"Four jumbo in every order," the waiter said.

"We'll have two shrimp cocktails," Mug said.

Jake, Amanda, and I each ordered filet mignon. Harvey ordered the garlic spinach without garlic and the onion mashed potatoes without onions, scallion if they had it. Harvey was a waiter's nightmare. Always had been. Always would be. Julius Caesar felt powerful in Rome. Harvey felt powerful in a restaurant ordering a Caesar salad with olives instead of anchovies.

"And a bottle of your Cakebread Cabernet," Harvey said.

He was such a food addict. Even his wine had cake in it.

"This is our first time in Connecticut," Mug said. "It's not as beautiful as they say."

"What did you expect?" Jake asked, clearly annoyed by her comment.

"More horses," she said.

"Mom, this is Stamford. It's a city," Jake explained.

"You should come in October," I said. "The foliage is breathtaking."

"We like Wisconsin," Mrs. Burglar said. "Have you ever been?"

"No," I said.

The waiter brought the wine, waited for Harvey to taste it, poured some in each glass, and lingered at the table.

Jake stood up. "I want to thank my parents for coming to Connecticut. I want to thank Harvey for this wonderful dinner. And I want to thank Marcy for giving up her ticket to *Hamilton*."

The waiter whispered to me, "You gave up a ticket to *Hamilton*?"

I nodded to the waiter and returned my attention to Jake's toast. I clinked my glass with a utensil.

Mrs. Burglar's spoon was already in her handbag.

Jake turned to Amanda, pulling her up. I thought how wonderful they looked next to each other, a perfect set.

The couple held hands, swinging arms back and forth.

Amanda was grinning. "There's something we want to tell you."

Say anything now except that you're pregnant, I thought.

"We're engaged!" Amanda said, then let out a shout.

They kissed each other for a long time. Probably a minute, but it felt like an hour, because we were watching our daughter in a serious embrace.

"I asked Mans a while ago."

"And I said yes!"

Jake reached into his pocket and brought forth a small velvet box. I could tell from Amanda's face that she had no clue he had brought the ring to dinner.

Jake opened the box.

"You're amazing," Amanda said. She leaped into his arms, her heels in the air.

People at adjacent tables started clapping. Tears ran down Amanda's face. Jake placed the ring on her finger.

I looked at Harvey. He looked at me. I looked away. I tried to swallow, but the lump in my throat had hardened into rock. I was thrilled for Amanda, but there was something else. Here was a moment Harvey and I had dreamed of, but sadness settled in. Amanda was starting out, and we were finished.

Don't think about yourself, Marcy. This moment belongs to your daughter. Shake it off. Now.

Amanda held out her hand so we could all see the vibrant emerald set in gold. Then we all stood, and she walked around the table, showing it to us one at a time. When she placed her hand in front of Harvey, I could hear him thinking, *"An emerald. Not a diamond. That's the ring?"* It wouldn't occur to him that Amanda might have asked for an emerald. She was a rock-hard Taurus. Her birthday was in May. The May stone was emerald. *Please don't say anything, Harvey.*

"Mazel tov," I said, crying and smiling at the same time. I had never had a daughter get engaged before, and I suddenly felt overwhelmed by joy. Then I had the odd feeling again, the bite of loss. She had gained a husband, and I was losing a daughter. I felt as though someone had taken her away from me and on to something definite, as though her life was now decided. It seemed so final. Yet look at Harvey and me. That had seemed final. I hoped what had happened to me wouldn't happen to her. I prayed it.

Mug came over to hug me. Quickly, I remembered that my daughter was marrying into either a family of crazies or a family of felons. Maybe both.

I could hear my mother: *"She's marrying a boy from Kenosha?"*

Jake's father could've been governor of Wisconsin and my mother would have looked down on him. Well, she was in heaven—she was looking down on everyone.

Mug was still hugging me. Her dress had a cap sleeve, and her armpits were wet. I could feel the stickiness of her deodorant, so I took a step back. I kissed her on the cheek.

"We're family now," she said. Then she walked back to her seat.

I was still standing when suddenly, I felt Harvey's arms around me, thicker than I remembered.

"We did it," he said. "Our daughter is getting married." He stopped just short of twirling me around.

How wonderful this would have been if what had taken place the year before had not happened. But it had, and I was in no mood to dance.

"Come on, Marcy, one twirl." I didn't want to ruin the celebration. I let him twirl me. As we sat down, he held my hand too long.

We enjoyed the meal, and Mrs. Burglar asked that her leftovers be wrapped for her to take home. She was taking the food back to Wisconsin? I hadn't finished my steak. The skin was left from my potato. She asked if I minded if she took my leftovers. Jake shook his head. I could tell he was embarrassed.

"What are the plans?" I asked Amanda once the waiter delivered dessert. I had ordered cheesecake with fresh strawberries and whipped cream on top. Amanda looked down at her ice cream parfait as though she didn't want to discuss what she had in mind. Right then and there, I decided that I wanted to make up for the unfortunate fact that my daughter was getting married while Harvey and I were at odds, and the way I could do that was to do whatever it took to keep Amanda happy for her wedding, to be a help and not a hindrance, to keep my mouth shut. I knew from the stories I had heard from friends, especially Dana, that nuptials could go nuclear, that walking down the aisle was no piece of wedding cake, but I was going to keep the peace no matter what.

"Please say you will get married in Wisconsin," Mrs. Burglar said. "I'm not a flyer—and those lines at security. On the way here, I nearly toppled over while trying to remove my shoes, and I was patted down."

Harvey had a question. "Do you wear an underwire bra?"

Mug looked at him quizzically. She nodded.

"Never wear an underwire to the airport. You were stopped because of the metal in your bra."

Mug was not paying attention. "They search nice American people like me but allow a young man in a caftan to sashay through security.

Those morons are examining *me* while the shoe bomber is on the loose."

"Mom, you can't say things like that," Jake reprimanded as Amanda looked away in embarrassment.

"Your generation! Politically correct this, and politically correct that. I'm just telling it like it is, Jake."

"No. You're telling it like *you* think it is."

It was getting uncomfortable at the table, and I decided I didn't like this whole in-law thing. Like my family didn't have enough issues. We had to marry into some more?

"There's a catering hall near our home in Wisconsin," Mug said, hoisting her wineglass.

"There are three weddings at a time, and everywhere you look, you see a bride coming or going," Jake said, still obviously annoyed with her previous remarks.

"I will not ask our relatives to fly to Connecticut," Mug proclaimed, her face reddening. "The wedding must be within driving distance. People have weddings in Wisconsin all the time."

"Hammers do not get married in Wisconsin," Harvey said.

I heard my mother. *"I always liked that Harvey."*

Amanda and Jake were silent. Like people who knew in advance that this would take place and had planned to shut it down.

"We haven't discussed anything," Jake said.

You haven't discussed anything? I know my daughter better than that.

Jake squeezed Amanda's forearm, which translated to "We agreed not to discuss venues tonight."

I assumed they didn't want to talk in front of Jake's parents. I understood that, too many cooks and all. But I was the bride's mother, the celebrity chef. I couldn't wait to get alone time with Amanda. To hear her ideas, to tell her how much I wanted this wedding to be the best.

After the kids left, Harvey and I stood curbside. He asked me for my ticket, passed it to the young valet, and walked back to me.

"I had no idea she was serious about him," he said. "She hasn't known him long."

"But you know him," I said.

"No. Not really." He paused, considering. "Well, I guess we have a lifetime to get to know him."

"We"? I thought. *We are not "we."*

"I know all I need to know about his parents," Harvey said.

"Well, I think they felt uncomfortable with the prices. Mad Maestro is steep."

"Not when I announced I was paying."

"Do you think the mother has a problem?" I said.

"No," he said. "She just likes to be the boss."

"Harvey, she stole all the tampons out of the bathroom."

"You're kidding."

"I saw her. And she took all the breath mints."

"Now those she needed."

I was feeling uncomfortable being relaxed with him. "I wonder what's taking so long? Did they go to Sweden for my Volvo?"

The valet pulled up with Harvey's sports car. He turned to me. "You have the Volvo, right?"

"Yes, I do."

"Sorry, but it won't start."

"What do you mean?" I said, confused. "It's a Volvo."

He shrugged. "What I said."

I looked at Harvey. Harvey looked at me.

"Can you jump it from my car?" Harvey asked.

"I guess," the valet said.

"Let's do it," Harvey said, and they drove Harvey's car to mine.

I was hopeful, but when they returned, Harvey shook his head. "The Volvo wouldn't start. We'll have to deal with this in the morning."

Even though he was trying to help me, I was put off by his "I'm in charge here" tone. I felt like saying what Ben used to say when he was a toddler: "You're not the boss of me."

"I'll drive you home," he said.

"No, no. I can call AAA now," I insisted.

"We're about to close the lot," the valet said, shoving his hands in his pockets as though to say his hands were done working for the day.

I didn't see much choice, so I got into Harvey's car.

"What about the ring?" Harvey said as he began to drive me home.

I pretended I didn't understand his inference. "What about it?"

"Who are you kidding? Jake bills six hundred dollars an hour. What did he do with the other five hundred and ninety-nine dollars?"

"The ring is stunning."

"If you like green."

I tried not to, but I had to laugh.

"Like old times," he said happily. "So, what were you saying about Jake's mother?"

"She stole a spoon off the table too," I said.

"It's not her I'm worried about."

"Whom are you worried about?"

"Our daughter."

"She's in love."

"With a guy who thought an emerald was a diamond."

"Maybe she asked for an emerald. And Harvey, you fixed them up."

"I didn't fix them up. I just said my daughter lives in Seattle. He must have taken one look at me and known she was a knockout too."

I laughed.

"I can't believe I'm losing my baby," he said. "I mean, this is it. It's so final. She's young. Maybe she could have done better."

"What kind of better?" I asked, wanting to see if we were on the same page.

"Someone like Jake but from a family like ours."

You mean like the family you dumped in the river?

"We'll never know," he said.

"Forget about the ring, Harvey. You're displacing your feelings."

"Tell me, is this how serene one gets when living with a professor?"

Now I was annoyed. "I'm not living with him. Besides, Harvey, we're separated. Why do you care what he does?"

There was silence, and then, as we stopped at a red light, he begged, "Go to a diner with me. Our baby just got engaged, and I would like to be with you."

He said it so sadly that I felt bad for him and for me. It was supposed to be a happy moment, but I felt loss. Like I was handing over a prized possession, and I had no idea how the new owners would take care of it. I didn't know Jake. I didn't know his parents, and they weren't what I would have expected. Suddenly, I was in business with strangers.

"Okay," I said.

Harvey pulled into the Happy Days Diner, a few miles from Atherton. The place had old-fashioned aluminum siding and flashing neon lights. We passed a rotating display of black-and-white cookies, linzer tortes, cheese Danish, apple turnovers, and immense buttercream cakes. We found a booth with a jukebox at the window.

Although we had just eaten at Mad Maestro, Harvey ordered my all-time diner favorite—rice pudding. He asked for a strawberry Belly Buster, their largest shake. When he left me, I had wished he would get fat, but I had meant maybe a fifteen-pound gain. At this rate, he was going to need a fire rescue team to lift him out of his bed. There was no point in saying anything. No one wants to hear a word about weight. Want to lose three hundred pounds? Tell your three-hundred-pound friend she has to take better care of herself.

"So what do you think?" Harvey asked.

"I was just thinking that I feel like I am going into business with total strangers. Who are these people? We meet them once, and they get our daughter?"

"I thought she'd marry into a family we had something in common with."

"They're Jewish. We're Jewish," I said.

"Marcy, they might as well be Eskimos."

The truth was, he was right.

I looked up as the waitress delivered my rice pudding. It was then that I saw Jon entering the diner. He took his hand out of his jeans pocket and waved. He smiled. Nerves shot through my body, a lightning bolt.

He came right to the booth. Although Harvey and Jon had never met, I could see from Harvey's face that he knew Jon was "the professor." When you live with someone for decades, sometimes you get to know them. On one hand, Harvey was surely not glad to see Jon. On the bigger hand, the hand the size of the diner, he would enjoy his chance to check the guy out. I was uncomfortable with Harvey inspecting Jon like second-rate merchandise not good enough for his business.

"What a coincidence. My kind of coincidence," Jon said sweetly as he smiled at me. The last time I felt that ill at ease, self-aware, and uncomfortable, I was in a Lamaze class.

I introduced them.

"Harvey, Jon. Jon, Harvey," I said matter-of-factly, wondering whether Harvey was what Jon had expected.

"Mind if I join you?" Jon said.

I gave him a look that said "What are you doing?"

Harvey wanted to size Jon up, so of course he patted the seat next to him, across from me, but Jon ignored him. He sat down beside me, as close as he could get.

"Interesting to meet my girlfriend's husband," Jon said.

"So, I hear you're a professor," Harvey replied.

"And a painter," Jon said.

"A lot of outside work in the spring I bet," Harvey said, just to be irritating. He knew what kind of painter Jon was. "Maybe you could give me a fair price on my warehouse."

"And I hear you're into lingerie," Jon said. "Anyone's in particular?"

I was pleased that Jon had handed it back to Harvey, but if I was ever going to die, this was the right time. I moved further into the booth, toward the window, hiding my face behind the jukebox.

"So I thought you two were meeting Jake's parents tonight."

"We did," I said, wondering if he thought this was a ruse. "We did," I repeated.

"How'd it go?"

"Amanda and Jake are engaged," I said.

"That's great!" Jon said to both of us. "Any plans?"

"Not yet," I said, hoping this scene would soon be over.

Jon could obviously feel my discomfort, and I could tell how disappointed he was to find me with Harvey and a rice pudding. "I only came in to get one of those big black-and-white cookies to go."

"And *I* only came in because my car wouldn't start at the steak house."

"What happened to the car?" Jon asked.

"Stuck, wouldn't move," Harvey said.

The waitress put the check on the table.

"I'll take Marcy home while you pay the check," Jon said.

Perfect, I thought. "Good night, Harvey."

"Quite an evening," Harvey said, although he was downcast and appeared pale.

I felt sad. I knew that normally this situation would have made me deliriously happy—a handsome man enters a well-lit diner on a cold winter night and whisks me off, leaving my duplicitous spouse waiting for the check. But that night, our daughter had become engaged. Where would this lead next?

Chapter 6

"Are you having some kind of neurological problem?" Candy had said when I told her I was bailing on *Hamilton*. Her cousin Donna had scooped up the ticket, but Candy wanted to go to the city with me. I agreed on another play, and that's how I wound up so far off Broadway I could have dipped my foot in the Hudson.

The theater, Fifth Stage, was on Forty-Eighth Street. "This isn't Off-Broadway," I said. "This is Off-Off-Off-Broadway." I finally spotted Fifth Stage, which was in a brownstone. "How many times have you been here?"

"I go whenever Kate does the design."

"Who's Kate?"

"My agent's daughter."

I grimaced.

"Think of it as supporting the arts," Candy said.

"Is it art?"

"Barely."

Once inside a vestibule, we saw a sign for the show and an arrow pointing up a steep staircase without a railing. I held on to a peeling wall as we climbed several flights. I caught my breath as we reached the entrance to the theater.

"You really have to love theater to go through this to see a show."

"Worse for you yet, the only bathroom is another floor up."

"That's okay. I'll hold it," I said. "You know, until we find a ladies' room on earth."

Candy's agent, Teresa, was at the door in a lemon-and-lime tent dress that seemed to take over the blackened space. She had a streak of silver in her ebony pageboy haircut. She wore hoop earrings the size of pancakes.

Candy introduced me as the executive director of the Guild for Good.

Teresa patted my hand. "I am well aware of the Guild. If I can ever help in any way, please call me."

We chatted for a moment, then looked for seats.

"That was nice," I said to Candy, as I found an aisle seat in the last row, Row E, and I let Candy sit first in the adjacent one. There were about a dozen chairs in the row, the final one against a wall covered in a charcoal-colored curtain.

"Don't even bother calling her," Candy said. "She never returns a call."

"She returns your calls," I said.

"Only because when I call her, she doesn't hear a phone ringing. She hears a cash register."

"That sounds like something I would say."

"I'm catching on," Candy said.

"Well, don't catch on too much. I like you the way you are."

The theater filled. We rose so a grandmother holding a cane with ribbons on it could pass. No sooner had we reclaimed our seats than Grandpa, sporting a white cap advertising Long Boat Key, appeared. We rose again. We sat again. We stood so a young couple could pass. They were waving to everyone they knew.

"I hope that's it. I'm done standing and sitting," I said.

"Why? We could use the exercise."

I didn't see how a woman bedding her personal trainer would need additional exercise. "So what do you like about going to these productions?" I asked.

"Other than it's easier than saying no to Teresa?"

"Yes . . ." *And thanks for dragging me along.*

"I feel invigorated when I see artists setting out in the world. I marvel at their promise. I wonder about their dreams."

"You envy their blank slates," I said.

"You can't buy a blank slate."

A man in gray slacks and a light-blue cashmere crewneck asked me if the seat next to Candy was taken. When I stood, I realized he was only about an inch or so taller than me, maybe five seven. He had a big face with big eyes, like the shortest movie stars always do. In fact, he could have been a movie star. His black hair was slicked back. Also, he was the kind of guy who looked like he'd just come out of the shower even though he might have been at work all day. He had my attention—and Candy's too. She scooted our jackets off the seat next to her. I placed mine in my lap.

He smiled at us. He looked like he flossed three times a day. I hated overly organized people. They made me feel so insecure.

Immediately, he struck up a conversation with Candy.

"Ellison Graham," he said with a friendly nod.

Candy said her name and introduced me.

He was so intent on her that I realized he had not found the seat randomly. He had spotted Candy and liked what he had seen.

I listened in. His son had a part in the play. The boy had attended Brown and, before that, the same boarding school as Candy's son, Jumper. On the basis of that information, I knew Candy would take an interest in him. School snobs unite. Candy was enthralled. I turned to my playbill and looked up his son, Ellison Jr. In his bio, he thanked "Dad, Mums, Lexie, my dog Elizabeth Taylor, as well as anyone who ever advised me to go into theater—including every sports coach at Bosley-Billingsworth." So the kid had a sense of humor.

"Did your wife see the play last night?" I asked, leaning over and getting to what I thought was the heart of the matter.

He looked at Candy. "I'm divorced."

"And she's divorced," I said, pointing at Candy. "What a coincidence."

Candy gave me a look.

I figured that as long as I had gotten started, I might as well ask him all the questions it would be discourteous for Candy to ask.

"Have you been divorced long?" I didn't want her catching him on the rebound.

"Long enough," he said.

Candy laughed—at me. "I hope you don't mind the inquiries from Lois Lane."

There was a request to turn off mobile devices. The curtain went up. When his son took the stage, Ellison Graham leaned far forward, with his hands clasped together. He didn't recline until junior exited. He did that each time his son appeared. I respected it and found it endearing. I decided I liked him.

The play was called *Enter and Exit*. I don't remember much about it except there was a lot of door slamming. At intermission, I wanted to make an exit myself. But I would have had to leave without Candy, who was busy with Ellison. She had mentioned to me more than once that she didn't have many female friends. Could it be because she ditched the girlfriend she dragged along as soon as she found a man she liked?

Candy was extraordinary at flirting. Ellison handed her his wallet so she could see a photograph of his daughter. She rubbed the soft leather deliberately back and forth between her fingers.

When Candy excused herself to go to the bathroom, I was surprised. I'd thought she would leak before she left this man. But for all

I knew, that was strategy too. I followed her. "I think somebody likes you," I said, as though we were in high school.

She grinned. "Looks that way."

Candy headed up the stairs to the bathroom; I waited on line for a soda. Moments later, she returned.

"Come into the bathroom," she said with a tug at my sleeve.

I wondered what the secret was, and I followed her.

There was one restroom. She opened the door, and we stepped in. But that's all the stepping we could do, because it was the tiniest lavatory I had ever seen. Bathrooms in Manhattan are small, but if you can wash your hands while sitting on the toilet, that's extreme.

"I'm spotting," she said.

"Spotting or bleeding?"

"The first."

Someone knocked.

"We're in here," I said, annoyed and worried about Candy.

Another knock.

"Can you please wait?" Candy said through the door as we stood face-to-face.

"We can go to an emergency room."

"In Manhattan? Not happening. I'll call my gynecologist tomorrow."

"Are you sure? What about a walk-in center?"

She shook her head.

I didn't know how much Candy was actually spotting, but I didn't think waiting was a good idea. From my experience, not dealing with a problem created more problems. But, of course, I could understand that she preferred to see her own doctor.

"I'll call my gynecologist tomorrow," she repeated.

"It's important. You shouldn't wait."

She bit her lip.

"What?"

"The spotting. It's not the first time," she confessed. "It happened in Italy. I didn't want to look into it there."

And you didn't see a doctor as soon as you got home? I thought.

"Don't look at me like that," she said.

"Like what?"

"Like you think I'm a fool."

But you are a fool.

"I'm going tomorrow," she said.

"Promise?"

"I promise."

I didn't believe her. I didn't trust her. I was frightened she would procrastinate longer, and if something was truly amiss, it would get worse, and soon it would be too late to do something about it.

There was banging at the door. I unlocked it. A woman who looked like someone from a bad dream was standing with her legs crossed, her eyes livid. "Two of you? Well, that must have been fun."

Candy and I smiled and started back to the theater.

"Ellison is interesting," she said.

"Did you ask him what he does for a living?"

"It's only been an hour. And for forty-five minutes, we were watching a show."

"Well, it's the first question I'd ask," I said.

"So when you first met Harvey and asked what he did for a living, and he said he was in brassieres, that wasn't a complete turnoff?"

"I guess not."

Mercifully, I fell asleep during the second act. I didn't worry about snoring—a sound effect could only make the play better. When I woke, people were clapping. Loudly, like friends and relatives. I was bored and tired and concerned about Candy, and I couldn't wait to get home.

The next morning, I drove to Candy's place. She answered the door in yoga pants and a loose sweatshirt.

"What are you doing here?" she said.

"I'm taking you to the doctor."

"I don't have an appointment. I haven't called yet," she said, embarrassed.

"I'll get you an appointment when we get there."

"How? Without calling?" she said. "Are you convincing him to come to my house too?"

"Just get in the car," I said.

"I can't go out like this." She pointed to the yoga pants.

"Eighty percent of women in America go out like that," I said. "I took the morning off from work. Just get in the car."

Her doctor wasn't in Atherton. He was five towns over, in Sandy Lake. She didn't say a word about driving herself or about the way I drove, which was not a good sign. When I came to a short stop at a railroad crossing, she jolted forward, then back, and then looked ahead. None of this was good. It meant she was worried. I thought maybe she had fibbed about spotting. Maybe she wasn't spotting; maybe she was bleeding.

Her gynecologist's name was Dr. Haverford. His name was embossed on the entrance to his office suite. To the side was a plaque with a list of his staff, names temporarily attached. Here one day, gone the next. Immediately, I determined that Candy was not seeing anyone but the doctor.

"Maybe if I can't see him, I'll see a nurse practitioner," Candy said.

"Leave it to me."

There were only a few women waiting in the room. It had chevron carpet and peach-colored walls. I approached the reception window and rapped once on the glass. The receptionist was an attractive middle-aged woman with frosted curly hair. She wore a necklace over a lilac turtleneck.

"I love your necklace. What is it made of?" I said, buttering her up.

"Amethyst," she said, fingering the stone on the chunky chain. She held it up, toward me.

I bent closer to the sliding window that separated us. "So tell me, where did you get it?"

"My boyfriend gave it to me."

"Special occasion?"

Candy was beside me. I could feel her take a deep breath, waiting for me to get to the point. The point was that befriending a receptionist—or, for that matter, the person assigning seats on the airplane, the front office manager at a hotel, et cetera—had always worked well for me.

"My birthday, yesterday," the receptionist said.

"Happy birthday!" I shouted as though she had just blown out candles.

The receptionist laughed. "What can I do for you?"

I moved my hand through the window to shake hers. "I'm Marcy. My friend Candy doesn't feel well and needs to see Dr. Haverford. We would have called, but there was no time."

I omitted the part where this medical emergency had been months in the making.

"I'm sorry, but he doesn't have a moment. He's leaving in a few minutes. I can fit you in with one of the technicians."

"I forgot to ask your name," I said.

"Janine," she said, clearly unaccustomed to anyone asking her name or making conversation with her.

"Janine, you seem so wonderful. Maybe you could just ask him. My friend lost her father," I whispered. "I am very concerned."

"What's the problem?" Janine whispered back.

"She's bleeding." I figured the worse I made it sound, the more likely the doctor would see us sans appointment. "Blood. Red. I hope you will help us."

"Well, since you're so nice . . ." She headed toward the examination rooms and whispered something to someone near the door. She returned to her chair, and she winked. "He'll see you."

I knew Candy was thankful I had talked our way into seeing the doctor, but that she wouldn't chummy up to land the last seat on the last lifeboat leaving the *Titanic*.

Then she surprised me.

"Thank you, Janine," Candy said. "And by the way, I love your hair."

Chapter 7

Christopher Kingston stopped into the office on his way to Vermont. He was a large and wealthy man who had been in finance but now owned a respected gallery. He was chairman of the Guild board, my boss.

"The new office looks good," Christopher said. "I should come more often."

"Well, you like to hold meetings in your gallery. And I enjoy going there."

His eyes landed disapprovingly on Cheyenne, who was at her desk, dipping her chicken nuggets in sauce. I introduced the two.

"Would you like coffee?" Cheyenne asked.

Christopher waved her off and turned to me. "Tell me about Art Explosion."

Art Explosion was our most lucrative event. I came up with the name because it was held in an old ammunitions warehouse. The proceeds supported creative programs in inner-city schools.

"We already have forty artists willing to display. Would you like to discuss it now?"

"No. We'll meet in the gallery next week. I can't stay long today. I'm heading to Burlington to see my son."

We talked about the Guild for a while. He asked me how my personal life was. I told him I was seeing Jon, who was also on the board.

He smiled. "Keep making the good choices, Marcy."

Easy for him to say—he was the kind of person who had always been the captain of his ship. As for me, I'd been a skipper. I had gone aboard the *Harvey* and sailed wherever my husband wanted to go. Back then, I had no idea there was any other way to do it.

After Christopher left, my phone rang.

"What are we going to do about Dad?" Amanda blurted before I could say hello.

"What happened?"

"He wants the wedding to be in Connecticut."

And so do I.

"It gets worse."

"Worse than Connecticut?" I said sarcastically.

"He wants it to be at the synagogue." She drew out the word "synagogue" like it had eighteen syllables.

"What's so bad about that?" I had already called the synagogue to see what dates were available.

"Mom, getting married in a temple is so 1979. I might as well wear a daisy crown in my hair."

"I wore a daisy crown."

"See. I'm right. Old-fashioned."

I pushed down my disappointment. I had always imagined a wedding at our synagogue, but if that wasn't what she wanted, it was fine with me. I wanted her to have what made her happy. I wanted everyone to get along. I knew it wasn't easy having parents. I had had two of my own.

"Where do people get married now?" I asked.

"In botanical gardens, on cattle ranches."

"You want to get married on a cattle ranch?"

"Of course not, but my friend Julia did."

"Why?" I asked.

"Her father is a neurosurgeon, but he owns a cattle ranch in Wyoming."

I heard my Mom: *"Being a doctor wasn't enough for him?"*

"So you want us to start herding cattle so you don't have to get married in a synagogue? I can see your father now—galloping on Little Joe Cartwright's horse, his toupee blowing in the wind."

"Very funny, Mom. You know what I'm saying."

I knew that Harvey was not going to go for any of her ideas, all of which would be laughable to him. But it was her wedding, ultimately her decision, so I went with the flow. "Do people get married in museums?"

"Yes."

"In art galleries?"

"Very popular."

"Christopher Kingston was just here. He owns the most beautiful gallery I have ever seen. I'll bet it holds 150 people."

"Mom, I'm not getting married in your friend's gallery. Besides, we want a destination wedding."

You're the new and improved Marcy, I reminded myself. *Shut up, and let her do what she wants. Get on with your life, not her life.*

"Honestly, I think you should get married wherever you want to get married. And whether it's on a cattle ranch or the Orient Express and one of us is murdered, it's fine with me."

"So, you'll talk to Dad?"

"No," I said. I didn't want to have to deal with Harvey.

"I was thinking about a resort in Kauai," she said.

"Hawaii?" What an insane idea. Had she gone nuts? Harvey would definitely put the kibosh on that one.

"Sounds nice, Amanda," I said. *Stop there. Don't say more.* On the other hand, maybe I could get my points across, help her see the light, if I remained more diplomatic than a UN envoy. "Hawaii might be too far, though, don't you think? It will take a long time to get there. What's more, airfare will be very expensive for your guests."

"Which would be great, because then a lot of people won't come."

"What did you say?" I asked.

My mother: *"She doesn't want people to come?"*

"Do you mean that you are inviting people, but you don't want them to come?"

"Just some people."

"Which some people?" I asked.

"There are people I have to invite, but I don't really want them to attend. If I hold the wedding in Hawaii, they won't come. On the other hand, someone like Dana would go to my wedding no matter where it was."

"Yes, Dana would, but Hawaii is a long and costly trip. I don't know how anyone from here could go there for less than a week. Her kids are busy. She might have to come alone."

"That's okay. I'm not inviting her family, just Calvin."

I was aghast. What was Amanda thinking? She had to be kidding. Dana's family was family. Dana's kids and my kids practically grew up together. What had happened to her heart?

"But we all went to Jeremy's wedding." Dana's son had married Moxie at a country club in Massachusetts, which was where Moxie was from.

"I—we—want a small wedding. It's bad enough that Dad wants to invite all of Bountiful and every person in the world who has ever sold a bra."

"Well, at least he doesn't want you to invite everyone who has ever worn a bra."

"Ha, Mom. Ha."

"Keep me in the loop," I said, practically feeling myself beg. "And if you decide to get married in a barn, muck it first."

It was one of those warm, clear April days I'd prayed for all winter. When I returned home from work, I went to the road to get my mail. Since bills for Harvey had been redirected to Five Swallows Inn, there were only magazines, catalogs, and advertisements in the box. *Your husband checks out, and even your postal experience changes.* I thought about the postman. I wondered what he thought was going on.

I started back down the driveway, thumbing through my pile until I landed on *AARP The Magazine.* I wished AARP would stop communicating with me. You turn fifty and get slammed on the head by an AARP card. And don't tell me about the discounts. I started requesting the senior discount at the movies when I hit forty-five, and sadly, no one ever questioned me about it.

Candy came up behind me.

"What are you doing here?" I asked. "Wait. Where's your car?"

"I walked here."

"You did?"

"It's only a few miles," Candy said.

"No one walks in Connecticut unless they have a dog or . . ."

"They're exercising."

"Are you exercising?" I said.

"No. I'm agonizing."

"Oh no. What did the doctor say about the results?"

"I have a tumor on the lining of my uterus," Candy let drop in one breath.

"Oh, damn," I said, moving my hand from my forehead to my chin. I held my chin only when things were really bad.

"Yes, damn."

I had to tell myself to stop shaking my head before I upset her even more.

"I can't believe this," she said. "Haven't I been through enough already?"

I wanted to ask if the tumor was malignant, but I couldn't get the m-word out of my mouth. I concentrated on the blacktop, the pavement. "I don't know what to say."

"Why don't you say, 'Is it malignant?'"

Because I refuse to release that word into the air, because I feel like it will spread.

"The answer is that I don't know."

"When will you know?" I asked, trying not to sound desperate.

"I have to wait for more tests to come back," she said.

"When does that happen?"

"Two weeks."

"We have to wait two weeks? How do they send the results? Pony Express?"

"You know who reads test results now?" she said. "People in India. Somewhere across the world, someone is deciding about me."

I imagined a man in India. He's at a screen all day, examining one tumor, then another. Swiping right for the next picture. He doesn't know Candy. He doesn't know a thing about her and what this could mean. He peers at an image of her uterus. He does it quickly because the day is almost done. He says it's not malignant, but it is. Or he says it's malignant, but it isn't. He goes home for dinner. His wife asks about his day. He says he's sick and tired of looking for tumors. He says that he is sorry he falsified his papers so he could practice as a radiologist.

"Come inside," I said. "We'll have a drink."

"No, I am just going to walk home. I might as well move my body while I still have a whole one."

"Stop. You'll be fine."

Why did everyone always say that? You'll be fine. About to be thrown off a cliff? Don't worry. You'll be fine.

"You're not walking home. I'll drive you," I said as though something treacherous would happen if she strolled through the bucolic Connecticut neighborhood, past the quiet houses with cedar play sets. "Let me give you a bottle of water."

"I'm not thirsty."

"Of course you're not. You're Candy."

She laughed and wiped a tear at the same time.

"You're not alone," I said. "I'm with you."

There's a saying: "Nothing is shorter than someone else's pregnancy." And nothing is longer than waiting for a diagnosis, cancer or no cancer.

Chapter 8

In May, Jake's parents hosted an engagement party in Wisconsin. It was for the Berger family and close friends, but we were invited as well.

I was in the airport in Connecticut, reading a book Jon had recommended, waiting for the plane. It was delayed. First, it was delayed in Charlotte. Then the crew was late. Lastly, the plane required a new part—which I preferred they took care of before I got in the air. I hit the Dunkin' Donuts outpost in the terminal.

I asked for a medium coffee and begged the server not to fill it to the top.

"No problem," she said. Then she passed me a brimming cup. As I opened the lid, I spilled some on my wrist.

I was wiping up the coffee with a napkin when I heard someone say to the server, "AARP. I get a free donut with a large cup of coffee, right?"

The voice was familiar. I looked up to my right and saw Feldman. His full name was Martin Feldman, but we always called him Feldman. He had started out as Harvey's accountant and eventually became his financial advisor. Harvey called him for everything—business and personal. When it came right down to it, he was Harvey's best friend.

Feldman was tall, looming over Harvey. Once, he'd told me he wore size fifteen AAA shoes. "Those aren't shoes," I'd said. "Those are skis." He bought conservative clothes at Brooks Brothers, which he referred to as Crooks Brothers. His wife was also tall. She smiled once, but her face cracked.

Although Feldman himself had amassed a fortune, it was his custom to take advantage of any freebie that might be around. He once told me it was because he had grown up in a tenement. I pointed out that there were no tenements in Kings Point, New York, and in fact, the great Gatsby had resided there.

"Marvelous Marcy," Feldman said.

I hated when he called me that. *Flatulent Feldman,* I thought.

"So how is Whitman, your new accountant?" he asked.

Parker Whitman was Candy's cousin. I had called him when I'd realized I had to protect my own interests. Then I'd fired Feldman and hired Whitman. It was a huge moment in my life. I hadn't felt so grown up since I got my period in seventh grade. I swear, the whole experience was like peeling off tight and sticky pantyhose after a tedious anniversary party in someone's shadeless backyard. Having had that experience too often, I understood why so many women no longer wore pantyhose—even when they were dressed up.

The Dunkin' Donuts girl handed Feldman his coffee and a French cruller.

"I love AARP," he said to me. "I remember turning fifty and receiving my card in the mail. What a milestone. I guess you're on your way to the engagement party."

"Yes. And where are you off to?"

"Doesn't anyone tell you anything? I'm going too. It was so nice of Amanda to invite me."

Amanda invited him? What happened to keeping it small? Keep it small except for the people Harvey insisted on? I had a feeling I was in a losing game, playing baseball without a mitt.

"You know, I like to feel that I had some impact on your life," Feldman continued.

Some impact? Feldman's financial advice was behind every decision Harvey made and was more than likely one of the reasons Harvey had not filed for divorce yet. And I was holding firm on Harvey owning the entire mess. I wasn't in control of much, but I was in control of that.

"There's the man," he said, pointing ahead.

I turned around to see Harvey topped off with his toupee. He was wearing a white Ralph Lauren polo shirt, but he had gained even more weight, and the little green polo horse was spreading. In fact, the green horse looked like it was having a foal.

Some time had gone by since I had last seen Harvey at Mad Maestro, after which we had run into Jon in the diner. I didn't know it was possible for a human being to blow up like a helium balloon in so little time, but apparently Harvey had pulled it off. The man was out of control. What had he been eating? Small countries?

Harvey brushed by Feldman and gave me a big hello.

"What a coincidence," he said, joking.

After all, it was a small airport, and we both were on our way to the same place. What's more, we traveled American regularly because Harvey was all about points. One year, he flew to London for the day just to maintain his Platinum status. He had flown from Connecticut to Chicago en route to Miami in order to pile up the miles.

Harvey asked the Dunkin' Donuts girl for a medium coffee with milk.

Feldman said, "Get a large. Say AARP, and we get a free donut."

"A large," Harvey said.

"AARP," Feldman chimed in.

"What kind of donut?"

Harvey told her chocolate frosted.

As she turned to get it, he whispered to me, "She's a 34D."

I had spent a lifetime listening to Harvey the Bra King guessing bra sizes. The worst of all had been when he sized up teachers during conferences at Atherton High—just the two of us, with the teacher behind her desk. Each time, I prayed the teacher would not be full-busted.

I wanted to walk away, so I said I was going to the restroom. I dropped by a newsstand for aspirin and a magazine to hide my head in.

Leaning against a wall, I called Jon.

"Where are you?" he asked.

"Waiting for the plane," I said. "I wish you were here."

"Ah, shucks," he said. "But I'm sure that once I meet Amanda, I will be at the wedding."

I could feel my anxiety rising. "That's months away," I said.

I hadn't spoken to Amanda about inviting Jon to anything. I wasn't ready for him to come to the engagement party. I didn't think he would be interested in schlepping to Wisconsin for the weekend anyway. I wasn't sure when or where the wedding would be, but I was certain that by then, Amanda and Elisabeth and Ben would know Jon, and he would be invited as my guest. Still, the idea of Jon meeting my children made me anxious. I wanted them to accept him.

"We could do the twist, maybe even the Macarena, at the wedding," he joked.

I imagined his boyish grin.

"You know the Macarena?"

"Of course. Isn't that the one that you dance to as the band plays 'Hava Nagila'?"

I laughed.

"What are you doing today?" I asked.

"Painting. I started early this morning."

I asked more questions. I didn't want to hang up.

When I arrived at the gate, my flight was boarding. The plane was full. I looked at my ticket. I was 10B, a damn middle seat. What lamebrain invented the middle seat? As I reached row 7, I saw Feldman in

10. He was by the window. Harvey was on the aisle. The middle seat was empty.

Now would be a good time to die.

I wondered whether I could be arrested as a terrorist suspect if I ran off the plane. How could a spell in Guantánamo be worse than sitting between Harvey and Feldman?

I stopped.

The attendant came toward me from the rear of the plane.

"There are people behind you," she said nicely. "You really have to sit down."

I can't sit down. Can I catch another plane? Or should I just spend the entire flight in the toilet?

Harvey looked up at me and beamed. He stood so I could pass.

"What a coincidence," he said. "I always hope to have a beautiful woman in the seat beside me."

Feldman laughed. "It's all because of me. I reserved the end and the window seats in the hope that the middle remained empty."

"Worked for me." Harvey grinned.

"There's no one like Marvelous Marcy," Feldman said.

I wanted to eject him from the plane without a parachute. Instead, I settled in and opened *People*. It used to be my bible. But now I didn't know *The Bachelor* from *The Bachelorette*. Feldman was fiddling with his iPad. Before takeoff, the attendant came by and asked him to stow it.

Talking over me to Harvey, he said, "It's nothing but malarkey. They claim an electronic device will interrupt airwaves, and the plane will blow up. But they've never proven it."

"Feldman, please put it away," I said.

"Marcy, nothing is going to happen."

"Stow it, Feldman, or I'm telling the attendant you're on an FBI watch list."

"Feldman," Harvey insisted, and his stubborn friend finally got the message.

Harvey leaned a bit toward me. He was already taking up a good part of my seat. "Marcy, would you mind raising the armrest? I could use some room."

I liked the armrest between us. I would've liked another airplane between us.

"I would rather not," I said, sticking my head in my magazine.

"First class was full on this plane, or I would be sitting there," Harvey said.

I thought if I raised the divider maybe he would leave me alone, so I did. Instantly, Harvey's body seemed to expand even more into my seat.

About forty-five minutes in, I put my chair back and pretended to sleep.

Harvey nudged me. "Do you want half of my sandwich?"

Feldman was leaning against the window, snoozing.

"I haven't been feeling well," Harvey said. "That donut is on its way down the chute."

Please don't share.

He gulped the diet soda the attendant had brought and asked her for another. He was thirsty due to diabetes.

In the old days, I would have been really worried about him. I'm a great worrier. The only reason I didn't make the US Olympic Worrier Team was that I was too worried about trying out.

Feldman was snoring. His snores were chortles.

"I hate the way he snores," Harvey said.

"He snores like someone is trying to kill him," I said.

Harvey laughed. "How do I snore?"

"Like you're choking on a porterhouse."

⌒⊚⌒

I would not want to be chased by a ravenous lion. But it would be better than seeing my mother-in-law in the lobby of the hotel. I knew

Amanda had invited Harvey's mother, Florence, to the party, but that was only because Harvey had insisted, and Amanda had assumed she wouldn't come.

Florence lived in Arizona. When I first became serious with Harvey, he told me straight out that she was a bitch. I thought that was a little harsh, but as I got to know her, I realized that it had been very gracious of him to say.

The first time I met her, she was visiting New York. We had arrived at her hotel to join her for brunch at the appointed hour. Harvey called her room. She insisted that we come up. It was a huge deal to meet his mother, and I wasn't crazy about doing it in her hotel room, but Harvey had pulled me along.

Harvey introduced me. I put out my hand, but she ignored it. Instead, she scanned the floor, where dress shoes, from patent leathers to rhinestone sandals, were scattered around. "Thank heaven you're here," she had said. "I need you to put away my shoes."

Speechless, I placed the shoes in the boxes that were strewn on the bed. As I did so, Harvey took a seat in an armchair, answering his mother's questions about the business.

"You missed those pumps," she said, pointing. "And don't forget to stack the shoeboxes in the closet."

Did you want that alphabetically by the name of the manufacturer?

When I spotted her in Wisconsin, I knew she hadn't seen me, so I slipped into an alcove. Then she turned toward me and raised her sunglasses. Florence had undergone so many face-lifts, her chin was somewhere over her forehead. From years of tanning in Arizona, her face was rawhide. The woman was as cold as an iceberg but looked like burned toast.

Seeing me, she smirked, then did a little hand wave, as though her wrist were broken.

She approached in her flouncy floral dress. Her hairstyle, a severe bob, hadn't changed since that first day with the shoes. She was wielding a silver cane. "Marcy, a hello would be in order."

"Hello, Florence," I said. All I needed to do to even the score for years of unkindness was call her Flo. She detested the name Flo.

"I'll bet you're surprised, and delighted, that I decided to attend."

"Well, it is a big trip for you," I said, attempting to be cordial.

"I came to see you."

She did? What now?

She tapped her cane. "I hear you've decided to leave Harvey."

I took a step back. "That's not exactly how it happened, *Flo*."

Flo, Flo, Flo.

"I assume you understand that you will not receive a cent from the Bosom."

She'd always called the company "the Bosom." It drove Harvey nuts.

"After all, my grandmother started the company back when I believe your ancestors were praying they would not be rejected at Ellis Island."

Nice, I thought.

Ben and his partner, Jordan, approached. Ben was good looking, and not just because he was my son. He stood six foot two, with curly brown hair, and he was born with a beauty mark above his lip. Recently, he had ditched his glasses for contact lenses. Jordan was midheight, toned, with a large, handsome face and dark saucer eyes. He wore his brown hair in a ponytail. I could easily imagine the logo from *GQ* above his head.

Although Harvey had told Florence that Ben was gay, she had never accepted it. When she asked how Ben was, she always asked if he had met a woman yet. After a while, Harvey had stopped correcting her.

"Grandma," Ben said, no hug, no kiss. "This is Jordan."

"Jordan?"

"Jordan is my partner."

"When did you start a business?"

"Not that kind of partner," I said.

She looked askance. Ben shook his head. Jordan was about to say something, but Ben shook his head again.

"Did you bring a date, Ben?" she asked.

There we go—over the top.

"Jordan *is* my date," Ben said strongly.

Florence looked up at the ceiling. "It's so difficult to hear in this lobby."

"Hear this," Ben said. "I am a homosexual."

"That means he likes men," I said.

Florence closed her eyes as though if she couldn't see, she couldn't hear.

The next person I marry will be an orphan.

⁓

The event was an open house, come anytime after five in the afternoon. I had no interest in sharing a ride with Harvey, Florence, and Feldman. Elisabeth, Ben, and Jordan had spent the day at the Berger home, bonding with Jake's friends. I hailed a cab.

The Berger residence was on a quiet, curved, tree-lined street with identical homes: pleasant, broad split-levels made of brick. There were many midsize dark cars parked in the double driveway, and more on the paved road.

As I stepped out of the cab, I pondered how dejected and lonely I felt arriving at my daughter's engagement party by myself. That's not easy when you've been married almost your entire adult life. Flashing before me were events I had gone to with Harvey—parties for newborns, bar mitzvahs, graduations, weddings. I used to feel frustrated and disappointed, because I would be ready to go on time, but he always came home from work on his own schedule. He would have to change his clothes. We would be late. It turns out waiting and being way tardy is better than going alone.

I wiped a tear from my eye, arched my back, planted a smile on my face, and knocked. No one came to answer the door, so I assumed no one could hear me. I opened the door to the sounds of music and laughter and walked in. There was a foyer with a coat closet and shoes on the floor. I removed my heels and stood in my stockings. I put my shoes back on and decided I would wait until someone told me to take them off. I searched the overstuffed closet for a hanger and hung up my belted spring coat in the far back so I would remember where it was.

I worked my way down the crowded hall, which was decorated with framed pictures of my future son-in-law growing up. Apparently, he had played all kinds of sports. He had a ball of some kind in his hand in almost every photograph. I hadn't thought of him as athletic. This was good. He could teach my future grandkids how to play sports.

A woman in her eighties stopped me.

"You have to be Amanda's mother. You just have to be."

"I am," I said with a smile, relieved someone had approached me. "I just got here."

"I'm Great Aunt Rose," she said brightly, cupping my hands in her palms. "I love your daughter. I just love your daughter. Oh, and she is so accomplished. And smart! I can tell that she was in line first when they were giving out brains."

"Thank you," I said. "I like her too."

"So do you think they'll have children right away?"

Let's get through the wedding first, I thought.

"Have you seen Amanda?" I said, ignoring the question about my daughter's reproductive plans.

"Yes, she's in the living room, unwrapping gifts. They got right to it. I know she registered, but I had to get her something thoughtful."

"What was that?" I asked.

As she whispered, her eyes sparkled. "I embroidered a cover for her Kleenex box."

"Wonderful," I said graciously. "Amanda sneezes a lot."

She smiled at me, pointing ahead. I walked through an archway to see the Berger family, neighbors, and friends on two deep sofas, some armchairs, and many metal folding chairs. Some were standing.

At the far end of the room, which was painted cornflower blue, there was a white brick fireplace with a mantel. On the slate mantel were tchotchkes, little things that my mother used to refer to as "dust collectors." Mug had probably stolen them. Every single one would have fit in a pocket.

Amanda was seated on a tall striped dining room chair, piles of gifts in front of her. Her hair was up in a ponytail. She was dressed casually in cream slacks and a matching shirt. Jake was beside her, unwrapping gifts. Elisabeth, Florence, and Feldman were on low chairs. Of course, Harvey was on the Bergers' fat recliner. Ben and Jordan were standing, looking on and making remarks to one another.

I waved to Amanda from the back of the living room.

"Everyone, my mother's here!" she said loudly.

There was silence as the guests turned to see me.

"All the way from Connecticut," Amanda added.

"A round of applause for Connecticut!" a stocky man yelled out.

I took a bow in response to the warm welcome. My family led the clapping.

"We're all happy you're here," a woman said.

"Three cheers," the man next to her added. He looked like her, so I knew he was her husband, because if you live with someone long enough, you look like him, even if you started out looking entirely different. I think it's the same with people and their dogs. If I ever had a dog, he would look worried.

Amanda returned to business. "This lovely wooden laundry rack is from Mug and Bernie," Amanda announced, chirpier than I had ever seen her, clearly wanting to endear herself. "And look, it folds just like an accordion."

She demonstrated.

Okay, so she is going overboard.

Elisabeth maneuvered her way around the guests and came to sit with me.

"Quite the gift," she said quietly.

I touched her knee. "I'll buy one for you when *you* get engaged."

"I did meet someone, but sadly, he dry-cleans everything."

"Underwear?"

"Well starched." Elisabeth laughed.

"Where did you meet?"

"At a conference," she said.

"Is this serious? Do I need to plan another wedding?"

"Are you kidding? After participating in this circus, I intend to elope."

That would be fine. Just invite me.

As Amanda opened gifts, I looked around the living room. Above the upright piano, the Ten Commandments were posted. I guessed Mug hadn't read the eighth one, "Thou shalt not steal." Then again, Harvey skipped the seventh, "Thou shalt not commit adultery." I wasn't merely casting stones. When did I last "honor the Sabbath"?

I went into the kitchen for a drink. Mug came in. She was wearing a boxy knit dress, navy with piping at the round collar, which I bet was from Talbots. To me, Mug looked about a size ten, but in Talbots she was probably an eight. Everything in there ran larger than in other stores. Buying a smaller size made customers feel good. I felt best at the Gap. At the Gap, I wore medium. My daughters wore small. It was good to know that on a bad day, if the supermarket wasn't cheering me up, I could fall into the Gap.

Mug hugged me.

I would have to grow accustomed to that.

I gave her a squeeze, clutching my purse, in fear for my wallet.

"Have you spoken to the kids?" Mug asked.

"About?"

"They want a band."

I had no idea why she was bringing up music when there was still no venue.

"Those bands are so loud. You can't hear yourself think."

I wanted to be friendly, but I didn't want to discuss the wedding. Talking about the wedding with her while the kids weren't there could lead only to misunderstandings. I diverted.

"Do you have anything cold to drink?" I asked.

She poured iced tea into a tumbler and gave it to me.

"I love those pictures of Jake growing up," I said.

"A DJ is good enough. Right?"

Okay, I give up. "The kids should have whatever they want."

She looked at me, annoyed.

I had no idea what I had said that was wrong.

"Whatever they want? Is that how you brought up your daughter? She gets whatever she wants?" Mug was still holding the tea pitcher, and she put it down hard.

Stay calm, Marcy. Bite your lip if you have to.

She became coarser, waving a finger. "My friend Rosemary told me that the groom's parents are responsible for the music."

I had never heard of that. I would have to consult Emily Post as to who paid for what. Not that it mattered. I knew Harvey. Amanda was his daughter, and he was as old-fashioned as he was generous. Harvey would shell out for the whole shebang, hoping that the in-laws would give a substantial gift to the kids. *Not happening here, Harvey.*

"A band is three times more expensive than a DJ."

Her estimate was low.

"I am not paying for a band."

Maybe the inside of her wallet had never seen daylight, but there was also a chance she just couldn't afford to help with the wedding. I decided to put her at ease. "Look, Mug. If the kids want a band, we'll pay for it."

"What about the rehearsal dinner?"

Since when did Jews rehearse?

"Really, there's no problem, Mug. I understand. I have the message."

She picked up the pitcher. "More tea?"

Do I have to pay for it?

I would do just about anything to get through this wedding in peace.

Minutes later, I was standing to the side by myself, eating fruit salad. Florence approached, her cane tapping up to me. Now what did she want?

"Marcy." She said my name like it was roll call in the Army.

"Yes, Florence."

She pursed her lips.

Just spit it out, I thought.

"I can't fathom it. I can't believe you are letting Amanda do this."

"Do what, Flo?"

"Marry a man whose mother gives her a laundry rack."

Chapter 9

The Library was a restaurant that had been an actual library until Atherton built a new one. There were books on shelves. The flowers on each table were made of printed pages. The place mats were laminated book covers. Each menu was in a Dewey decimal drawer. Mustard-colored tabs separated the small plates, salads, entrées, and desserts. I did not like small plates. I did not want a lamb lollipop. I wanted a lamb chop. One sea scallop on a dish does not look delicious—it just looks lonely.

Dana always picked the Library when it was her turn to choose a restaurant. I met her there, and when we were seated, she didn't wait for a menu. "Let's order the Tuscan salad," she said.

The Tuscan salad was amazing—roasted garlic cloves, olives, mozzarella balls, moist polenta croutons, ripe grape tomatoes, lettuce, and imported balsamic vinaigrette. Sounds simple, I know. But if the regular sous chef was off for a day, I could actually tell by the salad.

"We've built a friendship on this salad," I said to Dana.

"How many do you think we've eaten?"

"I don't know, but it's the only time we ever eat the same thing anymore."

Since becoming a grandmother, Dana had changed. She was obsessed with looking young. She no longer depended on her fast metabolism to do its work, and she had become fanatical about her weight. She'd sooner touch a hot industrial iron than a chocolate brownie. I missed the old Dana, the Dana who consoled me with party-size bags of chips. Friendship has limits. If she gave up alcohol, we were through.

When we met, I never knew which diet she would be on. On one of her plans, you could eat all the carbohydrates you wanted—for an hour a day. Dana ate some pasta. Then she puffed away on a cigarette. If I had sixty minutes to eat carbs, I'd pull up a stool at Sweet Heaven Bakery.

"I have news," I said. "Elisabeth is seeing someone new."

"Serious?"

"She just met him, I think. She said that if she ever does tie the knot, she's going to elope."

"Good thing, Marcy. You'll need years to recover from Amanda's wedding. If you think breaking up with your husband was a blood-sucking misery, wait until you live through marrying off one of your children."

"Jake's mother pulled me aside at the engagement party to tell me she was not paying for a band."

"She's not paying for anything. I know Harvey. He'll pick up the whole tab."

"She doesn't know Harvey. She doesn't know me."

"Well, get ready. You're about to spend every Thanksgiving with her."

"It's like I just went into business with someone I don't even know."

She nodded. She'd been through it all when Jeremy got married. She understood.

"How is Wolfgang?" I asked.

"Wolfgang," she repeated, clearly unhappy with her grandson's name.

"You got to name your children. Now they get to name theirs."

"I hate the way that works," she said as she moved the bread away from her and closer to me. "In any case, I hardly see him. He's three months old, and I've seen him three times."

"Do you ask to watch him?"

She shook her head. "I'm not changing diapers."

"Maybe Jeremy can bring him over when he's constipated."

A waitress in an apron with the cover of *The Old Man and the Sea* asked for our orders. Dana asked for her salad without dressing.

"Who are you kidding?" I asked. "The polenta croutons alone are hundreds of calories."

"Give her my polenta," she said to the waitress.

"Why don't I help you babysit?" I asked, thinking it might be fun.

"You would do that?" She was astounded, as though she'd met me yesterday.

"Sure, why not? You babysat Harvey's parrot when I was trying to unload it."

"Calvin is visiting his mother this weekend, but Jeremy and Moxie are coming to visit anyway. I'll offer to watch Wolfgang on Saturday."

"Great."

Dana clapped. "If I was next to you, I'd knock your shoulder."

"I know you would."

❦

On Saturday night, in my loosest jeans and a flannel shirt, I went to Dana's to babysit. Jeremy greeted me with a big hello. He seemed older than I remembered him, but then again, I had a permanent picture of him in my mind.

In it, Jeremy was sixteen. He had a mop of blond hair covering his eyes, a cutie-pie face. He had mentioned that he was looking for a job, any odd job, so I had said he could paint our guest room, which really didn't need paint. It took a week for Jeremy to finish, during which time I had provided well-balanced lunches, snacks, lemonade, and conversation. After Jeremy left, I had to call Paint Guy to repaint it.

As Jeremy took my coat, Moxie appeared. Since I had seen her last, at Wolfgang's christening, she had colored her yellow hair to a deep chestnut. For this reason, she looked whiter and pastier than ever. I figured she weighed about fifty-three pounds when she got on the scale with a fifty-pound weight in her hand.

Out of Dana's earshot, Moxie said, "If Dana diapers the baby on the wrong end, be sure he can breathe through his mouth."

Ordinarily, I might have laughed at this—but no way, not at Dana's expense. "She has three kids of her own."

"Jeremy says she was never home."

The girl certainly knew how to irritate me.

I waved her off. "She worked hard. She was a single mom."

"Between marriages."

Put a plug in it. Why don't you walk a mile in Dana's stilettos—bring up three kids and put them through college—before you call in the jury? "Don't worry. I won't let him crawl out to the highway. And neither will she."

"That's only because he doesn't crawl yet," Moxie said, deadpan.

"You know, Moxie, it means a lot to Dana to watch your son."

"Do you want to know the truth?"

Never say you want to know the truth. The truth hurts. And if it isn't painful, it's plain insulting. Think about it. Has anyone ever said, "Do you want to know the truth?" before confiding that you could have made it as a supermodel?

"I am taking a chance. I'm taking a chance that my family won't get lung cancer from Dana's secondhand smoke."

"She would never, ever smoke while watching your son."

"I'll tell Mom you're here," Jeremy said to me when he returned from the hall.

The portable crib was parked in the center of Dana's great room. The room was the epitome of comfort, with a taupe sectional, patterned pillows on the floor, a potbelly stove in the corner, and a sixty-inch flat-screen on the wide wall.

Wolfgang was in the crib, on his back, asleep in blue, one-piece footed pajamas. The mattress was covered with a Winnie the Pooh sheet. No blanket. Not one stuffed animal.

The house seemed a little cold to me. "Is there a blanket for Wolfgang?"

"We don't believe in blankets," Moxie replied.

"Is that a religious thing?"

"A baby can get caught in a blanket."

"My kids always had blankets," I said.

"They could have suffocated, Marcy."

"All three were at your wedding, so I guess they survived."

Jeremy came into the room, then Dana. She was wearing her go-to clothing—a billowy silk blouse, a wide belt, jeans, and stilettos. It was an outfit that said, "Baby? What baby? I don't see a baby."

"The movie is two hours, an hour for dinner. We'll be back by eleven o'clock," Moxie said, checking her watch.

"What about feeding?" Dana asked.

Moxie looked at me. "I'm unable to breastfeed," she whispered.

I decided to reassure her. "I gave my kids formula. Although I admit, I had to change the brand every time Ben got the runs. And he only got the runs when I had just bought a case of the new formula."

Moxie shook her head. "There's a bottle of someone else's breast milk in the fridge."

"Someone else's milk?" Dana said. I was curious too.

"I purchase milk from another mother."

"What?" Dana said.

"How do you know it's good?" I asked.

"She went to MIT," Moxie replied. "I pay extra for that."

"So, if the baby cries, give him the milk?" Dana said.

"Oh, no, I feed on schedule," Moxie said, removing her phone from her jeans. "See, here's my breastfeeding app."

I had never heard of such a thing. She had an app that told her when to feed her baby? I was lost in the Stone Age. I hated not knowing about that app. What else didn't I know about? Maybe someone had invented an app that would exercise for me.

"But what if he's crying before the app goes off?" Dana asked.

"We feed only on schedule."

Jeremy handed Moxie a coat. He was clearly in a hurry to leave.

"But what if he keeps crying?" Dana asked, not understanding.

"We don't want to spoil him."

"But he's just a few months old," Dana said.

Jeremy pulled Moxie's hand. "Okay, let's hit the road."

When they were gone, Dana rolled her eyes halfway to Europe.

"Now do you get it? I don't know if it's her or her whole generation. Rules, rules, rules. Moxie should have seen me—drinking and smoking— while pregnant with Jeremy. She never would have married him."

"I didn't drink, and I didn't smoke," I said.

"Another person who thinks I'm a lousy mother."

"No one thinks you're a lousy mother. Jeremy is great. The twins are in college."

"And take a look at your crew. Elisabeth is a doctor. Amanda, the retail genius, is getting married. Ben is in law school."

"We did a good job," I said. "But when did everyone grow up?"

Dana knocked my shoulder. "Let's watch a movie. I have diet popcorn."

"You mean cardboard popcorn."

"I am not going to be a fat grandma. Ugh. That word."

"'Fat'?"

"'Grandma.' What about *The Big Chill*?"

That movie was one of my favorites. It's about a reunion of college friends. I had seen *The Big Chill* more times than I'd seen my own face.

"Great," I said.

Dana ordered the film.

The movie title rolled. Wolfgang cried. Dana didn't budge except to put popcorn in her mouth.

I picked up the baby. He cried louder.

Dana said, "I can't hear the movie."

I thought she was going to come over and comfort the baby, but all she did was reach for the remote to turn up the sound. This from the woman who had wanted to babysit, complaining about how infrequently she'd seen Wolfgang.

"We've seen this movie so many times we could recite it. Go get a bottle," I said.

"Maybe it's just gas," Dana said. "There's a lot of gas in my family. My father once got thrown out of a bar for farting."

"Oh, of course," I said.

"No, it's true. He pointed to my mother and said, 'It was her.'"

"Get a bottle," I repeated, shaking my head in disdain.

Finally, she left to get the bottle. When she returned, she handed it to me, and I held it to Wolfgang's mouth. He wouldn't take it.

"Why didn't he screech when his mother was here?" Dana said.

"Because then his mother was here."

I rocked Wolfgang and passed him to Dana.

She touched his bottom, and then held her hand out. "I think he's wet."

"So change his diaper."

"That's why I invited you," she said.

I put a long towel on a counter to put the baby on. I opened the diaper, and the baby squirted me—bingo—in the face.

Dana started laughing. "That's my grandson."

I held the infant's legs with one hand and wiped my cheek. "That's right. This is your grandchild. You change the diaper."

Standing by as Dana struggled with the diaper, I noticed that the baby had a scarlet rash on his bottom. "There's the culprit," I said. "Look at that rash. It's on fire."

"I have some Vaseline," she said.

"Ointment would be better. Look in the diaper bag."

After I basted Wolfgang's cute little butt, Dana placed him back in the crib. I picked up a stuffed koala and a rubber giraffe, stationing both near his chest. He quickly tired of shrieking and fell asleep. Dana and I nodded at each other, proud of our job well done, and returned to the movie, both of us sitting on the couch.

"I have been thinking about something," I said.

"Can you think about it after the movie?"

"Do you think I am doing the right thing waiting for Harvey to file for divorce?"

She turned toward me. "Is he still paying the bills?"

"Generously," I said.

"So, why bother?"

"Why bother? Why did you file for divorce?"

"I divorced my first husband because I was bored by him."

"And the second one?"

"He was bored by me."

"No one can be bored by you," I said.

"That's true." She tossed a kernel at me.

"But I'm seeing Jon," I said.

"Does he care that you aren't divorced yet?"

"He's never said anything."

She shifted her eyes to the ceiling, shaking her head. "Then let sleeping dogs lie. And you have to admit, Harvey is a dog."

"What about the house?" I said.

"Marcy, I told you to stay where you are for now. But if you want me to tell you to pack up, I will."

"No. I want an honest opinion." As though there were anything else I would get from Dana. "How did this happen? Me. Separated from Harvey, restarting my life as Amanda is about to get married, and you, a grandmother? When my mother was our age, Harvey insisted she needed long-term care insurance."

"That whole generation was old."

"And what about us?"

"We're young, but our kids think we're old."

"And what about our kids?"

"An entire generation of self-involved brats who think they're entitled to everything, because we convinced them they were."

I laughed. We both forgot about the movie.

"By the way," Dana said, "I am trying to stop smoking."

"That's great, Dana."

"This is my first day," she said.

"Why today?"

"Because Wolfgang was coming, and I know Moxie doesn't want me to smoke when he is in my house. I'm dying for a cigarette. I puffed on a pencil this morning. But I know they hate my smoking."

"They *are* right about that. But in general, you know what I would do in your situation? I'd smile."

She looked at me quizzically.

"If the baby fusses and screams and won't take a nap, don't complain. If your new silk, full-retail blouse is stained by regurgitated breast milk—bought from a Phi Beta Kappa—tell Moxie what a joy it is to babysit. Dana, you're in advertising. Spin the story."

"I brought up three kids. But it's different being a grandmother. You just can't afford, can't tolerate, one thing going wrong."

"How was he?" Moxie asked as soon as she came through the door. Jeremy had his hands in his pockets, waiting to hear.

"Sleeping," we said from the couch in unison.

Moxie went to the crib.

"There are stuffed animals in here!" Moxie said, turning to Jeremy. "The crib has to be empty. If the giraffe wound up anywhere near his mouth, he could suffocate. And that bear. I don't believe it."

All right. So the girl is nuts.

"Mom?" Jeremy said, condemning Dana.

"Don't say a word to them, Marcy. It's a waste of time," Dana said as she left the room. I threw up my hands. Had she not heard a single line of my pep talk? Smile. Don't complain. Tell them what a joy it is.

Moxie lifted the baby out of the crib. Immediately, he cried. She stuffed him in a hoodie and hurried out of Dana's house. Jeremy picked up the diaper bag.

Before he left, he turned to me. "Tell Mom I said good-bye."

"Jeremy," I said from the couch.

"Yes?"

"Your mother and I raised six amazing human beings."

"I know, but Moxie is not like other mothers. She worries."

Chapter 10

Most Sunday mornings, Jon and I strolled through the endless farmers' market on the picturesque town green in Atherton. Facing the green, there was a white colonial-style church with a red door and a steeple. There were elegant, stalwart homes, the kind that the leaf peepers marveled at in autumn while wondering who was fortunate enough to live in Atherton. A few homes had historic plaques, but my favorite was the white house with gables that was shaped like a birthday cake. Before we were together, Jon had painted a picture of it, and he had the painting in his apartment. I hoped he would give it to me to hang in the yellow house, but I didn't tell him that.

In addition to local farmers, the outdoor market hosted crafters, and we knew quite a few of them from the Guild. There were also many young families, none of whom we knew; lots of toddlers waiting to have their faces painted; teenagers in jeans hanging in groups; and a middle-aged woman here or there interested in quilts. Some local organizations had information booths; others sold homemade cookies, coffee, and hot cocoa. The volunteer firemen gave kiddie rides in a fire truck.

Jon and I had a thing—we always wore jeans and plaid flannel shirts and Frye boots to the market. On cool days, we layered. If the weather demanded coats, we threw on old denim jackets. Always, I pushed my hair into a ponytail with two barrettes on the sides. Jon wore a straw hat and chewed on a piece of hay he found at the market. Let's just say we went into it 100 percent.

We selected ugly vegetables, because we didn't want all the ugly vegetables to feel bad. I thought this was original of us until Jon pointed out that he had ordered ugly vegetables for years. Jon was holding an eggplant that looked like it had dysentery. He was about to put it in my basket, which contained crooked carrots and other sad misfits.

"That one might be overdoing it," I said.

"You're hurting his feelings," Jon said, holding it up and looking it over. "On the other hand, maybe you're right." He put the eggplant back into the farmer's bin. "I'll go and get something for us to drink," he said, and then he headed toward the booth selling cider.

As I stood alone, my phone rang.

"We need to talk," Harvey said in a voice way too bossy, condescending, and annoying. His command made me want to hang up, but I figured he was calling about the wedding. I was hoping he wanted us to get on the same page. This would be best for Amanda, and also beneficial to me, because if Harvey was laying down the same law, it would be tougher for Amanda to blame me for everything she thought was a major injustice, the last outrage being that I had—oh no—asked for pictures of each table to ensure that there were photographs of everyone who attended.

"No one takes table pictures anymore," she had retorted.

"I was at a wedding last year, and they took table pictures," I had said. "In fact, I purposefully stood next to an overweight woman so that I would appear thinner."

"Did it work?"

"My shoulders looked narrow."

"Mom, there will be no table pictures. I will give the photographer headshots of the people who must be in pictures, and he will refer to those while shooting."

I had imagined the photographer looking down at his cheat sheet, searching for the people Amanda wanted pictures of.

"Okay," I said to Harvey. "I can be at Starbucks after work. About six?"

"How about the house?"

I was uncomfortable about meeting at the house, wary that Harvey would become too cozy. Apparently, he heard my thoughts in my silence.

"Marcy, don't be ridiculous. I just want to talk in private."

I could do this for Amanda. It wasn't easy for her to go through a wedding with separated parents. Or to go through anything with separated parents. I tried to think of one thing that had not been bad about this for my children. Could it be that it had drawn them closer to each other? I only wished.

"Fine. The house on Wednesday at seven is fine. But don't ask me for a cup of coffee. I will never make you a cup of coffee again. In fact, not making you a cup of coffee is my best life goal."

"I got it," he said. "What about tea?"

I laughed to myself. Then I said, "That's not funny, Harvey."

⌒୭

I was bothered by what had happened at Dana's, how Moxie had thought we had been delinquent about watching Wolfgang, so I called her to apologize. Moxie thanked me, and I could have left it at that, but instead I decided to put in a good word for my friend.

"Don't be hard on Dana," I said. "She took excellent care of the baby. I'm the one who put the animals in the crib."

"That's the least of it. You were watching an R-rated movie."

"Don't worry. We're over seventeen."

"We don't watch R-rated movies in front of the baby. *The Big Chill* has suicide, pot, and sex. Doesn't that single friend sleep with Kevin Kline?"

Moxie was nuts. What was worse, she had no sense of humor. So in the great daughter-in-law raffle, Dana had gotten the booby prize. Worse yet, there was no way she could ever get along with Moxie. Jeremy had married his antimother.

"You know Dana and I have never gotten along," Moxie said. "She poked fun at me, because I wanted the cocktail hour at the wedding to be forty-five minutes. She said I was classless, because she insisted on top-shelf liquor, and all I wanted was beer and some wine."

I couldn't imagine that Dana had said this directly to Moxie. "She said that to you?"

"No, she said it to Jeremy. He told me."

Thanks, Jeremy.

"When she visits, she always brings some huge, useless thing we don't need and don't have room for. One time, she gave us a painting some friend of hers had made. She acted like it was from the Museum of Modern Art. It was dreadful, an old fishing pier in Maine."

I knew the painting. It was by Jon. Dana had bought it from him at one of his shows. She said it was a gift for Jeremy. Now this was getting personal.

⟡

I had had enough of being Henry Kissinger and Madeleine Albright rolled into one. I was going to keep my mind on my work. The following day, a Monday, the best day to start a new habit, I was at my desk, filling out a grant application for the Guild. Around noon, Cheyenne announced she was going to McDonald's. She asked me if I wanted anything. I told her a small order of gout and clogged arteries. She returned with a Big Mac. When she came into my office to deliver it, she asked if I wanted to see what she had done so far on Facebook. I told her I would after lunch.

I ate my Big Mac alone in my office. Afterward, Cheyenne and I went into a room with a conference table. I sat next to her, looking at her laptop. She had done a lot in a short time, and I was happy.

"Do you want to have fun?" she said.

"Fun is my middle name," I said sarcastically. "Marcy Fun Hammer."

"Let's look up one of your old boyfriends."

I wasn't particularly interested in this. I shook my head.

"Oh, come on. People do it all the time."

"I don't need to look up an old boyfriend. I have a new boyfriend," I said with a thousand-watt smile on my face.

"You do?"

"Yes. And he's really great."

"That's good! I want to hear all about him, but let's look up the old guy anyway."

Cheyenne pulled the laptop closer. If only I had been like her, so direct, always going and doing just what I had in mind. I told her how I admired this.

"I'm a millennial," she said.

"Are you saying your entire generation is like this?" I asked.

"Not the losers." She took off her lime-green sweater, a sweater that matched the lime-green streak she had put in her jet-black hair. "Okay, just tell me the name of your college boyfriend."

"He dumped me," I said, as though it had happened yesterday.

"So when was that? During the French Revolution?"

"The Crusades," I said.

"Was he your first?" Cheyenne said, her eyes almost twinkling.

Taken by the moment, I did something dumber than a dinosaur's brain. I answered yes.

"How old were you?"

"Eighteen."

"You didn't have sex until you were eighteen?"

Had I lost my virginity too late in life? There was nothing I could do about it now. Except change the subject. But first, I had to defend myself by giving Cheyenne a history lesson. "Girls waited to have sex back then."

"No, that was the time of the sexual revolution."

"Not in Queens," I said.

She glanced up at me. "Let's find him."

"Oh, okay. Michael Goldfarb," I said. "Michael A. Goldfarb, if I remember correctly."

For a moment, I felt younger than the youngest millennial. "So, what if he answers? What will you write?"

"'Remember when we banged in college?'"

"That's a joke," I said.

"True, but let's look him up."

She typed, and then there he was—salt-and-pepper hair, silver glasses. I had long ago forgotten about the distracting brown mole on the side of his nose. I couldn't believe that by now there wasn't a way to remove that thing.

Facebook informed me that Michael had become a world-renowned photographer who specialized in animals of Africa. We watched his video of an elephant giving birth—first the sac, then the whole baby plummeting out all at once in a flood of amniotic fluid. Nice elephant, but where was Michael's wife? No wife? What about kids? So, what, if I had married him, I would be childless? And where would I have been while he was in Africa with the wildlife and his wild life?

Cheyenne was prodding me to send a friend request, but instead, I thought about Jon and how I was wasting my time with this non-sense. Who cared what had happened to Michael the grade-A loser, who pissed me off so bad that I wanted to knock his new girlfriend over the head with her guitar? Or that I had to go to the counseling office just so they could tell me I was suffering from "serious lack of boyfriend"? And it got worse. I was so depressed that my mother wanted to pull me out of school and take me home for the semester. Amazingly, I cheered up the moment she mentioned this idea.

I should've been thanking the heavens that I didn't have to troll Facebook and the rest of the World Wide Web for men. Badbatch.com. I had hit the good-guy jackpot. I was holding a four-leaf clover in a field of wilting weeds. I was fortunate to know Jon and start a relationship with him. He was my man for all reasons. I looked forward to seeing his blue eyes, his blond stubble, and his ponytail. I loved that his apartment was filled with books and paint and brushes and art, and that he had a canoe he built in his living room. I adored his sexy scrambled eggs and that he actually knew where to find a fuse box. I liked the way he smiled—and every kiss, from the first one in my house.

I shut the laptop and pushed out my chair.

"Party is over," I said to Cheyenne. "Let's get back to work."

Chapter 11

I had just gotten several days' worth of dishes out of the sink and loaded begrudgingly into the machine. I threw in detergent and pressed "Start," but it wouldn't go on. I revisited the problem two days later. The dishwasher was dead, but the rancid odor had taken on a life of its own.

I rang up Dishwasher Guy, who said he could be there at four the next day. I left work early, annoyed that I had to do so. I parked myself in my kitchen and waited. Four turned to five and then turned to six.

I had given up, aggravated, when he called. "Sorry to be late, but I can be there in half an hour."

"In half an hour" was exactly when Candy had planned to drop by. She wanted to go out for a glass of wine. When she came in, I told her we had to wait for Dishwasher Guy.

"They are always late," she said. "If they show up at all."

I uncorked a bottle of Pinot Noir. I lost track of time, but I could measure it in bottles. We were on our second when I heard a knock at the door.

Dishwasher Guy was handsome. He had a square jaw like Superman and short brown hair. He was wearing a red-and-black checked shirt and jeans. Not daddy jeans. I could easily imagine what came between him and his Calvins. I guessed he was in his thirties.

"My name is Evan," he said. "Do you want me to remove my boots?" I looked down at his buffed mustard-colored work boots, the laces at the top tied perfectly. "Because of the carpets and all."

"Oh, you should definitely remove your shoes," Candy said. And as he bent over, she pointed behind his back to his rear end.

"So let's see that dishwasher," Evan said.

I poured more wine. Candy watched from behind as Evan tooled about.

"I have binoculars," I whispered to her.

Evan's head was in the dishwasher when she said, "Evan, how about a glass of wine?"

"Sure, it's been a long day. Why not?" he said as he stopped looking at my dishwasher and concentrated on Candy.

I couldn't believe she was offering him a drink when he had been hours late, and all I had wanted to do was get my dishwasher fixed so we could go out.

"Marcy, do you have another glass?" she asked.

"No," I said, glaring at her. "They're all dirty because my dishwasher is busted, remember?" I pounced on the word "remember."

She went to a cabinet and found a goblet.

"How old is this machine?" Evan said.

"I'm not sure."

Evan disconnected the dishwasher, moved it, and turned the thing inside out and upside down.

"Too bad," he said. "Because this is a big problem."

"How big?" Candy asked, raising an eyebrow.

Shut up and let the guy repair my dishwasher.

"Big," Evan said.

He joined us at the table, took out a calculator, and typed in some numbers.

Candy filled his goblet.

He rubbed his big knuckles back and forth over his lips.

"Jeez, my lip is cracked," he said.

Candy said, "Have you tried vitamin E?"

"Vitamin E?"

"I have some if you want it," she said, reaching for her bag.

"Sure."

"I bought it just in case I met a handsome repair guy with a chapped lip."

Please tell me she is not going to smear it on his lips.

"Thanks," he said as she handed him the tiny tube.

Candy had had enough to drink. I corked the bottle and put it in the fridge.

"I have to go out to the truck to get a part."

"We'll be waiting," Candy said. "Don't be long."

"You've got to be kidding," I said when Evan was out of earshot.

"Oh, stop being such a killjoy. Loosen up."

"I think you might have had too much to drink," I said.

"I'm entitled to a little fun."

He came back in, and Candy said, "Do you want me to show you how to fix it?"

"The dishwasher?" Evan asked.

"No, your lip. You didn't put enough ointment on."

He lit up like the bright lights on a car on a dark road in the woods. He pointed to the crack with his index finger, tapping on it.

Candy moved closer to him.

Her eyes widened as I grabbed the vitamin E out of her hand. I could see that Evan was taken aback. He grinned at Candy, as though to say "That friend of yours is tough." Then he went back to work.

He reinstalled the machine, stored his tools, and asked politely for a credit card. As I handed him my card, he gave Candy a wink, and she gave him an inviting smile.

Business taken care of, she walked him to the door. She was gone for fifteen minutes.

"What is up with you?" I asked when she returned. "You were acting crazy with Dishwasher Guy."

"What could be wrong with me? My life is perfect," she said.

"Okay, then. Give me an example of that perfection."

"Here's one. I was married to a gynecologist, and when do I have problems with my uterus? After I divorce him."

"I am sure Brian would help you get any information you need."

"Brian has his own problems. He's been fired from the hospital in Colorado."

"Why? What did he do?"

"Sexual harassment. Not one, but three complaints. All from interns."

"I'm sorry, Candy."

"Forget him. I have to worry about me. My whole life, I am fine. I'm healthy. Then this hits when I'm all alone."

I felt a flash of gratitude. I had children who were adults. If I needed help, one of them would step up. Which one? I recalled the adage "One mother can take care of six children. But six children can't take care of one mother."

"Brian was my health advocate," Candy said. "Can you get a better health advocate than a man who's a doctor? Right now, Brian would put up a 'Do Not Resuscitate' sign if I had a nosebleed."

I pulled closer at the table and touched her arm. "I can be your health advocate." It seemed so little to do. So small in light of all we had been to each other when our parents became ill and our marriages fell apart.

"I need a hysterectomy."

I was blown away, far away. The past year, for both of us, felt like one thing after another. "What? When? Why? What's going on?"

She held her hand to her forehead. "It might not be a complete hysterectomy, but definitely removal of my uterus."

"Oh, that old thing," I said.

"Well, it's not like I'm using it," she said.

"That's the spirit." I didn't really know how long I could keep making uplifting remarks.

"But I feel it's what makes me a woman."

"It's inside. No one will even notice it's missing." Okay, I was done being cheerful in the face of tragedy. "What else did the doctor tell you?"

"I have a tumor the size of a Ping-Pong ball."

I imagined a Ping-Pong ball. Then I imagined it inside me. Suddenly, I couldn't remember the word that meant "nonmalignant."

"Hopefully the tumor is benign," she said.

Benign. Yes, benign. That's the word that means everything now.

Hearing about Candy's tumor made me dwell on how precarious life was. I couldn't swat it out of my mind. One day you're fine, then suddenly, who knows? That's what happened in my marriage. But being sick was worse. Candy just had to be all right.

⁀ꝃ

The next day after work, I drove home to meet Harvey. I sat in the car, staring at my house. The façade was light stone and colonial-blue clapboard. All the front windows were the size of doors. We had six bedrooms, six full baths. No better place to have diarrhea.

I thought that I should move. I should move while I was well, while I could enjoy it. But then I imagined Harvey living in the house, inviting our children over, having my family in the house *without* me.

I knew exactly how it would be. Harvey would order pizza. Elisabeth and Amanda liked vegetarian. Ben—meatballs. Of course, Harvey chowed an everything pizza—because Harvey had always enjoyed having "everything." I imagined the pizza boxes stacked on my kitchen counter, my children goofing around with one another. Everyone laughing. Not one of my kids thinking, *Mom always liked the crust.* Things are pretty bad when your own family won't save you some crust.

And what if Harvey remarried? The new wife would move into *my* house. I wanted to heave. I had gotten used to the idea of him with another woman when he fessed up to having a baby with that model. If they had a baby, it meant they had sex, right? But the thought of an all-new woman lounging in the hot tub in the master bath with him was excruciating, especially since he and I hadn't gone in that tub together even once. I imagined his second wife, That Bitch, brewing morning coffee in my kitchen. How dare she drink coffee in my house? I hated her mug, "Keep Calm and Marry a Rich Man."

Maybe what I had to do was stay in my house and defend it. Maybe I needed to buy a machine gun and stand in the driveway, ready to shoot.

Harvey pulled up. He was in his sports car, wearing khakis and a golf shirt. He looked around, like a groundskeeper. "We did a great job with the landscaping," he said.

"Harvey, we never touched a blade of grass. It was all Landscaping Man."

"But who hired him?"

Inside, I discarded the blazer I had worn over my pinstripe shirt, which was wrinkled after a day at work. I excused myself and went into the bathroom. I smoothed my hair, always trimmed slightly to maintain a length below my shoulder. I noted some despicable gray at the roots. Just looking at that gray made me age twenty years. I placed my palm on the offending roots. I planned to walk around just like that until I made it to a hair salon.

When I reappeared, Harvey was exploring the kitchen, looking around like he'd never before seen it. "I should've bought a new fridge, a larger one."

"Harvey, a football team could be stored in that fridge."

"Got any coffee?" he asked.

"Coffee? Never heard of it."

"Just kidding," he claimed. But he wasn't.

"What do you want to discuss about the wedding?" I said, getting down to business.

"I really need a cup of coffee." It would never occur to him to brew a cup for himself. In fact, I couldn't remember one time in three decades that he had touched a coffee maker. I had told him when he called that I wasn't making coffee, and I wasn't.

"Harvey, either make it yourself or drive to Dunkin' Donuts and get one. Oh, and bring one for me." I sat down at the head of the table. "Shoot," I said, my hands clasped in front of me. The sooner we got this over with, the better.

He waited a moment. He looked at my eyes, and then he lowered his head a bit. "I want us to get back together."

What? I had thought he might say this eventually, one day, but not sitting in the kitchen. At opposite ends of the table. While I had gray hairs on my head and thought I was there to discuss Amanda. The romance of it all!

No need to consider this one. "Don't think so."

"Marcy, there will not be a repeat incident."

An incident? He was calling it an incident? Having a baby with a woman younger than our daughters was an "incident"? I thought of it more as a hundred-car pileup involving several jetliners.

"Harvey, I can't get back together."

"Ever or today?"

I took a breath. I had to ask. "Why do you want to get back together?"

"Because we're making a wedding together. Because we're family."

I nodded. I missed those things too. Desperately. I felt the ache and wondered if it would ever fully go away.

"I'm a family man," he continued. "I made a mistake."

And there it was. The reason we were broken.

"Haven't you ever made a mistake?" he asked.

Yes. I made the mistake of trusting you.

I leaned forward. "Harvey, why don't we just get through this wedding? I just want to get through this wedding as a family."

He touched my hand. I shook my head. I stood up.

"I can wait," he said.

I looked him in the eyes. "You'll be waiting for a train that is never going to come."

"My train will come," he said confidently.

"Let's talk about the wedding," I said, ignoring his remark. "I want Amanda to have the event she wants. And I want us to get along to facilitate that."

He sat back, lifting the chair legs with him. "That is not a problem. I know what you think a wedding should be. And I know what I think a wedding ought to be. We are in total agreement."

"I was talking about Amanda."

"Marcy, she's a kid. What does she know? You know where I'm telling her to get married?"

"The synagogue? You're wasting your time."

"The Seascape in Florida."

"Really?" This was good news.

"Really."

"I love the Seascape. The beach is heaven, the building is gorgeous—and the food is great. What's more, the kids have so many great memories from vacationing there. It's a fabulous resort. And we've known the manager for so many years. It will be a pleasure to work with him."

"I've already spoken to him on the Q.T. I was amazed to hear that he has the Saturday night before the Christmas crush available. There was a cancellation."

The Seascape was perfect. Five stars. Maybe seven, in my opinion.

"So now do I get a cup of coffee?" he said.

Chapter 12

Before Amanda informed her company that she had accepted a position in Connecticut, she was sent to New York on business. She had a room at the Bliss. It was where movie stars stayed. When I arrived at two, paparazzi were stationed outside, waiting for Denzel Washington and George Clooney, who were about to start filming a movie. I waved to the photographers. Then I blew a kiss.

In the lobby, I spotted Amanda wearing all camel—a short camel skirt and a ribbed short-sleeve knit top that reminded me of the kind of poor boy sweater I wore in high school. Matching shoes and shoulder bag. Apparently, she had added camel to her repertoire of black, white, and cream."

She hugged me hello. "Do you want to have tea?" she asked.

"Tea? When did you start drinking tea?"

"When I noticed they have a high tea here, like the British, every afternoon. I checked it all out yesterday. Scrumptious. There are scones, cakes, muffins, and itsy-bitsy sandwiches." She held her thumb above her index finger, demonstrating what "itsy-bitsy" meant.

"I am sure the price isn't itsy-bitsy," I said.

"Mom, I'm a bride! We're here to discuss my wedding. Let's have fun."

The "tea" was in the lobby. It was a romantic setting, perfect for mother and daughter. We sat with a small table between us as the solemn young waitress, in a dress that was basically a body mold, presented a silver platter with four graduating tiers of delicacies—each no bigger than the swab on a Q-tip.

"Looks great," I said. "Is that salmon or a pink dot on that crust of bread?"

Amanda laughed as she helped herself to a muffin the size of a shirt button. A waitress brought over a pot of tea as well as cups and saucers with shiny demitasse spoons.

"This is delightful," I said. "Fifty or sixty of these tea sandwiches, and I won't be hungry for dinner."

Amanda nibbled on a sliver of cucumber topped with an eye drop of cream cheese.

"Pass a scone if it's not too heavy," I joked, anticipating what she had to talk to me about.

"Speaking of small things," she said. "I have a small favor to ask you."

"Ask away," I said, trying to imagine what she was about to request, hoping she wanted to go look for a wedding gown the next day and excited to tell her that I had already made an appointment at Palladium, a renowned bridal shop in Brooklyn, to do just that.

I imagined her trying on gowns. Would she go white or off-white? Long train, short train, or none at all? What about the veil? I'd be stationed on a plush love seat, sipping the cold champagne provided by a saleswoman so overly solicitous that I wanted to slap her, waiting excitedly for Amanda's appearance in each gown.

"What's that TV show?" I asked. "The one about shopping for wedding gowns?"

"*Say Yes to the Dress.*"

"Don't even ask. I would love to look for wedding gowns."

She wiped the corners of her mouth with a cloth napkin. "Oh." She cleared her throat. "Well, there's no need to go anywhere for that."

I was flabbergasted. "What do you mean?"

"I already found a dress in Seattle."

"Well, I'm sure we can find the same one and try it on in New York. And I want to pay for it. My mother treated me to my wedding gown, and I'm treating you to yours."

"That's so sweet, Mom, but I bought it already."

She bought a dress—*without me?*

"Amanda, who goes shopping for a wedding gown all by themselves? In all of those television shows, they always have the whole bridal party there. I saw one show where the mother-in-law was even invited. That bride was crazy, but—"

"I bought it, and they ordered it, and it's coming in in a few weeks. Naturally, the gown will need alterations, but I have time."

I was about to alter her head. Did Amanda think I would be too annoying? Have too much to say? So what if I did? I was her mother.

I thought back to when we had shopped for her prom dress. First, we'd visited Tryon's in Atherton. Tryon's was a small boutique specializing in junior sizes. There were three fitting rooms, each the size of a phone booth, with privacy provided by drawn curtains.

I'd waited on a bench in the center of the store, and Amanda had popped out to show off the dresses she'd felt she looked good in. I'd liked them all—until she'd sashayed in front of me in a red dress that was way too short. I hadn't said a word. I knew if I had, she would have wanted it even more. When it comes to sixteen-year-olds, prom dresses are like boyfriends. Just look as if you don't like a guy, and you might as well welcome him to your family.

As Amanda danced around the store, the college girl who worked at Tryon's emerged from a back room. "What do you think?" Amanda asked her.

"Too short."

Then she showed Amanda an alternate dress, a pink-and-purple strapless that covered her vagina, but Amanda wasn't happy with it.

We hit the other boutique in town, then went on to a big mall, where we went in and out of every store that wasn't named Casual Male. Amanda wasn't happy with any of the dresses she tried on, and I couldn't say she was wrong. When we returned home, my feet hurt. I was wiped out, and Amanda was disappointed.

"All my friends have their dresses already. I'll never find a dress. I'll have to stay home, and we already booked the limo."

Not only had they booked the limo, but I had also given my credit card, and although I was supposed to receive fifty dollars from each of the kids, I knew the likelihood of that happening was the same as my landing on the cover of *Vogue*.

"Let's go," I said. "We'll try more stores. We'll go to New York tomorrow if we have to."

"But I have school tomorrow."

"What's more important, school or the dress?" I said.

"Are you serious?"

The following day, we went to Lord & Taylor on Fifth Avenue, and Amanda found the world's most perfect dress.

I pushed the memory away and decided not to start something.

"You're going to love my gown," Amanda said.

I would have loved it more if I'd gotten to shop for it. "I'm sure it's beautiful, Amanda."

"I think I have a picture on my phone." She started thumbing through photos.

"No. I want to see it on you," I said, because I knew looking at it on her on a phone would reduce me to tears.

"It's lace over satin," she said.

"And it sounds gorgeous," I said as I reached for my handbag. "Excuse me for a moment. I must use the ladies' room."

I didn't need the restroom. What I needed was air. I went out the revolving hotel doors and sat down on a bench. My eyes were flooded. The dress broke my back. My daughter getting married would have been enough of an emotional ride on its own. She was grown up. She was starting a new life. She was going off with a man I hardly knew. But that was all complicated by the fact that Amanda was getting married just as I was about to get divorced. I wanted her to have what she wanted so I didn't have to fight with Harvey about it.

I worried that Jake would do to her what Harvey had done to me, and it wouldn't take thirty-three years. Furthermore, it infuriated me that she had no interest in meeting Jon. Did this mean she wasn't planning on inviting him to the wedding? I didn't want to dance all night with family and friends who felt sorry for me because they knew what Harvey had done. What was worse than a pity dance?

Crushed like a wineglass under a groom's foot, I took out my phone and called Palladium. I canceled the appointment I'd made to look for wedding gowns with Amanda. I took a breath. I swallowed. I rested my eyes.

I called Dana.

"Amanda bought a wedding gown without me."

"That bitch."

I laughed. "She really can be," I said.

"Remember, though, she's a bride, and she can't think of anyone but herself."

"No. It's more than that," I said as a tear dropped to my nose.

"What? Revenge for the breakup of your marriage?"

Until Dana said it, that hadn't occurred to me. "Is that what you think it is?"

"Who knows? Weddings bring out the worst in everyone. Judy the Realtor told me that her own daughter actually said she didn't want Judy dancing too close to the front of the ballroom, because she danced like a chimpanzee. And then there's Karen Anne. You know, from way back when we were on the board of the Atherton museum. Her future son-in-law told her she could only come to look for reception venues if she promised not to say a thing. And she was paying for the wedding! Marcy, don't care so much. Live your life."

"I had made an appointment to look for gowns tomorrow."

"Dope."

"If I'm a dope, every mother is a dope."

"You don't hear me arguing."

When I returned to the table, Amanda asked if I was all right.

"I'm disappointed," I said. "I would have liked to look for a gown with you."

"Mom, it wasn't any big thing."

"Not a big thing?"

"I guess Elisabeth was right. She told me you would be upset, but I liked the gown so much."

"I just want to be part of this. In fact, I had made an appointment for the two of us to look at gowns tomorrow. I just canceled it."

"You *are* part of it. I call you all the time and ask you what I should do," she said sympathetically. "Didn't I just call the other day and tell you to look online at the napkin rings I'm considering for my registry?"

"Okay, honey." I said it mostly because I didn't want her telling sad stories to her children—my grandchildren—about how I carried on about her wedding gown and ruined everything. And that I did it even after she'd asked me about the napkin rings.

Amanda patted my hand and then paused to sip some tea. "Can we talk about something else now?"

I nodded.

"I've been thinking about the ceremony. I want to ask you something, but I want you to be honest about how you feel."

No one wants anyone to be honest, ever. Honesty is the worst policy.

"Would you be willing to walk me down the aisle—with Dad?"

I wasn't invited to the bridal shop, but I was, thankfully, invited to the aisle.

"Will you be between us?" I asked, as that was the way I thought it should be.

"Isn't that how it usually happens at a Jewish wedding?"

"Then it's not like your father and I are actually walking together. We'll have a bride between us," I said, laughing.

"Exactly," she said, relieved beyond measure.

"Then of course the answer is yes."

"Thanks, Mom, really. Really, thanks."

I picked up a scone to take a breath.

"This is my last scone," I said. "I have to lose weight for the wedding."

"Right, Mom," she said, not believing a word I had just said.

I buttered the scone and smeared some jelly on it. "Amanda, I will do anything for the wedding that will make you happy. I don't know why you think any of this is a problem for me. It's not."

"Well, you didn't want to spend Dad's birthday with him. So, what am I supposed to think?"

"I didn't want to spend Dad's birthday with him, because I was trying to start my own life, my new life."

"Mom, it was one day."

"After thirty-three years of days." I tasted the scone. It needed more jelly.

"You know how he is about his birthday," she said. "He thinks it should be a national holiday."

"I do know how he feels. I thought about doing it, but I was petrified that if I spent the day with him, I would fall back into every old pattern I had."

As the words left my mouth, I felt proud of myself. I wished there were someone to pat me on the back. *Pat yourself on the back,* I thought.

"And that would happen because"—she paused to enunciate—"you still love him."

"I do love him," I said, "but as your dad."

"Bullshit," Amanda said.

The coarseness of her response stopped my train of thought. I said nothing for a few moments.

"Amanda, I think I'm doing well. I have a full-time job I like, I have Candy and Dana, and—amazing as it is to me—I have a boyfriend."

"Mom, you sound like a teenager. 'I have a boyfriend.'" She said the last part like a parrot. "After a dynamo like Dad, you're happy with an English professor?"

"Yes—and by the way, he's also a well-known artist."

"Well known where?"

"Amanda, I can do without the snide remarks."

"You're right. I'm sorry," she said, without conviction.

"Maybe we should get the check." *So I can drive home to my boyfriend, who is obviously not well known enough for my daughter.*

"No, wait," she said.

"What?"

"So the thing is," she said slowly, and then at the speed of light, "Jon can't come to the wedding."

"What?" I had been holding my napkin. It fell out of my hand. I saw where it landed, but I didn't pick it up. After that, my mind turned blank.

"I don't want him to be at the wedding."

I heard the words. I stared at Amanda. "I just said I would do whatever it took to get along with Dad, that I'd like to give you away with him."

"You're not *giving* me away. I hate that saying. It sounds like I'm in bondage."

"Okay, so we are not giving you away. We are getting rid of you, finally."

"About Jon . . ."

"Amanda, it never occurred to me that Jon couldn't come to the wedding. I've been talking about it nonstop. How do I not invite him now?"

"You're not doing the not inviting. I am."

"But there's more to it. I *want* Jon to be at the wedding."

"So you can dance with him in front of everyone and make this whole embarrassing situation even worse? Do you think it's easy for me to tell you this? It's not. I had to rehearse a thousand times."

I imagined her in front of her bathroom mirror, practicing while tossing darts into me.

"Mom, it's my day."

"Amanda, I assure you that you will have plenty of days."

"Not as a bride. It's my day. It's my day, and it should be exactly what I want it to be."

"It is what *you* want it to be."

"I just can't have Jon there. It will hurt Dad too much."

"Hurt Dad? I was the one who got hurt. Not Dad. Dad cheated on me. Dad had a child with an infant. Dad is fine. Dad is living in a five-star inn, getting a basket of warm muffins delivered each morning with the newspaper. How would you like it if Jake pulled such a stunt?"

"Jake would never do that," Amanda said.

I pointed a finger and then folded it back. "Do you think I thought Dad would?"

"I don't know what you thought."

"Don't put this on me. This is about you, Amanda. You have to grow up."

My sainted Jewish mother on high: *"Don't start with her, Marcy. Leave the boyfriend home. He's not blood. Your daughter is blood."*

"Mom, I have never even met Jon, and I don't want to meet him, because I don't want to have to invite him to my wedding."

I leaned back in my chair. "I feel like I'm choking."

"You can't be choking. The sandwiches were too small."

I didn't know what to say. I had no room to maneuver. The only zinger of a response here would be to draw the line, to say, "No Jon, no me." But I would never say that. I wasn't the kind of person who would ever make that call. I was going to my daughter's wedding, no matter what. I had a friend who didn't go to her son's wedding. Something about him never paying back a loan. She set herself up for a lifetime of misery. She has two grandchildren she has never met.

Suddenly, it occurred to me. The real reason Amanda did not want Jon at the wedding was that she wanted Harvey and me to stroll down an aisle together, to dance together, to get back together.

"Amanda, I have no plans to remain married to your father."

"I know. I know. But it's my wedding day, and I want my family around me. No strangers. Jon is a stranger. Where would he even sit during the ceremony?"

"In a seat?"

"In the front row?" she asked, almost squeaking.

"No. In another building, in another country, apparently. Is there a reason you don't like Jon?"

"He sounds way too nice. It can't be real."

"But it is real."

She moved closer and lowered her voice. "You really want to know what the problem is? It's the entire embarrassing situation between you and Dad."

"You're embarrassed? *I'm* embarrassed. No one is more embarrassed than me."

"I can't even tell my friends about it without turning the color of a beet. Dad having a baby and buying that woman a business in Argentina so that she'll never darken his door. Tell me the truth, Mom. Were you seeing Jon before Dad moved out? You sure found him really quick."

I could have said, "No, and you're being ridiculous." I could have said, "I knew Jon, but it never so much as occurred to me to do anything about him, because I was married to your father." But I had gone cold, and the big valves to my heart were cracking open.

"I can't discuss this anymore, Amanda. In fact, I have to go."

"But we're supposed to spend the evening together," she said.

"I've told you how much I want to help with the wedding, yet you bought your gown without me. You don't want to meet the man I am seeing. You haven't said a word to me about Grandma."

"What about Grandma?" she said, incredulous at my hysteria.

"My own mother, your grandmother, won't be at the wedding at all, because she's gone. She is missing everything. And your wedding would have made her so happy. And, by the way, as long as we are on the subject, I went shopping with her for my wedding dress. And we went out for lunch afterward. And we had fettuccine, because she loved fettuccine Alfredo."

I was sniffling like a sick kid. "And then we went home, and when my dad got there, we showed him a Polaroid of the dress. The photo was black and white, but that didn't matter, because the dress was white. And Grandma and Grandpa were crying, and I started sobbing, and Max the Maleficent came into the living room, and of course he made some snarky remark, and I wished I didn't have a brother, so not a thing has changed."

"Are you inferring I don't miss Grandma? I do miss Grandma. I miss Grandma every day."

"So you miss her. Would you invite her to the wedding? Or would she be in the column of people you are only inviting because you know they won't travel that far?"

"Now you're being insane. I loved—love—my grandmother."

Then I heard my mother. *"Knock it off, Marcy. You're a mother; she's a kid."*

"Who died and left me the grown-up?" I blurted, thinking aloud.

"She did, Mom."

Chapter 13

Back in Atherton the next day, I reverted to my most tranquilizing habit: cruising the supermarket. Touring the grocery store with a shopping cart in front of me had always been soothing.

I recalled when this form of therapy started. The kids were small. Harvey would show up late from work. I would be exhausted from a day of dragging around three children. At about seven o'clock, Harvey would have one foot in the door, and I, coat on and keys in hand, would announce, "I have to get something at the store."

"Can't it wait until tomorrow?" he would ask.

"Out of milk," I would respond, although there was practically a dairy truck in my fridge. I would say, "Dinner is on the table," and dart for the door. The cold night air on my face was an elixir. In my car, I would remove my gloves. Release my shoulders backward, rolling down several times. Move my neck around. Turn on the ignition. And head for Big Buddy. I would walk into the brightly lit supermarket as though it were Disney World. Better than Disney World—Disney World without children.

I'd put my handbag in my cart and stroll the aisles as though I were on the Champs-Élysées.

I could no longer go to Big Buddy, due to an unfortunate incident that occurred when I'd chased a woman down the cereal aisle immediately after Harvey had left. I chose Vegetarian's Paradise, which I had renamed Carnivore's Hell.

I was beside my cart, looking at apples, shiny ones, when I heard my name. I turned around. It was Samantha David, the town crier.

"Marcy, how are you?" she said. She wore a peacoat draped with a checked scarf large enough to cover a twin bed.

Nothing to report to the press, I thought.

"Hello, Samantha."

"I have never seen you here before."

"I'm a secret vegetarian. I only come out at night."

I noticed her staring at my shoulder bag.

"Is that leather? You own a leather bag?"

"It's okay, Samantha. I have no intention of eating it."

"Marcy, you're always so amusing! By the way, I heard you were dating."

What, was it on CNN? Banner on bottom: "Marcy Hammer finds man, exposes wrinkled knees."

"How wonderful. I don't know how women get the courage after so many years of being married. If Helmut left, I would just sit in my house alone, eating pizza."

I tried that. It didn't work.

"Did you go online? You're always so amusing. Even if your picture was so-so, I am sure you could compensate by just being funny."

"I have to go, Samantha. My hot, new thirty-year-old soul mate is waiting for me to come home and fry my pocketbook for dinner."

As I shot away from the produce section, I bumped into another cart.

"Marcy," I heard a baritone voice say. It was a voice that sounded as clear and strong as that of a radio announcer on an AM news show.

"Jerry, how are you?" Jerry Glassman was probably the nicest guy in the brassiere business.

"Not bad," he said. "All things considered."

I was wondering what "all things" were, but I didn't ask.

"Lynn left me," he blurted, shaking his head with regret.

Wow, I thought. *Is there anyone in America who is still married?*

"I didn't know, Jerry. I'm sorry."

"She said I was the reason she was fat."

"Well, then you should have stopped feeding her immediately."

I noticed his dimples when he smiled.

"Maybe she was right. When we met forty years ago, she was an itsy-bitsy little thing."

"I hate when they do that."

"What?"

"Hook you in when they're thin, then gain a hundred pounds."

He laughed. He had a nice laugh.

"You're cheering me up, Marcy Hammer. I like that."

He smoothed his thick, dark hair. I looked him over. He had been through a tough time, but behind his wire-rimmed glasses, there was light in his eyes. He wore a Patagonia running jacket over a black T-shirt, running pants, and Nike shoes. He was taking excellent care of himself.

"What about you?" he asked, mindlessly pushing his cart back and forth.

"Harvey's gone too," I said. "He told me we were having too much sex." Had I really just said that? The older I got, the bolder I became. Was it because I no longer felt like I had anything to lose? I thought back to junior high school, when I had watched every word, afraid of being made fun of, when I had walked down the corridor, uncomfortable in my clothes, in my body, fearful I might even be thinking the wrong thing. The result was that I hardly spoke for three years—and my peers made fun of me anyway. Once, I took a verbal assault just for wearing shoes that tied when the popular shoe was a loafer. I knew that. But Mom wouldn't hear a word about loafers. She said loafers were bad for my feet. Now they call such verbal shoe abuse bullying. But sometimes you are just bullying yourself. To tell the truth, I enjoyed being blunt. By the time I am seventy, I will be saying things like "Your fly is open. Think I'll zip it now."

Jerry moved closer. Our carts were touching. "I always thought Harvey was so lucky to have you. In fact, when I heard the whole story, I was positive he had lost his mind. Crazy what people do. You think you know someone, and suddenly, you wake up and realize you didn't have a clue."

He paused, thinking.

"Would you like to have a cup of coffee in the café?" he asked tentatively.

"Yes."

I pushed my cart behind his to the tables in the refreshment area near the cash registers.

"Black or with milk?" he asked.

"Milk and a Sweet'N Low," I said.

"No Sweet'N Low here. It's a health food store."

"Right," I said. "So just put in eight packages of raw sugar."

I sat at a tiled table.

"I saw Harvey last week," he said when he brought over our drinks. *What a treat,* I thought.

"We were at the LUMP Convention."

Ladies' Undergarment Manufacturers and Providers.

"So you're not retired yet?" I said.

"Trying to sell out, get a three-year employment contract. Then I want to travel. Have you ever been to Amsterdam?"

"No, but I like marijuana and red lights and Heineken."

"I'm going to start in Amsterdam, because my son lives there now."

I took a sip of the coffee, which had too much milk and definitely too much sugar.

Samantha David appeared. "Look at the two of you. Marcy, you didn't tell me you were seeing Lynn's Jerry. That's so funny—Harvey and Jerry—both in the bra business."

I didn't care what she thought. I sipped, hoping Jerry wouldn't encourage her with a single word.

"Nice to see you, Samantha," Jerry said as a clear fare-thee-well.

She winked at him and walked off.

"So, your son is abroad. Where is your daughter living?" I asked.

He adjusted his glasses. "Olivia is in Manhattan. She's married, expecting a baby."

"Fabulous," I said.

"It would be a lot more fabulous if Lynn and I could get along."

I gritted my teeth, ready to hear about his soldiering on.

"Lynn and I are still throwing rocks at each other. You may be getting along with Harvey now, but one day you'll see."

Why did people always have to say, "You'll see"? The thing you would "see" was nine times out of ten something ominous or at least not enjoyable. "You'll see" when your baby is two—and throws macaroni and cheese all over the restaurant floor. "You'll see" when your daughter starts dating—and you find a condom in the back seat of your car.

Besides, I knew Jerry was wrong. Although I often wanted to push Harvey out a window on the top floor of the Empire State Building, I had made up my mind that I was going to get along with him because of our kids. I didn't think this would be easy—I'm not that big a fool—but I was committed to being "the bigger one," as my mother had always called it.

"Tell me one problem, and I will solve it," I said. Just call me Judge Marcy.

"Lynn has a new boyfriend."

"Is that difficult for you?"

"Well, there is a problem."

"What's that?" I asked.

"Her boyfriend is my brother."

We chatted about his ex-wife and his ex-brother even longer. He glanced at the wall clock in the refreshment area, took a breath, and shook his head. "I'm sorry, Marcy. Unfortunately, I've got to go. I have a checkup with my dentist—to clean the bad taste of divorce out of my mouth."

I laughed. "Well, it's been great running into you. I hope things settle down."

"Wait," Jerry said.

I smiled, wondering what he was going to say.

"How about dinner sometime?"

Taken aback, I could feel myself blush.

"Thank you so much for asking," I said.

"And?"

"I'm seeing someone." I hadn't said that sentence since Nancy Reagan wore red at the White House. It sounded odd, yet it was eye opening, and I repeated it to myself. At Jerry's expense, I felt proud and cocky about it. That wasn't right. But I couldn't help it.

"It's true, then," Jerry said, shaking his head.

"What?"

"All the good ones are taken."

Good one or bad one, I did feel taken.

◌϶

Elisabeth called. "Want to go to the mall?"

Her call was a dead giveaway. She had heard the wedding gown story from her sister. Nobody went to a mall anymore. The mall was as passé as a Jell-O mold with fruit in it.

"I guess you heard," I said.

"Yes. I'm not looking for any brownie points, but I warned her not to buy the gown without you."

"Where would you like your brownies delivered?" I asked.

"At least she is not making you wear the maid-of-horror dress."

"I saw the picture you sent. It's not that bad."

"It's not that good either," she said.

"You can always cut it down later."

"I think you mean cut it up."

"What do you need at the mall?" I asked.

"I don't need anything, but Spiritual Experience is offering a free gift when you spend thirty-five dollars. I love those free gifts."

"Okay, I can go on Saturday. I'll meet you at ten o'clock at the counter in Macy's."

～9～

I took my time to dress nicely. When I finished, I looked in the mirror in my bedroom and saw that I looked pretty darn good in a denim skirt, a turtleneck, and navy flats. In fact, I looked young. I smiled at the mirror. I still felt lousy about my experience with Amanda, but Elisabeth had made me feel better. I knew she was busy and that her invitation was from somewhere deep in her heart.

When I showed up at the makeup counter, Elisabeth was trying perfume.

She held out her wrist. "What do you think?"

"You smell like a watermelon."

"That wasn't what I was going for."

She hugged me hello.

A salesperson appeared. She was a middle-aged woman in a white lab coat. Her badge said her name was Yolanda.

"Hello," I said.

"How can I help you?"

Elisabeth pointed to a sign on a stand depicting a canvas pouch. Below the sign were samples. Cotton-candy-colored lipstick, beige foundation with SPF 15 sunblock in it, apricot blush with a brush, black mascara, and beads that twisted open to release magical moisturizing oil.

"I see you're having a giveaway, and I want to buy something that would qualify me for it."

"You would have to spend thirty-five dollars," Yolanda explained.

"What costs thirty-five dollars?" my daughter wanted to know.

"Nothing really," Yolanda said. "Two lipsticks are thirty-nine dollars, if that helps."

"No. I want to buy something for thirty-five dollars," Elisabeth said.

"Well, it would have to be something over thirty-five dollars."

"Like what?"

"Our Reincarnated Face Mask imbued with chrysanthemum is forty-four dollars." She displayed a thimble of a jar. "It's best for dry skin. I see that your mother has dry skin."

"I'm not her mother," I said. "I'm her sister."

"Yes, she's my sister," Elisabeth said. "My younger sister."

Yolanda sized me up. I have to say I was having a good time.

"For you," she said to Elisabeth, "I would recommend Younger Than Youth. It's a serum and it's just thirty-nine dollars. So is our night cream."

Elisabeth shook her head. "If we need to spend thirty-five dollars to receive the free gift, something here should be thirty-five dollars."

"Elisabeth, let's just buy something."

"You're right. I'll take the serum and the cream, entitling me to two free gifts."

"Oh, I'm sorry, it's only one gift per person."

"Okay, then my younger sister here will take a serum, and I'll buy a cream, entitling us to two gifts."

As we walked off with our bounty, Elisabeth's phone went off.

"It's Amanda. You take it. I can't listen to one more thing about the wedding," she said to me, then told Amanda, "Here's Mom," and handed me the phone.

"What are you doing together?" Amanda asked as we walked to another counter.

"We're shopping, but right now Elisabeth is spraying perfumes."

Amanda spoke as though nothing had taken place between us. I went with it.

"Jake just told me he wants nine ushers."

"Nine? What, did he pick them off an unemployment line?"

"There are no lines anymore, Mom. You just go *online*."

"Really?" I said. "Even unemployment is easier now."

"Mom, concentrate."

"Why nine?" I asked.

"His two brothers, his three cousins, and his friends from camp."

"He still sees friends from camp?"

"Once a year, they meet in Chicago and go to a Cubs game."

"For a guy, that's about as close as it gets," I said.

"Well, it's going to look ridiculous. He wants them to wear tuxedos and top hats. They'll look like the cast of *A Chorus Line*."

"One," I said. It was my favorite song from the show.

"What I Did for Love," Amanda said, naming another one.

"You may have to do it for love."

"But I only want Elisabeth and Ben to stand up for me. No bridesmaids."

"You can do that. The only problem is everyone will think Jake has tons of friends and you have none."

"So now I have to worry that the people at my own wedding will think I'm unpopular? Mom, in high school, I was voted most likely to succeed."

"Well, your friend problem is not a big deal compared to the Dad problem."

"What Dad problem now?"

"Once he hears there are nine ushers, he will assume you are having a bigger wedding and want to invite more employees from Bountiful."

"Let me talk to Elisabeth," Amanda demanded.

"She wants to talk to you," I told Elisabeth, who now smelled like a botanical garden.

Elisabeth waved me away, shaking her head vigorously.

"She can't talk right now. She just died of perfume overdose."

"Your cousin Phyllis called to ask when we were going to talk about a flower girl dress for her granddaughter."

"Uh-oh." Now Amanda was in real trouble.

"What was I supposed to tell her? 'Not only is your granddaughter not my flower girl, but I wasn't inviting you to the wedding'?"

"What are you going to do?" I asked.

"No, Mom. What are *you* going to do?"

"Oh, don't get me involved in this."

"She's your cousin. Your cousin, your problem."

Elisabeth turned to me. "Just hang up. I want to go to lunch."

That evening, as I unpacked my gift from Spiritual Experience, the doorbell rang. It was Jon, and he was holding a bouquet.

I kissed him. "Wow. Thank you. Is there an occasion?"

"I don't need an occasion."

Ten points, maybe a thousand.

He followed me to the kitchen. "What's that?" he asked about the makeup on the table.

"Free prizes," I said.

"How do you get free prizes?"

"It's easy. You go to a department store with Elisabeth."

He rubbed his chin down to his neck. I adored the way his chin and neck were always rough.

I put the flowers in water. I used the splotchy brown-and-red vase that Ben had made for me when he was twelve. It was one artifact I would keep forever.

"You have so much fun with your kids. I don't know why you don't want me to be part of your family as well. I've always wanted a family," Jon said.

He had never said anything like this before. He was a widower, and I knew this was difficult for him to talk about.

"My wife had three miscarriages, Marcy."

I could feel my face warm with his pain.

"I should have been a father of three. But this is how things worked out."

I thought of him going with his wife to the hospital each time, his eyes welling. His dreams crushed. Then I imagined how Jon would have been if he had become a father. Showing his son how to put on a tiny baseball glove in the park. I imagined him at a high school game, in the stands, while his kid played first base. I didn't know what to say. I ached for him.

"I never told that to anyone," he said.

I took his hand. I rubbed his palm. "I am sorry, Jon, so very sorry." I could feel tears in my eyes.

"I want to be part of a family, Marcy. I would like to be part of your family."

"No, you don't. They are all horrible people."

"Marcy, this is not funny."

"I know. I know. I'm joking only because I don't know what to tell you." I touched his face. "I like your rough face," I said. I kissed his cheek.

"Marcy, I really want to discuss this now."

I backed away. "Okay," I said.

"You are compartmentalizing your life. You've got me. You've got your family. Two separate entities."

"Jon, I'm not a magician. I can't just turn my family into your family. It's going to take time."

"How much time? We've known each other for years. We started seeing each other in the winter. It's summer. How much time?"

"I'm not sure."

Who was I to deprive him of what he wanted? Especially when all he wanted was to be nice to me and to my children? I felt like some other person—not me, but some mean woman. But I knew my kids were not ready to treat him the way he wanted to be treated, like a friend. Jon was waiting. I had to say something.

I spoke softly. "I want to involve you, but I don't think it's time yet. I don't think I am ready. Maybe one day I will invite everyone over for a wonderful dinner."

"Maybe one day?" he said, color rising in his cheeks. "Perhaps I should stop seeing you until maybe one day."

"If you want to do that, I understand," I said, afraid he would agree. *Please don't let him agree.* A moment passed, but it seemed like half an hour. I held my breath.

"I don't want to do that," he said, shaking his head.

I felt a cool wave of relief, as though an entire ocean had passed by. He was right. It was time to let him meet the kids. But what would I tell him about the wedding? About Amanda and how she just didn't want him there?

"I'll set something up," I promised.

He smiled. "Ask me to do my trick."

"To Kill a Mockingbird," I said.

Chapter 14

Instead of hiding under her white, thousand-thread-count Italian covers until the impending date of the hysterectomy, Candy doubled down on everything. At first, I thought it was a show of good attitude, then I realized it was denial. She dumped Leonardo, her very personal trainer, because she said life was too short and she had to stop playing around. She saw Ellison Graham as often as possible. She joined my gym. I forgot to tell her that I went there only when dragged by wild horses. In fact, the last time I had gone was when I'd told Amanda I was choosing dinner with her and her in-laws over seeing *Hamilton*.

Candy went to the gym every single morning and made me agree to meet her there on Tuesdays and Fridays before work. She enjoyed the StairMaster. When I arrived, late on purpose, I would take the one next to her.

"Answer me one question," I said as I set my meter for a molehill pace. "Why is it you never sweat?"

"I'm accustomed to exercise," she said. "Besides, eventually I do sweat."

"Where?"

"My cleavage."

"That doesn't count."

"Why not?"

"That's sexy sweat."

"I'm going on a date with Ellison on Saturday night," she said.

"That's great, but are you sure you wouldn't rather be seeing Dishwasher Guy?"

"He was handsome. But I like Ellison. He's taking me to New York to see that play *Wilkes Booth: A Night at the Theater*, about the assassination of Abraham Lincoln."

"You've already seen that."

"True, but it was superb, and Ellison already bought the tickets. Besides, it's not like I have to act surprised at the ending. The time to live is now. After all, I don't know what the future holds after my operation."

I asked her what was involved, but I already knew, because I had read about it online. There is a problem, though, about researching diseases on the Internet. They always show the worst-case scenario. Like a photograph of someone with type 2 diabetes would depict a man with all-black, rotting toes on his left leg and no right leg at all. Sometimes I think medical sites obtain photographs of diseases by going to skid row and asking men with no access to medical care to pose.

I took a sip from my water bottle as I climbed and listened.

"It's called an abdominal hysterectomy. The surgeon makes an incision across my belly in order to remove the upper part of the uterus. He's planning to leave the cervix. I need two to three days in the hospital afterward. They say it takes about six weeks for full recovery. But it does leave a scar. I just hope it's not big. I told him I'd prefer a horizontal incision."

I couldn't believe she was worrying about a scar. What, did she walk around nude all day? Mostly, I was aghast that she hadn't checked any of this out online.

"There are easier ways to do it," I said. "I think you should consult another doctor."

"For example?"

"Laparoscopic or robotic."

"But why wouldn't he have suggested that?"

The conversation was getting serious. I thought it would be best if I stopped exercising, in order to talk to her . . . or in order to stop exercising.

"I don't know," I said as my workout came to a halt, but she kept going. "Maybe he's in a rut. You know how it gets when you're our age. You do something a particular way for years. You never think about doing it another way. It's like Harvey and the microwave. The microwave was tucked away in a corner forever. So, one night, Harvey goes to make popcorn and starts complaining that he abhors where the microwave is. Knowing Harvey, it was too far to travel from the cupboard where he procured the popcorn to the microwave. I was very annoyed, so I unplugged the machine and moved it. He said, 'I didn't know we could move it.'

"Go online and research the newest methods. Question your doctor. If he insists on doing it the old-fashioned way, go for another opinion. Absolutely no ageism here, but I prefer young women doctors."

"Okay. I will."

"Will you?" I can really be a pain.

"I said yes. There's something else that's bothering me."

"Your woes are my woes."

"I'm really worried about vaginal dryness afterward."

A man in a T-shirt that said "World's Best Dad" was on the machine next to her. He was about to put on his headphones, but instead he just held them in his hand. Vaginal dryness—such a showstopper.

"Candy, wake up! The tumor is probably sitting in one place. And it's only the size of a Ping-Pong ball. It could've been as big as a paddle. Eighty percent of uterine tumors are benign. Everything will be okay. Just say a prayer or whatever it is that people who never go to church do."

"Yoga," she said. "I do yoga."

"Assume a position, and be grateful."

"I am grateful. But vaginal dryness is problematic. It can be devastating."

It was certainly at the top of my concerns. Right after "I can't get this jar of applesauce open."

⟡

I had been trying to think of a way to introduce my kids to Jon. Not just because he wanted to meet them, but because I knew it was a healthy thing for me to do. So what if the kids judged him harshly because they weren't ready to meet him? How many of their friends had I not liked?

I thought about Elisabeth's first boyfriend in high school. He was so beneath her, she could have crushed him under her Reeboks. Then there was the girl with the waist-length blond hair whom Ben had dated his sophomore year in high school, before he came out as gay. Cassandra Klein. She never said hello when she came into our house. She'd be talking to Ben, and as soon as she saw me, she'd clam up, like her mouth had been wired shut. She had that popular-girl way of making even me feel insecure. I knew she was a "mean girl" in school, and I disliked that about her. I had heard from another mother on the PTO that Cassandra had been torturing her daughter on the school bus, poking fun at her book bag, probably the only one in Atherton that wasn't from L.L.Bean. Life was so precarious on a school bus. To tell the truth, I'd rather be dropped from the sky without a parachute than board a bus to Atherton High School. Lucky for me, I had always walked to school.

Jon was active in the Guild, and I had known him for years and years, but in all that time, he had never met anyone in my family. What if I had a boyfriend who didn't care who my children were? Who never asked a word about them? I'd never like that kind of man. I had to grow up and take my boyfriend home to meet my children.

As I mulled this over, Ben texted to say he was headed to Vermont. He offered to stop on the way to have breakfast with me at Kerry's, a breakfast and lunch place in Atherton. When the kids were young, we ate there so often Harvey called it "the annex."

It occurred to me that the casualness of this unscheduled event—as well as the down-home ambience provided by Kerry's plywood walls, Venetian blinds, vinyl chairs, wobbly benches, and harvest-gold Formica tables circa 1980—would shout out to everyone "This is no big deal." Even though it was. Although Jon had not brought up the subject again, I wanted him to meet my kids before it became a thing. If we all met on Saturday morning at Kerry's, the deed would be done.

"Of course I will meet you at Kerry's," I said to Ben. "I could use some of those banana-walnut pancakes."

"I know exactly what I am having."

"Let me guess. Western omelet with three pancakes and a side of corned beef hash." I prided myself on knowing what everyone in my family liked to eat. In a grocery store, I would purchase three kinds of cereal or three brands of bread just to be certain every member of my family was happy. When I spotted a mother in a supermarket calling home to see what her children wanted, I felt that if she really loved them, she would know without making the call. I'm not saying I am not crazy.

"You always know what I like," Ben said.

On that cue, I plunged in. "So Jon happens to be free on Saturday morning, and I am thinking I would bring him along. He's a big fan of Kerry's. Loves the waffles—with whipped cream. Asks for extra syrup." *That's enough, Marcy.*

"Sure, Mom."

Sure, Mom? It was that easy?

"I'll call Elisabeth and see if she can make it too," he said.

So much for it being easy. I knew Ben was dragging along his sister, who was always busier than an ant building a hill, because he had no intention of going to this "boyfriend-meeting thing" alone. Whatever. I liked my kids depending on each other. I knew it had helped a lot during the initial phase of my separation from Harvey.

∽

Jon and I arrived at Kerry's first, then Ben, who had picked up Elisabeth at her apartment.

"Jon, this is Elisabeth and Ben. Elisabeth and Ben, Jon London." I could have run through rapid gunfire and appeared less anxious.

Unfortunately, Kerry's, which was hidden in the back of a strip mall and rarely busy, was packed with people enjoying or waiting to enjoy breakfast before all the things suburban families did on weekends, most of which involved a child and some type of ball.

Elisabeth was jumpy, and the first thing she said was "Mom, I have a lot to do today. I'm sorry, but I don't have time to stand on line."

"I don't get it," I said. "There's never a wait here."

Jon pointed to the trophies on a table filled with fathers and sons. "Looks like there is some kind of awards breakfast going on."

I started rethinking my decision. Maybe I should have picked a restaurant that took reservations. Maybe I should suggest another place. The trouble was, I felt stressed enough without figuring out where we should go. No one was talking. And the silence between us was ringing like a school bell.

"It looks worse than it is," I said.

Ben assessed the situation. Jon said nothing, which was exactly the right thing to say.

"It's very nice to meet you, Jon," Elisabeth said, "but I can't stay. Maybe we will get together another time."

"You're going?" I asked. I think I squeaked it. I was so surprised and so let down.

"That group," she said, pointing out the stretch of fathers and sons, "will be here until next soccer season."

I could tell from his face that Jon thought Elisabeth had plenty of time. That the truth was that she didn't want to spend it with him. Jon strolled over to the self-service coffee.

I pulled Elisabeth aside. "Elisabeth, you're making Jon feel awful."

"I didn't plan on a three-day line for a pancake."

She always did like a "short" stack.

The three of us were silent until Jon returned with his coffee.

Ben said, "How about we just go over to Dunkin' Donuts?"

In New England, there's a Dunkin' Donuts on every corner. In the time it takes to eat one cruller, you're passing another Dunkin' Donuts.

Jon shook his head. "Why don't we just drive through?" he whispered to me.

I wasn't sure what to do now. But I knew what I should have done. I should have picked a restaurant that took a reservation.

"Elisabeth," Jon said, "I am so sorry about the wait. I understand how busy a doctor can be. I'm glad we got to meet, and I have to say you are even more beautiful in person than in pictures."

"Thank you," Elisabeth replied. "Well, I guess I could be a little late."

Jon smiled. Ben rolled his eyes. A friend of Elisabeth's walked in, and she fell into a conversation.

"Hammer. Party of four," the host, who was also a waiter and a busboy, called out.

"Not too bad," Ben said.

"I know the maître d'," Jon joked. "We went to catechism together."

"I thought you were Jewish," Ben said.

"That was a joke," Jon told him as we headed to our table.

Ben smiled at me as though to say "This guy isn't half-bad."

As we sat at the table, holding menus, Elisabeth continued to chat up her friend. I waved to her. Finally, she bothered to join us, ordering a short stack, as I expected. When our heaping platters arrived, Ben, Jon, and I dug in, as though the last time we'd seen food, it had been dropped on our encampment from a Red Cross helicopter. Not Elisabeth. She took out her cell and stared at it, as though reading a text.

"Oh, I really have to go," she said. "Ben, can you give me a ride?"

Jon glanced at me. I glanced back.

"No. But I can call an Uber."

I was so relieved that Ben wasn't leaving with her.

"Well, Jon, it was nice to meet you." She should have added, "Even if I was colder than gelato." She pushed in her chair and headed out the door.

Don't get me wrong. I didn't expect Elisabeth to greet Jon as though he were the Dalai Lama. Pleasantries would have more than met my expectations. But those pleasantries needed to last at least a half hour.

"Patriots fan?" Ben asked Jon to drum up conversation.

At least Ben was being gracious.

"Not really," Jon said.

"Me neither."

"Red Sox?" Jon asked.

"Yankees," Ben replied.

And then, from that one word, Yankees, the two revved into a discussion of players, scores, the old stadium, and the new stadium.

The bill came. Jon grabbed it.

"Thanks, Jon," Ben said. "Next time, it's on me."

"Then I will order the filet mignon," Jon joked.

"At Burger King?" Ben said.

We walked out into a beautiful day, and Ben went to his car.

"He's great," Jon said. "I enjoyed meeting Elisabeth, but I am sure not as much as she enjoyed meeting me."

"I am so sorry," I said. "It's going to take time." I blew out a breath. "Elisabeth is uncomfortable. What am I supposed to do? She's a grown woman. She's a doctor. She has patients."

He turned and stared directly into my eyes. "You should have planned this better."

"You're blaming me?" He pushes to meet my kids, then he holds me responsible when it doesn't work out?

"How often did you go out as a family to a place like Kerry's for an important occasion?"

"Just on weekends for breakfast."

"So you thought you would just get it over with. Not make a big deal. Is that what I am to you? No big deal?"

He was right. I had been so intent on getting the big meet-Jon moment over with that I had not thought at all about how he would feel or what would be best for him.

"Slapdash won't do. Either I'm important, or I don't need any of this. I have no baggage. No kids. No ex-wife. My life couldn't be simpler for you. I am not dancing at the perimeter of your circle."

I bit my bottom lip. I nodded. "You're right. I'm going to make this up to you. I am going to take a stand."

Ever since Harvey left, I had been working on that. I was taking stands all over town. Just the day before, I had fired my house cleaner. Not because she did a bad job. I used to call her the magician. It was because she stole my credit card and bought a television with it. She claimed it was for her son to take to college, to put in his dorm room. What really steamed me was she went totally top of the line. What? He was going to college with a seventy-two-inch television?

"Marcy, it's not always about taking a stand. Sometimes it's as simple as making a reservation."

The next day, I called Elisabeth.

"What was your problem?"

"I don't know. It was just weird."

"It may be weird. But it's my life," I said.

Silence.

"Elisabeth?"

"I'm sorry, Mom."

I was happy she was sorry.

"Tell you what," she said. "Why don't we try again? Ben can come to Connecticut another time, and we can all have dinner at the house. Or, better yet, why doesn't everyone come to my apartment? We can have drinks and cheese, and it will be relaxing."

I tried not to overreact, but I knew she could hear in my voice how thrilled I was.

Later, I walked upstairs and sat on Elisabeth's bed. Although my children had been gone for years, it was only recently that I had asked them to come home and claim their possessions—posters with pronouncements from Einstein and Freud, locked diaries, dusty textbooks, stuffed animals with missing body parts, prom pictures in front of limousines, term papers, college sweatshirts, party dresses short enough to be mistaken for blouses, ragged T-shirts purposefully ripped at the necks and bearing names of bands that no longer existed, and pictures of elementary school friends they hadn't seen since the first day of middle school. The list went on and on. I didn't live in a house. I owned a long-term-storage facility.

In her quest for success, Amanda had lived in four cities since high school, and her Day-Glo-pink bikini swimsuit was still in the armoire in her room. Elisabeth had hired a U-Haul but only because it was less irritating than having me on her back, when at the time, I was already a hump about her dating a married man. Ben had shown up with a duffel bag.

Yes, my kids had taken what they wanted from their rooms, but they had forgotten about the basement, which was loaded with the souvenirs of our lives. I had possessions that hadn't been looked at since Jimmy Carter couldn't get the hostages out of Iran.

I considered whether I had the heart to go down to my basement, which was the entire length and width of our house. Wisely, Harvey had decided to finish only half of it and leave the rest for storage. This worked well when the kids were in their teens. They were able to have a birthday party in the finished part and sneak off into the storage area to make out. I'd bet that they still didn't think I knew about this. But how else to account for sweaters I found crumpled in corners near the dusty, old furniture from Harvey's mother's house?

I left Elisabeth's room. I went downstairs and stood at the precipice. I put my hands on the knob to the basement door and took a step onto the charcoal carpeting.

At the bottom of the stairs, there were cartons and cartons of Bountiful merchandise and a life-size portrait of Harvey's mother. There were file cabinets, most of them in a color of green that didn't even exist anymore. I wondered why my husband, who owned a warehouse, needed to store the blight of his business in our house.

Beyond Harvey's stash, I could see cross-country and downhill skis. Looking at it all, you would have thought that my children had never walked on anything but snow. From Elisabeth's first Barbie tricycle to Ben's treasured ten-speed, the bicycles reminded me of a family—a large one at that. Then there were the souvenirs of life, all randomly tossed: Amanda's menagerie of stuffed animals, textbooks, pom-poms, and sombreros. A six-foot cork bulletin board with a prom picture and a pink invitation to Elisabeth's sweet sixteen.

I stared at the door to the portion that was actually supposed to be for storage and knew it was too much for me. I parked myself on the basement steps. How would this monstrosity ever be cleaned out? But more important, why did I care? If something had been in the basement all these years, why would I ever need it? It was all just stuff.

If I moved out of the house and Harvey moved in, the basement and everything in it would be his problem. The ultimate revenge! Harvey would be the one who had to clean up. Beg the kids to take their stuff. Or, at minimum, call a service to do it. But I knew he wouldn't do that until he had gone through everything. The memories of Bountiful Bosom could not simply be pillaged.

But there was more. What could be more freeing than leaving everything behind? I imagined myself in a new place with new things. Things I picked out in my own good time. That would be honestly, truly starting over—from scratch. I hadn't moved in over thirty years. *Moving* was my move.

I called Judy the Realtor. I told her my plan. Because we were friendly, she asked why I had finally made the decision to move. I told her it was easier than cleaning my basement.

We settled on a price point to start negotiations. She asked when I wanted to move in.

"Whenever they want to close."

"They'll want to close right away," she said. "After all, the property is empty, and it's owned by an estate. The other Realtor told me the estate needed the cash."

"Estate? You mean 'the children' own it."

"Marcy, it is always a great buy when you are buying from a dead man's kid."

Yellow house, here I come.

Chapter 15

Jon and I went to the movies during the week, because on Saturday there was always a line. Like most couples, Jon and I had developed an entire set of rituals. I was amazed how this had happened in such a short time. Our most ritualistic behavior took place at the movies.

We both disliked fountain sodas. So I always carried our canned drinks in my bag. I know full well you're not supposed to bring food and drinks into a movie theater, that they make most of their income from the refreshment stand, but after years of marriage, I did have some serious Harvey in me.

The first time I suggested bringing our own sodas, Jon was horrified. Until he met me, he just didn't drink at the movies. But once we started doing it, he liked it. He said it washed down the popcorn. By the way, we always got a large. Jon didn't like as much butter as I did—enough that the bag leaked—so I also brought a container to divvy up the popcorn so he didn't have to wallow in my butter.

On a Saturday night before I took ownership of my new house, we decided to go to a movie. This time (it was his turn to pick, so we had to see something where everyone was being pillaged), I didn't have cans of soda in the house, so I poured orange juice into a water bottle. As I was about to leave the house, I caught sight of the Ketel One on my counter and topped off the juice. We slipped into our seats just as the previews were ending and we were being warned about turning off our cell phones, which I always had to do at the last moment. I handed the bottle to Jon, who was already holding the popcorn, and he put it in the holder between our two seats. The movie started with the star shooting his way out of a building, and Jon nudged me. He pointed to the bottle as he took a slug. I mouthed, "Vodka." Halfway through the movie, when the star was shot but we knew he wouldn't die, because he was the star, we started giggling. I hit Jon in the leg and whispered, "Stop." But he couldn't. A woman behind us tapped my chair.

Then I began to laugh. I heard someone a few rows back say, "Quiet. It's a movie." That's when Jon and I lost control. We both stood up and hurried out of the theater. We sat down on the first padded bench against a wall and laughed uncontrollably.

"Never drive drunk in a theater," Jon said.

"And never yell 'Vodka' in a crowded one."

"Is there any left?" he asked.

I shook the bottle. Empty. "Get a grip, and we'll go back in."

"I don't want to go back in," he said.

"You don't?"

He put his hand on my tights and then moved up my denim skirt.

"We both know the bad guy is going to die in the last frame."

Instead of going back into the movie, we walked to the parking lot for Jon's car. "You make the movies so much fun," he said. "I've been looking for someone like you."

I looped my arm around his and huddled close. For a moment, I closed my eyes, even though I was walking.

He mentioned my move, and I opened my eyes.

"I can go to Maine, borrow my brother's truck, and move every-thing for you," he said, trying to be helpful, as usual.

Moving was something I had to do on my own. First off, I didn't want to feel as though Jon and I were moving into a house together. We weren't. I wanted this to be my thing, my accomplishment, and the true starting point of my new life. I knew that if I could close the door of the house I had lived in my entire adult life—the house I had brought my kids up in, the house my mother had visited—and drive off, I could accomplish anything.

"Thank you so much," I replied sweetly, "but as I mentioned, I am only taking my clothes and some personal items, so I can move it all. I'll just do it piecemeal. I don't need help."

"You're saying that now, but you will change your mind."

I knew I wasn't going to change anything . . . except houses.

"I'm ready, willing, and able," he insisted as he walked in front of me, then turned to face me. "You know how able I am, right?"

I laughed, but I needed him to back off. In fact, Jon not backing off was the single most annoying thing about him.

I could hear Mom. *"He wants to help. So that's so bad? What—you want a man who lets you schlep? Then go back to Harvey."*

"Mom, Harvey never made me schlep. He always hired someone to do the schlepping."

I touched Jon's hand. "I have to do this myself."

"You're very brave," he said.

I took his hand. I loved when he said something good about me. I wanted it to continue, so I said, "Why am I brave?"

"Marcy, you are pushing forward. You could have just stayed where you are. In a very large and beautiful home with memories of everything that ever happened to you."

I am brave, I thought. *I'm practically a Navy SEAL.*

Dana called to give me the name of a moving company. I told her I was mostly taking clothing and, of course, important things like the vase Ben had made at camp. She was aghast.

"Are you nuts? You're leaving *him* with the goodies? I don't care if you want all new accoutrements. At least sell the furniture before he takes it and you don't get a cent for it. Besides, you have silver and good china and . . ."

"Calm down." Her concern was giving me the hives.

"There are going to be things you want, and maybe you won't be able to get them later. I wanted all the record albums when I divorced my first husband. But he wanted them too."

I hadn't heard the words "record albums" in years, maybe thirty plus. "You're dating yourself."

"I meant cassettes."

"So who made off with the albums?"

"We alphabetized all the performers, and we each got every other one."

"So he got . . ."

"Captain and Tennille."

"And you scored . . ."

"Eric Clapton."

Way to go, Dana. "Who took the Monkees?" I asked.

"He did."

"Micky Dolenz was so cute."

"The point is I wish I had walked away with all the albums."

Chapter 16

The key to the new house was in my hand, and my hand was shaking. I had not lived in a place that was my own since I had attended graduate school in my twenties. Back then, I had rented a studio in Greenwich Village. I had kept my clothes and shoes behind a curtain of beads. My finest piece of furniture had been my desk, which I had pushed against a wall in a corner to stop it from wobbling. My living conditions changed radically when I met Harvey. He was older than me and well established in his family's business. A week before we tied the knot, I moved into his apartment in a doorman building with a courtyard. It was on the Upper West Side.

We resituated to Atherton, mostly because Feldman insisted we needed to purchase a house for the tax deduction. A lot of my life decisions came about that way. Deduct, deduct, deduct. I had preferred a cozy country home like the one I was about to move into. Harvey had insisted on a behemoth.

After a while, I grew to love my Atherton home and all the memories we created in it. The sounds of the kids trampling noisily down the stairs to a dinner of spaghetti and meatballs and garlic bread. Dozing off at the kitchen table at three in the morning while Ben was completing his science fair project, a solar system made of Silly Putty. Piling into the family room, the fire roaring, the hot buttered popcorn in a ceramic bowl, watching a video together on a snowy Saturday night. There was another thing that was important to me—I loved that my mother had been in my house. Her spirit, her being, had touched everything. It was as all-encompassing as air. This was something I would never be able to say about the residence I was clutching the keys to now.

Often, now, I recalled the sounds of Mom's slow, cautious steps on a staircase. She herself had lived her adult life in a ranch home, everything on one floor. She had never become accustomed to and didn't like what she saw as the inconvenience of a home with two levels. When my children were infants, she would call several times a day to remind me to be careful when carrying the baby down the stairs. "Hold on to the railing" was her mantra.

This new house wouldn't have Mom in it, but then, it wouldn't have Harvey in it either.

Never in my life did I think I would ever be this grown up.

I stood inside the yellow house with the Yankee-blue door left open. I lifted my arms out. I jumped once up and down on the beautiful oak-plank floor. I had always adored broad planks, but Harvey had thought they reminded him of a farm. So moo this. I bent down and ran my hand over the polished wood. I wondered who else had touched those floors. Who had lived in this house? Did they have children? Were they happy?

I wondered if anyone had ever died in the house. I felt myself shake. What if someone had died in the house or, worse, been murdered? *You can do this, Marcy. Stop with the morbid ruminations that make you think you can't.*

I looked at the walls with nothing on them, just a coat of white paint that covered so many other coats of paint that had decorated the house. I wondered what colors the house had been before.

I heard my mother. *"White gets so dirty. Paint a color."*

But what color would I paint? I needed paint chips. Pronto. And it was going to be easy to choose from infinite shades of blue, because I had Candy to help me. Even Jon. I decided I had made a good decision becoming close with artists.

Then I thought, *I'll hang Jon's art on my walls.* I had to ask him about it.

I peeked into the living room on the right, the redbrick fireplace in the center of the longest wall. There was a mantel of gray slate. I decided immediately that I wanted one of Jon's Maine abstracts above the mantel. I thought about the one that Moxie disliked—the pier in Maine. I liked that one more than ever now. Maybe Jon had another one that was similar.

I turned my head to the dining room. There was enough room for a table that seated six to eight. I could have a dinner party, or I could have a large affair with everyone roaming about. *Come for cocktails,* I thought. *Join me on Saturday for cocktails, hors d'oeuvres, and scrumptious desserts from Sweet Heaven Bakery. Join "me."*

I loved the way that sounded.

Most of all, I prized how the house was delightfully void of my history—no furniture, no pictures, no mementos—a clean slate. Excited, I stamped my feet until a heel came off my shoe. I picked it up and looked at it and laughed.

I decided I had to see what it was like to be in every corner of the house, so I took off my shoes and walked heel-to-toe the entire perimeter—downstairs and then upstairs. In addition to a living room, dining room, and kitchen, the first floor had a laundry room, a half bath, and a bedroom I would use as a home office. Upstairs, there was a large, light-filled master suite to the right, a smaller room to the left, and another full bath in the hall.

I sat down at the bottom of the stairs. I cried. Happiness. Relief. I looked at my watch. It was four in the afternoon. I called Candy and

Dana and Jon and left messages for them to come over. Candy was the only one I reached. She said she was with Ellison. Was it okay if he came too?

I carried the suitcases of clothing I had brought from the car into the house. I went back out for the kids' college graduation photographs. I had taken them off the walls of the old house. But I had left the hooks up—for Harvey. Harvey would head up the stairs his first day back in the house and see hook, hook, hook. If only we had had more kids so I could have left more hooks.

I had a few other favorite pictures, including one of Amanda and me. We were on a weathered two-seat rocker in the fall. I looked peaceful in a fisherman's sweater. Amanda was three or four, with big eyes, a big smile, and little pigtails.

As I reached in the back seat for my parents' wedding picture, I heard a honk. I turned to see who it was. I saw Jon in his Subaru.

Jon stepped out of his car in jeans, a T-shirt, and a baseball cap. "I brought a gift. And of course, I need a grand tour." He carried in three large paintings wrapped in paper and blankets. In the living room, he unveiled each one. "I'd say these walls need some color."

As we were deciding where the paintings should go, we heard a car in the driveway. It was a Porsche. I could see Candy and Ellison in the front seats. They waved as they got out.

Jon extended his hand to Ellison, who was wearing a sports jacket, a T-shirt, and corduroys. Candy wore a skirt and blouse as usual. I was thrilled they had come.

I had a new house—and a new kind of family as well. No, I would not be alone.

As always, Candy had brought gifts. She had flowers, a basket of fruit, and a bottle of champagne. But she had forgotten glasses. I pointed that out. She said the champagne wasn't for drinking. It was for christening the house. Jon cracked it open against the front door. Then he chased me around the yard with what was left of the champagne.

I tagged Ellison, then screamed, "You're it!"

The game began. We chased each other like kids.

Finally, Jon yelled, "Marcy, it's time to come home for supper!"

He went to his car and carried an old red-and-white Coleman cooler to the porch. It was filled with four beautiful new glasses, green grapes, duck pâté, French bread, and two bottles of wine.

"Thank you, Mr. Thoughtful," I said. "You are one of a kind."

We relaxed on the porch. Candy raised her glass. "To the house of Marcy."

Chapter 17

Jon and I drove to Elisabeth's. She lived nearby, in a former factory town that had been transformed by young artists and hipsters. You could buy anything you wanted in town as long as it was organic, vegan, and gluten-free.

We climbed the three flights to her one-bedroom apartment. After she welcomed us, we maneuvered our way around her ten-speed bike in the foyer.

"I'm sorry, Jon, but I have nowhere else to keep it."

"I have a canoe in my living room, dead center," Jon said.

"You do?"

"He does," I said. "He made it himself."

"You know how to make a canoe?"

"He's a Renaissance man," I said.

"I guess he is," Elisabeth said, smiling as she stood at the counter and poured wine into our glasses. Elisabeth knew Jon was a professor and an artist, but there was something about the canoe that made her think Jon was unique, thank heavens.

"I'd like to invite you over sometime," Jon said.

Elisabeth sipped her wine. "Can I sit in your canoe?"

"Your mother certainly does."

My nerves were soothed. This was going so well. I couldn't wait for Ben to come. Nobody was easier than Ben. He was like me. He wanted everything to be pleasant. Mr. Congeniality.

We stood at the counter. Elisabeth had assembled a groaning board of cheeses, olives, pâté, and crackers. There was also a display of fruit. She began talking about one of her patients. Lucky for me, Jon had an aunt who had the same disease.

There was a hard bang at the door, then another and another.

"Hold your horses!" shouted Elisabeth as she hurried to the door.

Ben blustered in. He was in a drenched raincoat and hiking boots. He could have been in the shower and would have had less water on him.

"I guess it started raining," I said.

"Sudden and torrential," Ben said, wiping water off his face. "And there was no parking nearby. I had to go all the way down to the movie house."

"Take off your boots," Elisabeth said.

"I'm not taking off anything," Ben said in an angry tone that was so unusual for him, I thought it came from a ventriloquist.

Jon was king of social cues. He glanced at me and then glanced away. He plucked his wine from the counter, backed up silently, and went to the couch. He sat back like a voyeur.

"Have you heard the latest?" Ben said to no one in particular.

I shook my head.

"The boots," Elisabeth said.

"The boots," he said, imitating her.

Jon moved to the corner of the couch. I felt as if he were in the wrong movie.

"I come bearing family news. I just spoke to my ignorant sister in Seattle."

"And?" Elisabeth said. If he was about to bad-mouth Amanda, she was willing to help him get to the point.

"Guess where she wants to get married?"

"Where now?" I said.

"She wants to get married in Fortuda, the island near Bermuda."

"Someone hand me my shorts and knee socks, please," Elisabeth said.

As for me, I said nothing, because I was well aware that we had an audience, and this wasn't the play I wanted him to see.

"That's all you know about Fortuda?" Ben said.

"I've never been there," Elisabeth said. "By the way, the boots. And you're dripping on my wood floor."

Ben ignored her. "Fortuda is antigay."

"What do you mean, antigay?" I said.

"A gay person cannot get married on a cruise ship registered in Fortuda. Not only are they homophobic on land. They're homophobic in the ocean. Amanda is so insensitive. How is it that she was brought up by the same people as me?"

"Give me the raincoat, Ben," Elisabeth said.

Ben handed her the raincoat.

"I had no idea," I said. "And I am sure she has no idea. Did you tell her?"

"Of course I told her. Just now on the phone. You know what she said? She said we were all out to ruin her special day."

"Oh, not with that 'special day' again," Elisabeth moaned.

"She had the sympathy of a hawk for a carcass," he said. "How about a drink?"

Elisabeth went to pour some wine.

"A *drink*," Ben said.

She made him a martini. "Olive?"

"Yes. Stuffed. In my sister's face."

"Ben, you have to calm down. I am sure Amanda did not know about the discrimination in Fortuda. I am sure that once she has a moment to think, she will reconsider her plans."

I noticed Jon's eyes shoot from me to Ben, awaiting his response.

"I was so steamed, I just hung up. No one can talk to her about this wedding. Besides, do you think she cares about anyone but herself? Me, me, me! It's the only opera she knows."

Elisabeth laughed. I could see Jon holding it in.

Ben was pacing in his wet shoes. However, Elisabeth was now enjoying this indictment of her sister too much to be bothered by some soggy boots. "Amanda not only looks out for number one, she doesn't think there's a number two."

I defended Amanda. "Stop. I'm sure she didn't know about the discrimination."

"Don't be naive," Elisabeth chimed in.

"I told you that I told her," Ben said as he took a chug of his drink.

"Slow down, Ben," I said.

"She's deaf when it comes to other people," Ben snapped.

Jon remained on the couch, not saying a word, holding his chin in his palm, watching the ball being slammed back and forth, like he was at Wimbledon.

"Let me read to you from this tour guide for gays." He took his cell phone out of his jacket pocket and read. "If you choose to go to this island hell, you should keep a good distance between you and your partner."

"That's outrageous!" Elisabeth said. "Amanda chose Fortuda out of the air. She can select another island that's just as ridiculously expensive and time consuming to get to."

Ben held out his phone. "Good. So tell her."

"You have to talk to her," she said.

Ben put the phone away. "She's the most selfish person alive. I should have stopped talking to her when she busted my Walkman in high school and wouldn't pay to replace it."

"I replaced it," I said.

"She's still a bitch."

"Enough."

"And you know what else?" Ben said, "I don't see *her* here tonight."

Jon stood, and I could tell it occurred to Ben for the first time that there had been an audience for our family drama, that Jon was present. That Jon had heard Ben at his worst.

"Hi, Jon. Welcome to the family," Ben said.

❦

Elisabeth lent us an umbrella. It was no longer pouring, just raining slightly, as Jon and I found his car. I reached for his hand. I felt terrible that the night had turned out the way it had.

"I am sorry," I said. "This wasn't what I expected. I really, really apologize. If you are willing, and I wouldn't blame you if you weren't, we'll do it again another time."

"Are you serious? I loved it," he said.

What? He had to be kidding.

"I loved watching your family. I loved being with your *real* family. I loved your kids being real in front of me. And it was the first time I witnessed you as a mother. You're good at it."

"Thank you," I said, feeling warm and proud and appreciated. I squeezed his hand.

"So, what are you going to do?" Jon said as he held open the door for me.

"She's not getting married in Fortuda. But I'm not mixing in." Harvey would never, ever agree to a place that discriminated against Ben. Besides, he had told me that day in the house that he planned to steer Amanda to the Seascape in Florida. I was staying out of all this.

"Good decision," Jon said, then he shut my door.

It was so insanely wonderful to have someone I respected tell me that I had decided the right thing, to have a partner to share even the rotten experiences with. As he got into the driver's seat, I thought about how lucky I was to have met Jon. After Harvey left, I couldn't imagine how or where I would meet another man. I kept imagining myself in a low-cut dress at singles' night, the kind in bars—worst of all, suburban bars that had names like Peaches—sitting in a row with a hundred other divorcées, all blond, chitchatting with the bartender.

The next morning, I called Amanda.

"I know you," she said as though she had been right about forecasting Hurricane Katrina and had told everyone to leave New Orleans a week in advance. "I know you put Dad up to it."

"Up to what?"

"He just called. He told me that he wouldn't foot the bill for a wedding in Fortuda."

"He did? Amanda, I didn't say a word to Dad."

"Oh, yeah, right."

I decided to drop it and let her blame me. Why not blame it on Mom? Everyone put it on Mom. I certainly had, but at least I stopped after she died. Not everyone can say that. My cousin Leona was still pointing a finger at her mom for making her wear braces in high school when everyone else was already done. Until this day, Leona said it was the reason she never had a date. I didn't think so. I thought the reason Leona never had a date was that she was a bitch. Who cared what Amanda thought? As long as she got married somewhere that wasn't an affront to gay people everywhere.

"Amanda, there are plenty of places to get married, places that aren't offensive to your brother—and by extension, to us."

"That's not why I'm upset. I'm upset because I was done. I had a place—the Buckingham Palace Resort in Fortuda. Now I have to start all over again. Ben gets everything he wants—just because he's gay."

What was she? Ten?

"Elisabeth is the star, because she's a doctor. Ben is the favorite, because you always have to worry about how problematic it is to be gay in this world. It's not that problematic when you reside in Chelsea in Manhattan. You know what's difficult in Chelsea? To be heterosexual, that's what."

"Are you done with this ridiculous rant?"

"If you're done meddling . . ."

"I didn't meddle, and what's more, this is a decision you should have come to on your own."

"So, what? Now you are calling me insensitive?"

I had no clue, no idea, how to assure Amanda that if all three children needed me at once, I would divide myself in thirds. Also, I didn't think this was a good time to ask her when she herself was going to meet Jon.

I'd had enough for one morning. I said good-bye to Amanda. I felt like talking to someone my own age, so I headed over to Candy's. When I arrived, Candy was in overalls on the damp and shady edge of a pond in her yard. We chatted as she planted mats of very dark moss. Until that very moment, I didn't know anyone planted moss. I thought it was a weed. Candy told me that many people planted moss and she thought that it added a sense of calm and stillness to a garden. In that case, I definitely needed some moss. She asked me if I wanted her to plant moss at my new house.

"Of course," I said because it would make her happy. "But does it require upkeep?"

"No, that's why it's perfect for you."

"How are you doing?" I asked in a soft voice, as though if I said it softly, it would result in what I wanted to hear.

"There's bad news," she said.

"What?" I said, putting my fingers over my mouth.

"Can you hand me that moss?"

I did what she said. I picked up the moss on an edge, as if it were a dead bug.

She shook her head. "The tumor on my uterus is malignant." She stood up from the ground and removed her gardening gloves.

I shook my head. I couldn't stop. But I had to stop before I caused her to cry. "It can't be," I said. "There is no way this can happen. I won't allow it to happen."

She looked at me as though I was the one who was ill. "Hopefully, the doctor will remove it and find the cancer hasn't spread."

I was worried. I couldn't think. I forgot where I was, or I wanted to forget or just not hear anymore.

"Marcy, you could help here." She was loading her red wheelbarrow.

I tried to make her laugh. "Moss is gross," I said, pronouncing "gross" like "moss."

"Have you ever seen a hillside of British moss?"

"No, of course not."

"Well, if I survive this thing, we're going."

I'd go look at moss. I'd go look at anything, as long as she was going to be okay.

Chapter 18

Amanda, Harvey, and I were at a speck of a French restaurant on a corner in Greenwich Village. An elderly French woman kept post from a bistro chair positioned at the door. Her head hung low, as though she was snoozing, but I had a feeling she wasn't missing a thing. My bet was she was the owner and that she had turned the place reluctantly over to her children. She wore a leopard-print wrap dress, beige hose, and heavy black shoes.

As we entered, I looked around. The walls were painted yellow. White lights were strung across the room. The red vinyl bar had five seats facing a long glass shelf chockablock with liquor bottles. On the far side of the bar was a small black-and-white television hanging from the wall. The happy bartender and a waiter—in striped French sailor shirts—were thoroughly enjoying a game of soccer.

A middle-aged couple in bright casual clothing, almost neon in color—confirming they were tourists, not New Yorkers—had walked into the restaurant before us. They grabbed two stools at the bar and asked the bartender if he could switch the channel to the Mets game. So much for international relations.

A young hostess led us to our table, which was covered with white paper and had crayons sitting in a cup next to the salt and pepper. She handed us old-fashioned menus. I asked for French onion soup. Harvey ordered croque monsieur. Amanda went for the country pâté. We all had iced tea.

"You are going to be so excited," Amanda said, brimming with happiness.

Harvey and I looked at each other.

"We have decided where we are having the wedding."

"The dude ranch?" I said.

"What dude ranch?" Harvey asked, bewildered.

So she never even told Harvey about the Colorado idea, I thought.

"The Seascape!"

Harvey broke into an ear-to-ear grin.

"Jake just loved it, and we met the manager, who told him so many great stories about Dad."

I was as amazed as I was happy. "The Seascape is lovely," I said. "Do you have a date?"

"The Saturday night before Christmas."

I thought this was wonderful, especially since Guild for Good was closed the last two weeks of December.

"Don't forget to have the pigs in the blankets," Harvey said. "At the cocktail hour."

"Dad, we are not having hot dogs rolled in dough."

"Why not?"

"We are doing tuna tartare."

I had no opinion on men in penguin suits passing pigs in a blanket during the cocktail hour. I was more interested in potato latkes. I wanted something about the wedding to be traditionally Jewish, and because she had told me that she had chosen not to be married by a rabbi, I thought crispy mini potato latkes with a choice of applesauce or sour cream just might make up for the prayers.

Harvey perseverated on the pigs, and Amanda told him once again they were out of the question.

"Who's paying for this wedding?" Harvey asked. When in doubt, pull purse strings.

"It's not about money, Dad. It's about personal style."

"You wanted the wedding at a resort. It's at a resort. You wanted everyone to fly to a state no one lives in. We're flying. Amanda, this whole thing stops at pigs in a blanket."

Harvey really enjoyed little hot dogs rolled up in dough. I used to keep them frozen in our freezer and pop a few into the microwave whenever he was in the mood. He would become very upset if I didn't also have the brown deli mustard he liked.

"It's my day," Amanda said. "And I am not going to ruin it, ruin everything, with tacky little hot dogs from Hebrew National."

"I understand," I said, wondering why Harvey couldn't leave the hand-passed appetizers alone, since he now had the wedding exactly where he wanted it.

"And Dad, by the way, Hebrew National isn't even kosher anymore. No super-religious Jews eat Hebrew National. They should take out the word 'Hebrew' and just call it 'National.'"

Amanda cooled down as the waitress delivered our orders. Then she turned to me. "Well, Mom, if you understand about the hot dogs, maybe you will also understand about the potato pancakes."

"What about them?" I asked, hoping they would be crisp and wouldn't turn out too greasy. When they were oily at home, I blotted them. But at the wedding, nothing could be done.

"I know how you love them, but if we have potato pancakes, we might as well dance the hora."

"Are you saying you are not dancing the hora?" I said, bewildered.

My daughter was a Jewish girl marrying a Jewish boy. What did they have against a celebratory dance that had been used at weddings and bar mitzvahs the world over for more than 5,700 years? Okay, so maybe not 5,700 years, but as long as I remembered. Even those who just stood back and clapped to the music had a good time. I especially liked the part where friends lifted both bride and groom in chairs and everyone danced around them. At our wedding, Harvey and I were hoisted up and down as we each held on to the ends of a white napkin. I felt it was a symbol of us always being connected. Oh well, so much for that. What was wrong with Amanda? Had she not seen *Fiddler on the Roof*?

"No hora," she said flatly.

Harvey and I looked at each other. I decided to let him take over.

"I think Rabbi Straus will be happy to fly down and perform the ceremony," Harvey said.

"And no rabbi," she said.

"First, no hora, and now no rabbi?" Harvey said.

I was surprised Harvey hadn't been apprised of the rabbinical situation. Just what was Amanda telling him about?

"Who's going to marry you? A minister?" he asked.

"We are being married by Jake's psychiatrist."

"I never heard of that," I said, confirming my dinosaur status.

"You would have to be crazy to get married by a psychiatrist," Harvey said.

"He is becoming ordained online for the day. We don't want to be married by a perfect stranger. We don't want to hear meaningless blah, blah, blah. No one knows us better than Dr. Genesis."

"He knows Jake. Does he know you?" Harvey asked.

"Yes. We've gone to couples counseling."

Couples counseling? She hadn't even married him yet, and they went for counseling? I hoped once they were married, they never had sexual or financial problems or disagreed on whether to buy a baby crib that converted into a twin bed. *Okay, stop making fun. Maybe if you had gone for counseling, you would still be living with your husband and still be listening to his endless talk about underwire versus no-wire bras.*

"We feel that Dr. Genesis will say the poignant things we want to hear at the ceremony. He will keep it intimate and personal."

It's a wedding, not a sex act, I thought.

"Does Dr. Genesis know Jake wet his bed until he was seven?" I asked.

"How did you know that?"

"His mother mentioned it to me when I called to tell her how wonderful it was to meet her. Not that it's anything to be ashamed of."

"Of course he knows. That's the whole point," Amanda said. "He knows us."

"Rabbi Straus knows you," I said, evoking the name of the rabbi at the temple we long ago attended regularly but now visited only once a year on Yom Kippur.

"Rabbi Straus does not know me."

"Yes, he does. He can tell the story of how you put the sign for the women's bathroom on the men's bathroom in fifth grade."

"Mom, this is not funny."

Harvey threw his napkin down on his sandwich. That's how I knew he was really angry. Harvey always finished his food. He'd croak before giving up a croque monsieur. He pushed out his bistro chair and stood up.

"Amanda, dance the damn dance. And there better be pigs in a blanket."

Harvey walked past the old French lady sitting at the door and out of the restaurant (he has a penchant for walking out), leaving me sitting with Amanda.

"He is so ridiculous," she said. "Positively ancient. You know that's why he hasn't even tried to bring Bountiful to its deserved place on the Internet. I could set him up in days. But no."

"This isn't about your father," I said.

"Oh, wow, now you are defending him?"

"You're marrying a Jewish boy. Why wouldn't you want to celebrate your traditions?"

"I didn't want to tell you this, because I didn't want to upset you, but I guess it's time to let the cat out of the bag."

No, no, I thought. *Keep the cat in the bag. Suffocate the cat.*

"Jake is an atheist. And I'm thinking of becoming an atheist."

"What does that mean?" I knew what it meant, but I needed time to breathe.

"He doesn't believe in God," she whispered.

"What's God got to do with Judaism? We're talking tradition. Do you think eating a bagel is a religious rite?"

"Mom, I don't want to argue. I am having a hard enough time dealing with the fact that I am getting married, and my parents are separated. Is nothing for sure in this world?"

Go ahead. Hit me with a poisonous arrow.

I turned toward the business of my French onion soup. But it had grown cold. I didn't expect my daughter to be an atheist for longer than it took to pray for the next thing she wanted. After all, normally, before she'd started planning a wedding, she'd been very smart and had a lot of common sense. I decided I wanted to get along with Amanda and that I wouldn't say another word about any of her decisions.

"Maybe just step on the glass," I said.

"Mom!"

Barefoot, I thought.

I sat back, disgusted. The whole wedding was maybe three hours. Why had three hours become the debacle of a lifetime anyway? The wedding was ringing in my ears, frustrating me like a honker of an alarm in my car that wouldn't go off no matter how frantically I searched for the knob that would silence it.

I still hadn't told Jon that he was not invited. I was waiting for a good time, but I knew there wasn't one. *"Thanks for the wonderful dinner, Jon, and by the way, Amanda would rather take in toxic fumes in a locked closet than have you at her wedding."*

Amanda thought we were all torturing her, and if I heard her say one more time that it was "her special day," I was going to strangle myself with a blue garter belt after swallowing something old—Prozac in a ten-year-old pharmaceutical container.

⤳

When I got to the sloping lot on Eighth Street where I had parked, I stood outside and called Jon. I read the pricing chart as I waited for him to pick up. Parking was twenty-five dollars an hour. For twenty-five dollars an hour, you would think they would have taught my car a second language.

Finally, Jon picked up.

"It's me," I said like a little lost dog. I loved saying "It's me." You know you are extremely close to someone when all you have to say on the other end of the phone is "It's me."

"How did it go?" Jon said immediately in a breath. Imagine a man who wants to know what happened to you before telling you what happened to him. I had dreamed the impossible dream.

"It was like being at a basketball game," I reported disappointedly.

"How bad could that be?"

"I was the ball."

"Tell me."

"Amanda says she is now an atheist. She doesn't want anything at the wedding that would remotely remind anyone that she is a Jew."

"What about Harvey? No mistaking him for a Baptist."

"It's not funny," I said, feeling weepy. "She doesn't even want potato pancakes."

"That heathen," Jon said, pretending to be outraged.

179

I had to laugh. The laugh made me feel better. "Do you think I'm being ridiculous?"

"Of course not," he said.

"Are you sure?" I asked as a car shot out of the parking lot too close to where I was standing. I moved farther to the side as the driver in a baseball cap stalled his old Buick to give me a finger.

"Move over, Mama," he sneered.

"I'm not your mama, Grandpa!" I said to the driver.

"What's going on?" Jon said.

"Bad driver." I felt like a heap of dung. "Is it okay if I come over? I should be back in Atherton in a couple of hours."

"See you when you get here."

∽ඉ

I climbed three floors. Jon met me at his door. He unbolted the lock and let me in. He was wearing a flannel shirt, jeans, and a big smile on his face, like he had a secret he was bursting to tell.

"What smells?" I said. "Is something burning?"

"Oh no," he said as he rushed over to the stove in the galley kitchen and removed a sizzling frying pan. "Sit down a minute," he called out.

I sat on the chair by the window. I checked my phone. Candy had left a message about a doctor's appointment she wanted me to go to with her. I texted back that of course I would be there. I looked outside to the alley, where kids were playing, dividing into teams for something. I wondered why life couldn't be that simple. Then I remembered that it was no picnic playing games as a child. I was a klutz, and I always got picked last. When I was chosen next to last, it was only because there was a girl who was chubby. Then she would be last, and I would feel awful for her.

"Okay, come to the kitchen," Jon said.

On the counter was a small jar of Mott's applesauce. In his hand was a speckled platter stacked with potato pancakes.

I melted. "You're too much," I said. "Don't tell me you made these."

"Ran down to the supermarket and bought a few boxes of Golden frozen."

"I love the frozen ones," I said.

He handed me a fork. We ate until there was only one pancake, blackened, left.

"Don't eat that one," I said.

"Why not?"

"Let's save it for Amanda."

"I've been thinking . . ."

"Don't do that," I said. "It's dangerous."

"When was thinking dangerous?" he asked.

"When I was thinking my husband was trustworthy."

He looked at me seriously.

"I have a suggestion. Maybe we need to go to synagogue," he said.

"What?"

"Your issue with Amanda is her lack of interest in Jewish traditions."

"Bingo," I said.

"But when is the last time you went to synagogue?"

"I went on Yom Kippur to atone for my sin."

"Just one sin?"

"Oh, wait. I just thought of another one. I may have, maybe once in a whole year, said something bad about another person."

He laughed. "I think I know you better than that."

"Well, I only count it as a sin if what I said wasn't true or, worse yet, if it wasn't funny."

"That can get the sin count down, all right."

"I was also xenophobic."

"Fear of strangers?"

"No—fear of Zen," I said. "What about you?"

"Honestly?"

"Well, if you are not honest, you will have to atone for that too."

"I don't respect my mother and my father."

"I thought your parents were gone."

"They are. But I don't visit the cemetery."

"Oh," I said quietly, as I knew he was being very revealing, and it was probably hard for him to say what he had just said.

"The truth is, I don't want to go alone."

"I will go with you. I mean, if that's okay."

"Really? You would? A day at a cemetery is not exactly a day at the park."

"I like dead people. They don't answer back. That's with the exception of my own mother. I hear her talking to me most of the day."

"What is she saying?"

"Go buy a new sweater. Marcy, be nice to your brother."

"I wish I had known her."

"You know me. You know her."

"Is that true?"

"Look how I am handling this Amanda-is-getting-married ordeal."

"I think you are exaggerating. Ordeal?"

"Well, that's what my mom would have called it."

"Okay," he said. "So we will go to the cemetery."

"You are so romantic. You stop at nothing in that department."

"And we will go to synagogue," he said.

"What's your Hebrew name anyway?" I asked.

"Yakov ben Chaim. What's yours?"

"Rose Fitzgerald Kennedy."

He twisted the lid on the Mott's and put the jar in the refrigerator. His refrigerator was full. I liked that. I especially liked that I knew he had filled it himself. That he took care of himself.

"You know, I used to go to synagogue a lot," I said. "Especially when the kids were growing up. Before we bar mitzvahed each child, we had to attend Saturday services ten weeks straight. The rabbi wanted to make sure we knew the ropes. Plus, I sent my kids to Jewish camps. You know the kind—team sports are optional."

I took the platter to the sink and washed it. Then I scrubbed the burned pan.

"I can do that," he said.

"No, you made the pancakes."

"So you went to synagogue for your kids, but have you gone for yourself?"

"Wow, Jon. I didn't know Jews proselytized."

"Well, I am just saying maybe you are being a tad hypocritical about this Amanda thing. Maybe Amanda doesn't know how much this all means to you."

"Believe me, she knows. She understands that Judaism has nothing to do with religion."

"Judaism has nothing to do with religion—is that a quote from the Torah?"

"Deuteronomy," I said as I turned off the faucet and faced him.

"You mean like the cat with that name in *Cats*? It sounds familiar."

"Jon, I know what I am talking about."

"Okay, she's your daughter. You would know."

"When's the last time you went to synagogue?" I asked.

"I went to a service yesterday morning," he said.

"You went to synagogue on a Thursday?"

"Ten people are required for a service, so if they run short, they call me, and I dash over. No big deal. It's across the street."

"That's really nice."

"Lots of people do it."

"If lots of people did it, they wouldn't be hard up for a tenth person in a synagogue that has five hundred members."

Jon shrugged. He went behind the counter and turned the faucet, as I had left it dripping. I stepped behind him. I rubbed his neck in circles with my fingertips. He turned to face me.

Together, we moved to the living room and fell onto his couch.

⁓

I was at home, reading Sunday's *New York Times* in bed. I was up to the style section, the wedding announcements. Was there anyone in the world who did not graduate from Harvard Law, whose father wasn't a partner in a hedge fund?

I wondered whether Amanda was planning for an announcement in the *Times*. I thought how it would read: *"The bride's father owns Bountiful, the brassiere empire. Her mother works as executive director of the Guild for Good. The bride's parents separated when her father announced he was having a baby with a lingerie model who wore a 32DD. This wedding is being held at an inconvenient time."*

I heard a buzz. There was a text from Amanda.

Save-the-date card?

I typed back. ???

When to send?

Three months before.

What if you don't want someone to come?

Like?

Almost everyone Dad has invited.

I heard Dana's voice from the bottom of my staircase.

I have to go. Dana's here.

"Put down that *New York Times*, and come talk to me," Dana said.

"No. You come up here."

"Come down."

What was this? A contest to see which one of us could be laziest? She had no hope of winning. "Come up."

"Meet you halfway," she said.

I met her on the stairs. We each sat on a step. "What's going on?"

"Calvin wants his mother to come live with us."

"Whoa. In your house?"

"No. In your house," she said dully.

"Very funny."

"He doesn't want to move to Boston."

I held back a smile. I was sure Dana could expand her business no matter where she lived, so I was happy to hear she was staying in Connecticut.

"He claims I can handle both offices from Atherton. He wants to build one of those freestanding mini houses on our property and have his mom live in it. It's a trend now. You build a three-hundred-foot shack with a pinch of a kitchen and a bathroom with a handicapped toilet and a shower stall, and that's where you stash the declining relative you'd rather not live with."

"I thought that was what nursing homes were for."

"He says she's not yet ready for a nursing home."

"Well, she is his mother," I said. "He wants to take care of her. He wants to do the right thing. Look, it could be worse. He could want her to stay in your house. After all, you have three empty bedrooms."

"That's what he wanted. But I refused. Do you know what she did the last time she stayed with us? She went through my cabinets and tossed out all the dishes that didn't match."

"But you're like Jon. None of your dishes match."

"Exactly. You know what else? She combined all the cereals."

"What?" I said to that ridiculous notion.

"She poured every open cereal into one big plastic bag, tied a knot in it, and put it back in the cabinet. I had Raisin Bran in my Rice Krispies."

"It's a cruel world, Dana, a cruel world."

"Not as cruel as my daughter-in-law is to me."

"Things are bad?"

"Actually better. I'm doing everything I can to earn points with Moxie. She's allowing me to babysit again this Saturday. She needs a sitter on Saturdays so she can be in Connecticut. She's going to some classes here."

"For what?"

"She's training to become a certified psychic."

"You have to train to become a psychic? Couldn't you just see into the future and know what to do?"

Dana shrugged. "Who cares? I see an opening. It's my chance to look like a hero. I told her to bring the baby to Connecticut, and I will watch him. The problem is, I have so much on my plate—babysitting, the agency, the twins, and now my mother-in-law. As much as I hate to say this, and I never said it before, I am not thirty anymore."

"That's right. You're thirty-one," I said.

Dana knocked my shoulder as we laughed.

"I'm glad we're laughing," I said. "Because I doubt I'll be chuckling it up tomorrow."

"Candy's operation?"

"Yes." I was so sad at the thought of what Candy had to go through. I could feel it deep in my body.

"I'll call you at the hospital. You'll be at Saint Mordecai, right?"

I nodded. "Let me ask you something," I said. "If there are so many things you can do to avoid cancer, how is it Candy did them all and ended up like this? She exercises. She eats the right things. I think she would faint if I held a potato chip in front of her."

"You have chips?" Dana said, excitedly.

I sighed and shook my head. "What happened to the I-will-not-be-a-fat-grandma diet?"

Chapter 19

Once Candy was admitted to Saint Mordecai, I went to the cafeteria to wait. Candy and I had spent heaps of time there back when my mother and her father were sick.

I knew I should eat something healthy, because that was what Candy would want, so I bought a banana and an apple when I really wanted a bag of Fritos. It's amazing how much junk food there is in hospital cafeterias. It's like they are feeding you just so they will wind up with more patients. I mean what's with the fried chicken, the oily French fries, and the Salisbury steak soaking in gravy?

My phone went off, and I looked to see a number I didn't know. I didn't feel like talking to anyone I didn't know, so I almost let it ring, but then I picked it up.

"Good afternoon, Marcy."

Good afternoon? I didn't know anyone who said "good afternoon" as a greeting over the phone. I thought I was about to be sold insurance.

"Ellison Graham here."

"Oh, Ellison. Hi."

"I have been trying to reach Candy, and she hasn't returned my calls for three days, so I thought I would give you a call and make sure she's okay."

My guess was she didn't want to worry Ellison, but I really hated being on the spot.

"Is she?" he asked.

"Is she what?" I said, stalling, trying to decide what I should or should not tell him.

"Marcy, is she okay? I don't know why she isn't calling me back. We had a great time when we went out on Saturday, and then I heard nothing. It's unusual."

"I'm sure she's just busy," I said.

"Have you seen her?"

"Of course, of course."

"Okay, well, will you tell her I am trying to reach her? In fact, tell her I am very disappointed, and that if she no longer wants to see me, she should have the courtesy to tell me so."

I didn't want him to think Candy was ill-mannered or, worse, that she didn't care for him.

What if she got out of surgery and I told her he had called, but I hadn't told him she was ill, and he broke up with her, and it was my fault? He was perfect for her, and I was not going to be the one to ruin it.

"Ellison, I know she wants to see you. She likes you."

I felt so seventh grade. Like I should be scribbling "Mrs. Candy Graham" on lined, three-holed paper.

"Tell her I called."

"I will."

I ate my banana, then my apple, and then I returned to the cashier and bought the large bag of Fritos I'd wanted in the first place.

I hit redial.

"Ellison, it's Marcy. Candy is in Saint Mordecai Hospital for surgery. I'm in the cafeteria, waiting for her."

"Surgery? What kind of surgery?"

"She didn't want to tell you." Then I lied. "It's nothing big, but I thought you should know since you called."

Half an hour later, Ellison was standing at my table by the window in the cafeteria. He didn't ask a single question about what was wrong with Candy. He just sat and waited with me. I tried not to talk much, because I was afraid I might slip and say what the problem was.

"Do you want some Fritos?" I said, holding out the bag to him.

He shook his head. "No, thanks. I don't eat chips."

I was right. He was perfect for Candy. Then, suddenly, there was Jon.

"Jon? What are you doing here?" I asked.

"I was in the neighborhood," Jon said.

"I'll bet you were."

I could hear Ellison thinking, *"Marcy's boyfriend knew about the surgery, but I didn't?"* Someone else might have said that, but not Ellison. He was tactful.

"How much longer?" Jon asked as he joined us at the table.

"I don't know. They always tell you less time than it is going to take."

"Pass the Fritos," he said as he sat next to me.

Dana called.

"What are you doing?" she said. "Is she out yet?"

"No. I'm waiting. Jon and Ellison are here."

"I just left the agency. I'm on my way."

I thought about how Candy always thought she had no family to care about her. But it seemed she did have a family, a new kind of family. And I did too.

There was a text from a nurse. Candy was out of surgery. She was in the ICU and would be taken to room 1012. I was filled with anxiety as I realized that was the room her father had been in the day I ran into her at the hospital for the first time. I remembered that room as though it were the one I had grown up in. Candy had decorated it for her father. She had brought him his own quilt. She had installed matching curtains. There had been framed photographs of her son, Jumper.

I left Jon and Ellison in the cafeteria and went directly to the nurses' station. There were two women behind the desk. One appeared crotchety and exhausted. The other one had her hair in braids on top of her head. She was wearing scrubs featuring all the characters from *Frozen*. I asked if I could speak to her privately. She came out from behind the desk. I told her I loved *Frozen*, but the truth was, I had never seen it. She said her daughter loved Elsa and wore her Elsa costume to day care.

I explained about Candy being assigned her father's room and how I didn't think that was going to go over well. She said that Candy was already in the room, asleep. I asked if she could have Candy moved before she woke up. She said that was highly irregular, and the hospital was at full capacity.

I smiled at the nurse, knowing I wasn't going to let things go just like that.

I hurried to the gift shop. There was a *Frozen* balloon. I bought it and went back up to ten.

"This is for your daughter," I said to the nurse.

"You think moving your friend is that important?"

I nodded. "Yes."

She called over two orderlies.

⁓

Candy was still asleep. I looked at my phone. Jon and Dana were in the lobby, but Ellison was gone. A text said, I'll wait until she tells me herself. I wondered whether he was annoyed that not only Jon knew about the operation but also Dana.

I waited in her room. A few minutes later, Candy opened her eyes.

"You're here," she said with a struggle of a smile.

"I'm here," I said. "Dana and Jon are downstairs."

"Oh, I can't believe they came."

"You have a following," I said. "Do you want water or anything?"

"No. I am happy you are here."

"Someone else was here."

"My cousin Donna? I don't know how she knew. I only told you."

"Ellison," I said.

"You told him?" she said from her stupor. I swear my comment could have overcome the lingering effects of anesthesia.

"He called looking for you, and I said you were in surgery, but I didn't say anything else."

She smiled, serenely, and fell back to sleep.

Later, I found out that the tumor the size of a Ping-Pong ball was actually the size of a tennis ball. It was easy to remove, malignant but contained. The doctors suggested radiation as a precaution. I told Candy I would take her to radiation when she needed to go. She said I was a horrible driver and that Ellison had offered to take her as well.

Chapter 20

Amanda called while I was at Jon's apartment. She was kvetching about Elisabeth. She said Elisabeth was thinking small—once again—planning the bachelorette party in a restaurant in Manhattan when what Amanda wanted was a four-day event in New Orleans. None of the bridesmaids lived in the Big Easy, but apparently, they were all willing to take days off from work and drop a grand on airfare and some more on hotel rooms and beignets. Agree to be a bridesmaid and you might as well declare personal bankruptcy at the same time.

When I hung up, I held my hands to my head. I would have pulled my hair out, but with each wedding "incident," I was running out of hair.

Jon looked at me and said, "Let's get out of here. Let's go sit on the rocks in Maine. Then we'll go to Portland, and you can meet *my* family. As far as I know, none of them are planning a wedding. My eldest niece is fourteen."

I was excited to meet his brother, his brother's wife, and the girls. I asked Jon for the age of each of his nieces and bought gifts at a store that specialized in teenage treasures like lip balm kits and fuzzy fur pillows.

We took Jon's Subaru, crawling local routes dotted with white-steepled towns no bigger than pinheads on a map of New England. We looked like typical Maine tourists in jeans and polo shirts—mine navy blue, Jon's green. We wore brown baseball caps with moose antlers, and were swaying to the music on the radio. The song was "Girls Just Want to Have Fun." And I was. I was having fun.

Jon didn't need a map, but I was enjoying the one with advertisements featuring attractions. I had plucked it from a stand at a tourist information stop in Massachusetts.

I had always been a big fan of tourist information stops in New England. When the kids were young, Harvey would pull over at the "Welcome to Whatever State" sign, and Ben would take a copy of every appealing brochure and free tourist magazine in the place. He'd say, "Look, Mom, I have mail." Also, I really liked the vending machines—especially the selection of ice cream. Often, it was Blue Bunny, the brand name that could double for the alias of a porn star. Who names ice cream Blue Bunny? I needed to know, so I looked up the company. It turned out that no one makes more ice cream than Blue Bunny. Their ice cream sandwich is the best.

The map covering my lap in the car had funky advertisements with lots of curlicues for attractions, lodgings, and eateries along the road.

"We should stop at 5,000 Souvenirs," I said, joking as I looked at a group shot of balsam potpourri, beaded moccasins, pine tree deodorizers, moose T-shirts, and lobster-cracker sets.

"Yes. And if we buy a souvenir, they will have to replace it or change their name."

"To 4,999 Souvenirs," we said in unison.

Jon stopped at a beach on the rockbound coast. Without saying a word to each other, we both jumped out of the car, thrilled to be at the ocean.

All the time I'd lived with Harvey, I'd forgotten how much I loved going to the ocean. But Jon had made the ocean mine again. It's hard to find fault in a man who gives you an ocean. Each time we went to Maine, I loved it more.

We walked for a while, then Jon returned to the car for two chairs. He placed them next to each other, facing the sea, but far back.

I wondered why he always sat so far back, why he did not place the chairs closer to the water. I guess he could hear me thinking.

"In Maine," he explained, "when the tide rolls in, there is often no beach left, so I sit back to start with."

I thought about that. I thought that I would rather sit close to the water and then retreat when I had to.

"So you sit far back, even when you don't have to?" I said. "That's crazy."

"Why?"

"It's not that big a deal to move."

"What would you do?"

"Go to the front and only move back when it is absolutely necessary."

"Okay, let's try that," he said.

We moved the webbed chairs close to the water, a yard from the current surf.

On the beach, I saw a mother and a father and a toddler in a windbreaker. The boy ran in circles near the shore, kicking up seaweed, picking up rocks. After a while, he sat down on his knees to shovel sand with his hands. The parents joined in. I heard the father say, "We're digging a hole to China." I used to say that to my kids. My dad used to say it to me.

I thought, *This is life. This is what life is all about. Life is a family on a beach.*

But I had a new life.

"Do you like it here?" Jon asked smugly, knowing the answer.

"I could sit here forever," I said. "Or at least until it snows."

"Can you sit here long enough for me to run into town to get sandwiches?"

"Turkey with lettuce, tomato, and mayo on rye," I said.

"Bread, no wrap?"

"I'm an old-fashioned girl."

He kissed me. "I'll be back soon."

I stared at the ocean, thanking it for Jon.

I closed my eyes and fell asleep in the hazy sun.

Suddenly, a huge wave rushed over me. My jeans and the bottom of my shirt were wet. Before I could stand up, my chair turned, and I tipped over. As I sat in the wet sand, I heard laughter.

I turned to see Jon standing on the strip of cement dividing the parking lot from the beach.

"Tide's in!" he called.

I laughed.

"You're shipwrecked!" he shouted as he approached me, holding our lunch in a bag.

"I guess I sat close enough to the water," I said.

We grabbed the chairs and started walking away from the tide. He went to the car and returned with a beach towel as well as a hoodie from the back seat.

After I dried off, I put on the faded Price College sweatshirt. I liked that it was his go-to sweatshirt, sitting in the back of the car, helping him through life's emergencies.

"Are you too cold to stay?" he asked.

I didn't want our time at the beach to end, so I said I was fine.

He placed both chairs against the rocks.

Engulfed in the sweatshirt, I noticed everything he did for me. He did it effortlessly. I didn't have to ask. Or worse yet, repeat myself. Repeating myself was the worst of all. I hated asking for favors, so I rarely did, but on occasion I had no choice.

"Elisabeth, before you leave, can you see why the TV won't turn on?"

No verbal affirmation. A while later, I ask again.

"Elisabeth, you'll check the TV, right? I think it's something with the remote."

As she is about to leave, I am forced to repeat myself.

"Mom, I don't have time now. I have to go."

With Jon, I had the feeling someone was taking care of me, and it had been such a long time since I'd felt that way that I was overcome by the thought of it.

"Are you too cold?" he asked.

I shook my head. "Actually, I feel exhilarated."

We sat on the chairs in the thickening haze. The horizon was now difficult to see through the fog. I had something I had to tell him, but I was procrastinating. Putting off telling people important things was a habit of mine, a habit that often got me into trouble.

"This is perfect," I said. *If only I didn't have to tell you something that will ruin it.*

"Don't tell me anything that is going to ruin it," he said.

"How did you know I had something to tell you?"

"Marcy, your face is an open book."

"Look at me," I said. Then in jest, I smiled so wide my cheeks hurt. "Chapter thirty-four. Marcy is happy."

"And you know what?" he said as he held my chin and looked into my eyes.

"What?"

"Happiness looks good on you."

I decided I wouldn't tell him about the wedding. It was much better to torture myself thinking about telling him. I was on a mental roller coaster ride, and my face must have changed completely.

"Okay, what is it?" he said, frustrated, dropping his hands.

Get it out now, Marcy.

The big blurt. "Amanda would prefer it if I didn't invite you to the wedding."

I tried to read his eyes, but he looked at the ocean. "Why not?"

"She says it's not right, because Harvey and I are still married. She says it will be too disruptive."

"That's me," he said as he pointed to himself. "I'm very disruptive. You never know when I will bop down the aisle in the buff at a wedding. Immediately before the bride, of course."

"Come on," I said as I watched his face deflate.

He stared at me as if to say "Explain this one, and it'd better be good."

"Maybe it's about Harvey. He *is* her father. I don't think he's doing well. All he thinks about, apparently, is getting back together with me."

"Well, if I go to the wedding, he will realize that is not going to happen."

"Harvey is tough. When he wants something, he goes and gets it."

"Well, when I want something, I keep it. Besides, I think Amanda is using Harvey as an excuse. She's the one who doesn't want me at the wedding."

"Could be," I said softly. If I said it softly, would it hurt him less?

"Listen, Marcy, I need to know. Are you planning to let your children come between us?"

"No," I insisted, shaking my head. "They have nothing to do with us."

He responded with a guffaw. "You have got to be kidding."

"Why?"

"Because they have everything to do with us. I saw you looking at that family, those happy parents with the little boy. You were mesmerized, as though they had the answers to life."

"Look, I think Ben and Elisabeth like you. At least, they haven't keyed your car yet."

"And Amanda has yet to meet me."

"It's not about you—personally. She wants Harvey and me to walk her down the aisle."

I could see the hurt in his face. *When is Amanda going to grow up?*

I stalled by taking lunch out of the brown bag. We ate quietly, watching the beach, staring at the horizon. A woman jogged by with headphones. She looked so determined. A teenage boy threw a ball, and his terrier ran for it and brought it back.

I balanced my turkey on rye on the arm of the chair. I threw up my hands. "To be honest about the wedding, I'm confused. I wanted you to come. I kept thinking how much fun it would be. I thought about us dancing. I knew Amanda would ask the band to play a lot of old-time rock 'n' roll. And, considering the way Harvey carried on in the recent past, I didn't think it would matter to a soul whether we were divorced or not. I just didn't think anyone would care. But apparently, Amanda does care. And now I think it may be wrong to put my good time ahead of her feelings."

He stared at me.

"So I guess you shouldn't come," I said, relieved for me but knowing I had just put a dagger in Jon.

He stood, wiping his hands on his jeans. "Why didn't you tell me that weeks ago?"

"I don't know. I just couldn't say it. You've been watching me make all these plans, and it seemed hurtful, like you were the only kid in class I wasn't inviting to my birthday party."

"I am the only kid you aren't inviting."

I stood up and I lost it, rat-a-tat, like a machine gun. "Why do you care so much? Have you never been to a wedding? It's a bride and a groom. It's no big deal. And why are you making this so hard on me? I'm in a bind. It's an awkward situation. If I were you, I would be thrilled I wasn't invited. Why aren't you relieved you don't have to go?"

"You know what?" he said. "I think you're correct. I don't belong at the wedding. You and Harvey are not divorced yet. And, until you divorce Harvey, nothing is right."

"What are you talking about?" I said, even though I knew exactly what he was talking about.

He came closer to me, lowering his voice, pointing his finger. I had never seen him point his finger before. "No more discussions about when I will meet Amanda or whether I will or will not be on the sacred guest list for the wedding."

"I'm sorry," I said, about to reach for his arm.

"Marcy, I don't think we should see each other anymore," he said.

Suddenly, I felt as if the beach were a sinkhole and my shoulders were barely above the sand.

"Because you're not invited?" I said, as though that wasn't reason enough.

He pointed his finger again. "Because you're still married."

"Jon, I am sorry."

He put his sandwich back in the bag and folded his chair. "Nothing to be sorry about, Marcy. You simply pointed out the obvious. Guess what? I'm not interested in seeing a married woman. Harvey did you wrong, so wrong. And amazingly, you still haven't called a lawyer. What's with that? Take a good look in the mirror, and think really hard."

I was wet and cold and uncomfortable. My jeans felt heavy. As he headed to the car, I reached for the back of his polo shirt. I pulled on it, tugging. He turned.

"Get a divorce," he said.

Silently, he piled the chairs back into the car. The beach and the ocean looked dark, but I knew it wasn't about the sky. It was about me. I was dark. And cold. I had hurt him. Badly. And it was hurting me.

We got into his car without a word. Jon pulled out of the beach lot and followed the local road to Route 1. He didn't turn on the radio. It was so quiet. We passed someone mowing a lawn, and the sound might as well have been an A-bomb.

"Let's talk about this," I finally said.

He shook his head. He turned on the radio, loud.

I scrunched against the passenger door, feeling awful, trying not to cry, worried that I had lost him and that we would be over, done, kaput. I didn't want it to be over. It couldn't be over.

I hoped he would still head for Portland, despite what he had said on the beach. But he turned right, toward New Hampshire, toward Massachusetts, toward home.

We didn't speak until I asked him to stop at a rest area in Massachusetts so I could go to the ladies' room. As soon as I was out of his sight, I began sobbing. When I composed myself, I went to the ladies' room, and then I called Candy.

"I told him he wasn't welcome at the wedding," I sniffled.

"What did he say?"

"He was very hurt. Then he wanted to know why I hadn't seen a divorce lawyer."

"But you did. You saw Grace Greene, way back when Harvey told you about the baby. You didn't like her. You decided you would wait until Harvey filed first."

"I didn't say that to him." I sniffled again.

"Pull it together, Marcy."

"I will."

"This isn't exactly cancer."

I couldn't believe I had been crass enough to cry to her about my problems.

"Believe me, I know."

As I put away my cell phone, I watched a couple walk out of the rest area. He wore a brown bomber jacket and cuffed khakis, a loose fit. He rubbed her back. She grabbed his sagging ass.

I wanted to be part of a couple. I wanted to be a part of Jon's couple.

When I returned to the car, I placed my hand over Jon's as he turned the key in the ignition. "I want you to know that I consulted a lawyer months ago. Her name was Grace Greene. Everyone recommended her.

But Greene didn't just want the shirt off Harvey's back. She wanted his back. Besides, I wasn't ready to divorce him. I had only seen a lawyer because Dana insisted."

He was silent.

"Jon?"

"Okay, well, maybe it's time to find another lawyer, one you feel comfortable with."

"But I have this thing in my head. I want Harvey to file first—he left first, he files first. I didn't fail. He failed. None of this was my idea, and I want everyone to know it."

"Marcy, you could wait a lifetime for him to file. You could be in a nursing home, playing bingo, by the time Harvey decides to make a move. Maybe it's less expensive for him to remain married. Who knows?"

I certainly didn't.

"You're right," I said, nodding. "I'll call my accountant and ask him for the name of a lawyer."

"That's a good place to start," Jon said, but he continued driving home.

ᔕ

On Monday, I called Parker Whitman, who was Candy's first cousin. Candy had recommended him when it became apparent I could no longer depend on Feldman.

"I feel so lucky to catch you in the office," I said when the receptionist with the clipped voice put him on the line.

"How can I help you, Marcy?"

"I need a lawyer."

"What kind of lawyer?" he asked.

"A divorce attorney."

"Grace Greene," Whitman said.

"I saw Grace Greene right after Harvey left. The woman made Stonewall Jackson look like putty. She was ready to pummel Harvey and destroy my relationship with my kids to ensure I came out on top. If Grace Greene were a tool, she'd be a sledgehammer. She's a little mad dog for me."

"You want a puppy, Marcy?"

"Of course not. But I don't want to wind up not speaking to Harvey. I've worked so hard to keep everything copacetic, and in the middle of that, my daughter decided to get married, and we are making a wedding together. I feel like Al Pacino."

"You feel like Al Pacino?"

"In *The Godfather*. No matter how I try to get out, they keep pulling me back in."

"Take my advice. Hire Grace Greene before your husband does."

"She's not Harvey's type. She's doesn't need a bra."

"Marcy, you're Candy's best friend, and Candy is the only remaining cousin I would have a vodka martini with, so I am advising you as though you were a member of my family. And please don't become weak and even think of mediation. He has his own business. This is complicated. He could be hiding money almost anywhere. His dealings must be looked into by a first-class forensic team."

I needed an entire team? I imagined accountants in football uniforms and clutching calculators and briefcases, wearing eyeshades instead of helmets.

When I called Greene's office, the receptionist remembered me. She said Attorney Greene was busier than ever. She had nothing open for three months, until the New Year. Perfect—after the wedding. She added that if there was a cancellation, she would call me. *No need to do that,* I thought. But I didn't say it. I would leave this to fate.

That done, I condemned myself for my insensitivity. What a prize fool I had been for blubbering to Candy. I wondered what I would do if I were in her situation. Would I just crumble, staring vacantly at cable news all day? Or would I summon my strength, battling on with relentless optimism? Who was I kidding? I had never had an optimistic thought in my life. I would need someone to pull me up. And I knew Candy would be the person I'd lean on. She wouldn't ask if there was something she could do to help. She would jump into action and help.

I tried to think of something I could do for her. A new day spa had opened in town. I decided to treat her to a massage. When I arrived at her house to present the gift certificate, she was on her way out for a walk.

When she opened the envelope, she thanked me. "It's just what I need."

"I put a lot of research into this. The reason it says 'Massage with Clyde' is because Clyde is their best-looking masseur."

"Perfect."

"How are you?" I asked.

"Honestly, I'm worried."

"How worried?"

"I started going to church."

"That's great if it helps," I said, relieved that she was seeking support.

"Maybe I should go to a mosque and a synagogue too."

"Can't hurt to cover all the bases."

She filed the gift certificate in her pocket. "Want to go walking?"

"Do I have to?" I said.

She knew I was kidding. She smiled and pulled me along.

☙

I was in touch with Candy every day. I absolutely had to check in. I phoned every morning, and I texted her from work. When a friend is suffering and you call regularly, you chatter about the minutiae of life, as though illness is the last thing of concern on the list. It's not "How are you?" It's "How are your tulips?" On the other hand, when you call

203

just every so often, you're left with awkward conversation. "Seen any good MRIs lately?" Some days, Candy went on about the picture book she was working on or talked about Ellison. Other times, she got off the phone quickly, and I knew she was suffering from her treatment.

One Saturday morning in October, the kind of clear day when New England foliage is at its best, I stopped by her house to bring her healthy snacks.

She had taken to eating nuts, which a nurse had recommended. Being Candy, she counted them out, consuming five at a time. I bought four kinds—macadamia, almonds, cashews, and walnuts.

When I arrived, she was sitting with her legs crossed on her all-white sofa in her all-white living room, which had vibrant and colorful images on every wall. She had been buying art since she had sold her first picture book. She was just like the room. She was dressed in white, with a scarf around her neck that reminded me of a painting by Jackson Pollock.

"I want to know one thing," I said. "How do you wear a scarf when you don't feel well?"

"It makes me feel better."

I joked. "If I put a scarf around my neck on a bad day, I'd use it to kill myself."

"How are we friends?" she asked, touching the scarf lightly at her neck.

I sat next to her. "How is it going?" I asked quietly.

"I just hope the radiation is working," she said.

"It's working. You look radiant." I picked up a pillow and hit her knee with it.

"Jumper is coming home from boarding school for the weekend. I am taking him into the city."

"Are you sure you should schlep into Manhattan?"

"I have to. He doesn't know I am ill."

She had to be kidding. "But he's a teenager. You can tell him."

"I don't want to," she said.

"But how will he learn how to deal with life, how to help, if you shield him from reality?" I said, remembering that Jumper had not been at Candy's father's funeral.

"I want to get through all of this without him knowing a thing. I will not upset him."

Candy had so many family secrets that it was amazing her family had anything to talk about at all.

∽

When I was driving home, Amanda called.

"Mom, I need an opinion."

"Okay . . ."

"I'm not inviting Uncle Max."

"So you ask for an opinion by giving an ultimatum?" I said. Max was my younger brother. After my mother's funeral, he drove off in her car. I hadn't heard from him since, but I heard the skies rumble—my mother insisting he be invited.

"You can't do that. Grandma won't allow it."

"Grandma is not here, Mom."

Oh, she's here all right. She's here in my head.

"But he's such an airhead. He won't return the RSVP card, and then you'll have to call him."

Now she was getting to me. "I wouldn't have to call him. You would have to call him."

"He's your brother."

"I'm not calling him."

"By the way, what do you think of plus ones?"

"Whose plus one?"

"Anyone's. Like if someone is dating, there should be a plus one, but I think they have to be living together."

"I have an etiquette book right here," I teased. "It says that you need to be leasing an apartment under both names to be invited with a plus one. Proof of residence is required."

"No really, Mom. Like my friend has been seeing this guy for one month. Do I have to invite her plus one?"

"It's not a big deal. Just invite her with a date."

"But if she breaks up with him, he will be in all the pictures."

"And if she divorces him thirty or more years later, he'll be in a lot more pictures."

"Oh, and about a hair stylist. I'm planning to fly Jessica in, the stylist who owns the salon I went to when I lived in Seattle."

Fly in a stylist? Did she think she was a rock star? Clearly, she was getting carried away. Harvey was rich, but he wasn't Bank of America.

"That's ridiculous," I said. "The hotel will get you a perfectly wonderful stylist. All you have to do is call and speak to her about what you want in advance. The Seascape is a five-star resort. Anyone they recommend will be fabulous."

"Really? You think?"

"I don't think, I know."

Apparently, I had given her the wrong answer, because she said, "Maybe I should ask Elisabeth for her opinion."

"Believe me, she will absolutely agree."

We were getting along so well on the phone that I decided to ask her again about Jon coming to the wedding.

"What about Jon?"

"What about him?"

"We were discussing plus ones."

There was a moment of stony silence, like in a World War II movie, right before the enemy attacks, then the soldiers suddenly rush, and the machine guns go rat-a-tat, rat-a-tat.

"Look, Mom, you're not even divorced, and you want to bring this man, this Jon? It's inappropriate. I don't want him there. I can't deal with him glaring while you and Dad walk me down the aisle. But now there's more. After we talked about this in New York, I discussed the whole situation, top to bottom, with Jake. He is apprehensive and concerned that his parents would be embarrassed if you brought a date."

I would embarrass a woman who stole tampons?

"She steals," I said.

"Who?"

"Mug or Cup or whatever her name is."

"What did she steal?" Amanda said in a voice that was as good as saying, "You're ridiculous, Mom."

"Tampons."

"I know," Amanda said, laughing.

"You know?"

"Yes, of course. She gave them to me. It was sort of sweet."

Sweet? Amanda really was in love. No point telling her about the tip for the restroom attendant.

"By the way, since Jake's parents are so old-fashioned, how do they feel about your father having a child with someone besides me?"

"They don't know. Jake thought it was better not to tell them." I could hear her deep breath. "Mom, this is extremely difficult."

"For everyone," I said. "But we have to accept what has happened. Don't you think I wish we weren't having this conversation? I never envisioned this. It never even occurred to me."

"Mom, I am really sorry, but I do not want Jon at the wedding."

I wanted to holler at her as though she were small, to command her to go to her room, to tell her that maybe I had an inconvenient boyfriend, but her father had an even more inconvenient baby. To inform her that even her siblings did not want to hear one more selfish, shallow word about her wedding. I wanted to throw my iPhone across the office. And damn Apple. I wanted it to break.

Instead, I said a weak good-bye so she wouldn't think I had hung up.

Chapter 21

Cheyenne and I were discussing the signage for our annual fund-raiser, Art Explosion, when we suddenly heard a baby screaming in the hall.

"Wow! Some woman has her hands full," I said to Cheyenne.

"Maybe it's a man who has his hands full."

"Like anyone has ever seen a man with a crying baby in an office. Actually, now that I think of it, my husband used to bring infants to his office all the time. Then he had a baby with one of them."

"Do something," Dana said as she stood in our doorway with Wolfgang in her hands. She was holding him like he was something she really wanted to give away.

"Dana? What are you doing here? What's wrong?"

"I know I somehow brought up three children, but being responsible for my grandchild is different. I shudder at the thought of something happening. I put the baby in the car to go for a ride. He starts screaming. I stop the car. I notice he has a rash on his neck. I'm not giving this baby back to Moxie with a rash."

"Calm down, Dana. You're losing it for nothing," I said.

Cheyenne looked at the baby's neck. "That's not a rash. Probably, you had the car seat strap too tight."

"Oh no, I could have strangled him! Then what would Moxie say?"

"It's nothing. It will go away on its own," Cheyenne said.

Dana handed her the baby. "I was great at this when I had my own kids."

I nodded. She certainly was.

"But this baby thing is no longer for me. I want to take care of him, but I could land five new accounts with the energy it takes to care for one baby."

Cheyenne was tickling Wolfgang. He was laughing now. She hoisted him in the air. "Sky-high baby!" she shouted.

"You really like kids," I said.

"Love them. I watch kids all the time. The mothers in my neighborhood call me Super Sitter. They say it the way you would say 'Superman.'"

Dana perked up. And it wasn't from the coffee.

"Also, I think we should take off one of these sweaters," Cheyenne suggested. "He may be warm."

"Where do you live?" Dana asked.

"Twelve Oaks."

"We're practically neighbors."

Cheyenne placed Wolfgang on the floor. Then she sat down next to him, and they played with the office keys and then some paper coffee cups. Although Cheyenne was doing nothing more than rolling the cups, Dana was mesmerized.

"Would you be interested in watching my grandson?"

"Of course. He's adorable. I love chubby babies."

Uh-oh, I thought.

"He's not chubby," Dana said.

"She meant healthy," I said.

"When are you going out?" Cheyenne asked.

"Oh, it wouldn't be for when I go out."

Really? What would it be for?

"It would be for when I watch him."

I leaned back against the office wall and crossed my legs in front of me, just waiting for the ultimate Dana.

"I don't understand," Cheyenne said.

"Well, I babysit about once a week, usually on Saturday. You could come over, play with him, feed him, and bathe him. The usual."

"Okay," Cheyenne said, looking at Dana strangely. "Where would you be?"

"In the house, of course. I want to watch him, but . . . you know. Anyway, my daughter-in-law comes to Connecticut on Saturdays and drops him off at ten and picks him up at about six. So you would need to come at ten after ten and leave by, let's say, ten of six."

"She comes after Moxie and leaves before Moxie returns?" I asked.

"Exactly. That way, Moxie won't know I have a babysitter."

"So I wouldn't be Super Sitter. I'd be Secret Sitter."

"No. You would be both," I said.

Just then, Candy stopped in, carrying a small basket of fruit. It reminded me of the day I had met her in the hospital when our parents were ill, and she had brought a platter of cookies for the staff.

"Hi, Candy. What's with the fruit?" Dana said.

"I'm between treatments. I feel okay. I knew Marcy was working Saturdays, and I felt like doing something nice for someone."

I smiled. "I hope that feeling doesn't pass."

"Are there many more treatments?" Dana asked.

"I'll be done in time for the wedding," she said curtly, being Candy and not inclined to discuss her medical condition. "How about some fruit?" she said, holding up the basket.

I took the basket from her and removed the red cellophane.

I bit into a red Honeycrisp apple. I told her to come into my office so Dana could finish talking to Cheyenne. Once inside, she moved some cups on my desk to the side to make room for the basket. They all had coffee stains inside.

"How long were those mugs sitting there?" she asked.

"See that one?" I pointed to one with lipstick on the rim. "Marilyn Monroe."

"Did you ever hear of Kid Met?"

"Of course, the children's museum in Chicago."

"They're mounting a show of children's illustrations next spring. They asked me for one!"

She deserved some happiness. I thought about what she had been through in the past year alone. She was a human soap opera.

"There's more. Ask who else is in the show."

"Who else is in the show?"

"Dr. Seuss. Of course, he has an entire gallery, and I have one illustration."

"Oh my, you're in a show with the Cat in the Hat." I recited a few lines from the book.

"Yes, the Cat in the Hat and Walter the Walrus. Ask who else," she said.

"Who else?"

"Elephant and Piggie—you know, in the books by Mo Willems. Of course, he will have a room full of his work."

"So what? You have an illustration. You're insanely famous!"

"It's months away, but promise you will go with me to Chicago."

"I'm there. I'm so there. Your dad would have been proud," I said.

She glanced at the ceiling. "He's up there. He knows."

"For sure," I said. "He definitely knows."

∽⏾

After work, I went to Carnivore's Hell for therapy. There was a banner in the window: "We are happy to deliver orders over $100." I thought,

A hundred-dollar order from an "organic" market? What was that? One box of frozen riced cauliflower, a Hass avocado, and a coconut water?

My phone rang. It was Amanda. She was packing up her apartment in Seattle for her move to Connecticut. She had a wedding question.

I didn't mind being interrupted at home or even at work, but when the wedding began cutting into my restorative grocery time, I was troubled. I had just learned how to shop for one person, and it took a lot of concentration. And it was annoying because it was clear to me that the smaller the package, the more the product cost.

"Mom, what's with Uncle Max?" Amanda said as I turned into the frozen foods aisle.

"Where do I begin?"

"He still hasn't returned the RSVP card."

"You knew that would happen."

"But I'm trying to get a count."

"Did you invite him with a date?"

"Yes. After speaking to you, I decided to invite most single people with a plus one."

Plus one bimbo, I thought, knowing my brother's choice of women.

"So call him," I said.

"I don't want to call him. You have to call him."

"We went through this once already. It's your wedding."

"He's your relative."

"What's that, a new rule? If someone doesn't return an RSVP card, the closest relative has to suffer?"

"Mom, you're the one who said we had to invite him because of Grandma."

"So she should call him," I said.

I could hear my mother from heaven: *"He's your brother. Be the bigger one."*

My entire life I had heard that line from my mother: "So he trashed your favorite doll, pushed you down the stairs. He's your brother. Be the bigger one." Then she would spout her version of an eye for an eye: "Sometimes you have to look away." I had looked so far away I needed binoculars.

"Uncle Max is the least of my problems, though. There's a lot on my mind. I'm in a tricky situation with meat."

"What about meat?"

"Jake's mom insists on meat for a main dish, not just seafood. She says that unless there is a meat selection, it's not a proper celebration. She keeps e-mailing pictures of roast beef, lamb chops, and New York strip."

"So have a choice for the main dish."

"First of all, a lot of my friends are vegetarians. Plus, the wedding is in Florida, where the fish is fresh and delicious. I'm standing firm," she said.

"Make Mug feel better. Tell her you denied your father his pigs in a blanket."

"Wow. You're worried about Dad. I like that."

"He's paying for the wedding. The man is entitled to one pig in a blanket."

Chapter 22

When I rang to tell him I had progress to report, Jon put the issue of my marital status on the back burner. I asked him to call a truce and come over to my house. He agreed.

I prepared chopped salad, cheese manicotti, and fresh asparagus in Béarnaise sauce. I had a large fruit tart, courtesy of Sweet Heaven Bakery, ready for dessert.

When I opened the door, he grinned sheepishly and handed me a bottle of wine. I grabbed his hand and pulled him through the door.

Jon uncorked the wine. We went into my new living room and relaxed on the futon I had bought online. I thought I could use the futon in the living room until I found my dream couch, and then I would move it into one of the bedrooms. We put our wineglasses on the temporary plastic cocktail table I had purchased the same day. The white walls were bare because I was waiting to paint—and waiting for Jon to cool down completely before I asked him about warm colors.

"Jon, I want to tell you something."

He wrinkled his brow.

"I called a divorce lawyer."

"What did you call her?"

"No, really. I called Grace Greene again. She is the one I told you I had contacted when everything first happened. I thought she was too tough, that I would wind up at war with Harvey, which I do not want to be. After all, I have to consider the kids. I don't want to be invited to one birthday party while he gets invited to the next."

"I can see that," Jon said.

"But I called my accountant. And even he recommended her. It seems that because Harvey has such a large business and so many accounts, I need someone who has a lot of experience. I guess it's easier anyway since I already met with her. Believe me, that was no fun."

"Okay," he said. "When are you planning to file?"

"I meet with her after the wedding," I said.

He laughed. "Of course, after the wedding. It seems we have BW and AW. Before the wedding, after the wedding."

Yes, I thought, *you are right.*

"Well, I have news myself." He seemed happy.

My eyes widened as I wondered what it could be.

"I have a very tempting offer."

"From who?"

"From Price College."

I was excited for him. It's the best when something really good happens to someone you care about. Just the best. "You've been promoted to head of your department?"

"Better."

"Really?"

"They're creating a new campus, and Dean Prybutok wants me to set up a department of English. Guess where?"

I shrugged because I had no idea.

"In Japan."

"What?"

"Japan," he repeated.

I had no clue why he thought I would be happy about a job in Japan. If he was moving to Japan, he might as well move to, I don't know, Japan.

"I would be there for a little less than a year," he said.

"What year?"

"Starting in late December."

"Jon, Japan is literally on the other side of the world."

"You're not happy for me. I don't believe it," he said.

"I *am* happy for you. I'm not happy for me."

"Then come to Japan."

"It takes, like, days to fly there."

"Part of the deal is two round-trip tickets."

"So you would come home once?" I said as my voice went soprano.

I'd been trying to keep our relationship light, but not this light. Not light enough for him to take off for a year without me. Besides, when I had run into Jerry in Carnivore's Hell, I had realized I had no interest in seeing anyone but Jon.

"No. I thought you could use one of the tickets."

"So you want me to visit once?" *Now that's what I call not going steady.*

"I want you to come with me." A warm smile sat on his face, emphasizing the lines around his chin.

"To the other side of the world . . . for a year?" Surely he had lost his mind. But it was nice he had lost it, because he was inviting me to live with him. No matter how ridiculous the concept was.

"Wow, Marcy. I didn't think you would say yes immediately, but I never thought you would think the idea was ridiculous." To create a break in the conversation, he stood and faced me as I sat on the futon.

All I could think was that he would meet a sex kitten in a kimono. He would reside in a high-rise that was full of geishas. The geishas would treat him like a samurai warrior. In no time, he would forget about me.

"Come with me."

I was nothing short of dazzled.

"Come with me," he repeated.

"Where in Japan?"

"Tokyo."

Marcy Takes Tokyo, I thought. I had wanted to change. Committing to Jon. Moving to the other side of the world. Now that was breaking out. But then I heard the old Marcy, the real Marcy, the Marcy I was born as, speak, and I wondered why it was so difficult to change.

"I can't. I have a wedding to plan, a wedding to go to. And what about my job? I was just promoted. I think I can go national. The Guild for Good could unite artists throughout the country. And what about the little things? I have to go to Chicago in the spring with Candy to see her show. I promised."

Suddenly, as I said all of this, I realized that I had, in fact, made a life for myself. I had struggled off the ground on shaky legs and stood up and could reach for anything. I thought back to when I had forfeited a career for Harvey. But that wasn't just for Harvey. That was for my children. And the truth was, I wouldn't take a moment of the time I had spent with them back.

"And, and, and," he said in disappointment.

I had been so busy congratulating myself, I hadn't thought about what a wonderful offer he had made and how much I had hurt him by saying a flat-out no. He sat back down on the futon. His disappointment filled the empty living room.

"I'm sorry," I said. "Did you think I could drop everything in my life? I did that for Harvey, and look at the way things wound up."

"I'm not Harvey. And if I were, I would strangle you with your own brassiere right now."

"Kiss and make up," I said.

He shook his head. "Not on your life. I was so excited to invite you. I thought you would be thrilled. I should have known. First is your family and the wedding, the damn wedding."

"Don't say that."

"Why not?"

"Look, Jon, it would have been better if my daughter wasn't getting married in the middle of my divorce. But she is. And she's happy. And I am not doing anything to stand in the way of it."

"If only it was that simple."

"How do you know what 'it' is anyway? I can't just pack up and leave. There are so many things I want to do."

"You can leave the day after the wedding and meet me there. I could leave then as well, but as I recall, I am not invited. Unless, of course, that has all changed."

I shook my head.

He rubbed his chin the way people do when thinking. "Marcy, I am not in any way suggesting you should miss one minute of Amanda's wedding."

"It won't work," I said. "What about my job?"

"Oh, Marcy, you'll take a leave of absence. Call the boss. Call Christopher Kingston, and ask him if he knows someone who can fill in for you. He loves you. He knows me. He will make this work. Or just come for three months. People take leave for three months all the time."

My head was reeling. "You sound just like Harvey. Put your petty career on ice and move to Connecticut, where you can be subservient for a few decades. Then, when it's time for you to live a life, you will be underqualified for everything."

"Harvey, Harvey, Harvey," he said.

"That's what his parrot used to say."

"What parrot?"

"Harvey had a parrot. And all it could say was his name."

"If I had a parrot, it would say your name."

"I know," I said.

"So come to Japan."

"It's impossible."

"So what are you saying?"

"I don't know what I am saying. I am saying I can't go live in Japan."

"No. What are you saying about us?" he pressed on.

I shrugged, defeated.

"First, you don't want me to meet your kids. Then I am not invited to the blessed wedding from hell."

"Don't call it that," I stammered.

"Marcy, you are just not ready for a relationship with me. I am done paddling this canoe alone."

I was thunderstruck. How could he say that? "Are you nuts? Paddling? You're not paddling."

"What the hell does that mean?" He stood up and walked across the room to the fireplace. He looked downright self-righteous. I got up and went over to him.

"For months, you accused me of locking you out, of pushing you away, of putting my kids first. What did you say? 'I want to meet your kids. I want to be part of your family.' Or some such nonsense. Then, voilà! You do this. You, without a word about it to me, take a job on the complete other side of the world. Not for a month, not for a semester, but for almost an entire year. And, as though that isn't enough to throw our relationship into water so deep there is no getting back to shore, you just assume that I will go along, because what the hell else have I got to do?"

His face became sullen, pale. He scratched his neck, like he had poison ivy.

I stepped back. "Jon, I understand this is an amazing opportunity, but how could you accept this position without saying a word to me about it? How could you assume that I had so little going on that I would just pick up and be thrilled about an endless supply of Kobe beef?"

He stood still.

"Kobe beef is delicious," he said.

"Joking is my way out. Not yours."

He looked out the window for a moment. He turned back to me. "Marcy, I should have never made this decision without talking to you."

He was agreeing with me?

"You're right," he continued. "I was wrong."

Had I just heard a man say he was wrong?

"I should have talked to you when the dean made the offer."

"Yes, you should have."

"I should have told the dean, 'I have to discuss this with Marcy.' He would have said, 'Who's Marcy?'"

I laughed.

"And I would have said, 'The woman I love.'"

Chapter 23

It was late on a clear and cold Sunday afternoon in November. I took a walk on the road near my new house. Mostly, I thought about Jon. I wanted things to work out with him. But I knew from the breakup of my marriage that there was no way to predict or govern what another person would do. I was heartsick that Jon was leaving for Japan, but we would visit each other, and the older I got, the quicker time went by. Soon a year would feel like half an hour. I could rationalize anything.

When I returned from my walk, I saw a vision, my dream come true. All three of my children were on my porch, chatting in the white slat chairs, rocking back and forth.

I stood on the road for a moment and watched. I glowed inside and out.

"What a wonderful surprise," I shouted, running up to hug each one of them.

"You see, you don't know everything that's going on," Elisabeth said. She was wearing a new toggle coat. I liked it. I would've liked her in a burlap sack at that moment.

"All three of you at once. Am I dying, and I don't know it?" I said. "Is this farewell, Mom?"

"We're allowed to drop by without an occasion," Ben put in.

"I love your porch," Amanda said. "Why didn't we ever build a porch at our house?"

I was about to give a one-word answer, but instead there was a chorus: "Dad."

"It's amazing he didn't want a porch," Ben said, "considering how much he likes to sit."

"Too easy a shot," Amanda said.

"He moved back into the house last week," Elisabeth said, looking at my face for a reaction. I tried my hardest to act as though she had just mentioned that snow was usually white and tended to fall from the sky. I doubt I was successful.

"He hired a guy to help him find the washing machine," Ben said, trying to lighten things up, concerned about my reaction to the news. And it was news. Harvey hadn't said a word to me about it.

I held steady. I had my new house, and my three children were on the porch. I was happy.

We went inside. The paintings Jon had brought over weren't hung yet; they were leaning against a wall in the hall. I hoped that someone would say how impressive Jon's work was or just that it was impressive that someone had done so much work. Any crumb would do.

In the kitchen, Amanda turned the conversation to the wedding. "Dad asked me to invite Hungry Hannah." Hannah had worked at Bountiful since women wrapped their bosoms in rags.

"That's nice," I said, taking pretzels out of the cabinet and pouring them into a bowl.

"She fitted me for my first bra. Remember, Mom?"

"No mother ever forgets taking a daughter to buy her first bra."

I placed the snack on the kitchen table.

"Okay," Amanda said, "tell me when you took me."

I thought for a moment. I couldn't remember. Uh-oh.

"That's why it's best to be born first," Elisabeth said. "No mother ever remembers anything about the one born second."

"So, what should I say?" Ben pointed out.

"You were the first boy," Amanda said. "That's different."

"Yes, he's our boy," Elisabeth said, pretending to pinch Ben's cheek.

I brought out glasses and a bottle of good wine. We all sat down at the table. Amanda uncorked the Pinot Grigio. "Tell the truth, Mom, did you have me because you looked at Elisabeth and said, 'I know I can do better'?"

"No, Amanda," Elisabeth said. "She had you because she thought she could strike gold again."

"How about if I make dinner?" I said. "I could make pasta."

"Great," Ben said. "Do you have stuff for a salad?"

As Ben and I prepared dinner, Amanda went on about the wedding. She really had become a one-trick pony.

"Where should I seat Hannah at the reception, Mom?"

"Here we go again with the wedding," Elisabeth said.

"Put her with Feldman and the brassiere brigade, of course."

"You mean table 34C," Elisabeth cracked.

Harvey had won. There were going to be two tables of his business associates, but I knew Amanda had stationed those tables next to the kitchen door. As for me, I had asked Amanda to invite Max, Cousin Leona and Steve, Dana and her family, and Candy. I knew Ellison couldn't make it because of a business trip.

"I really need help with the seating plan," Amanda said. "Where do I sit Hatfield and McCoy?"

"Who?" Ben asked as he sliced tomatoes.

"Dad's cousins. They don't like each other," I said as I searched for the penne in the top cabinet.

"I've never known why," Amanda said.

The water began to boil in the large pot. I hadn't used a large pot in forever. I was so thrilled about the size of the pot. "Follow the money. It's always about money. Someone dies. Someone is left out of the will. Someone gets angry. Everyone meets to talk—then no one speaks again."

"Well, what should I do?"

"Put a few of Dad's cousins with Jake's family."

"I can't."

"Why not?" Elisabeth asked.

"Jake doesn't believe in mixed tables. He wants our family on one side of the room, his family on the other, and our friends in the middle."

How nice—a human Berlin Wall.

"Where are we sitting?" I asked.

"We'll be at one table. Table one, of course. You. Dad. Elisabeth. Ben. Jordan. Grandma Florence. Jake. Me."

I was touched. I had thought for sure she would sit with her friends or alone with Jake in obnoxious wicker peacock chairs. Not that a bride spent downtime at a wedding. I couldn't even recall eating at mine.

"What about Jake's parents?" I asked.

"They want to eat their prime rib with family and friends from Wisconsin."

Ben put the salad aside. "By the way, Mom. How is Jon? I have to say that I liked him."

"He wasn't what I expected," Elisabeth piped in. "But he's very interesting."

They both turned to Amanda.

"The bride is the only one who hasn't met him," Elisabeth said.

"Shut up, Elisabeth," Amanda blurted.

"Stop," I said firmly. "He's going to Japan the weekend of the wedding."

"For a weekend?" Ben asked.

"For a little less than a year." *Who knows what will happen?*

"What's in Japan?" Ben asked.

"A job."

"Why haven't you told any of us about this?" Elisabeth said. "I thought you really liked him."

"I didn't feel like talking about it."

And I didn't want to give Amanda a reason, other than the wedding, to celebrate.

Amanda looked around my kitchen. "Why don't you have anything hanging on your refrigerator?"

Like what—finger paintings?

"In the other house, you always had the fridge covered with stuff— report cards, awards, and so many photos. You even had pictures of Dad when he had hair."

"Don't take it personally," I said. "Magnets don't work on stainless steel."

"No way," Amanda said, appalled.

I went to the drawer and found a magnet that said, "Everyone needs a Jewish mother." I held it to the fridge and then let go. We watched it fall to the wide-plank floor.

"What's the point of a refrigerator that can't be used as a bulletin board?" Ben asked.

"Except for keeping food cold, there is none," I said.

When the four of us sat down for dinner, I felt like saying a prayer. But my prayers had already been answered. Now my new home was home.

Chapter 24

Jon stayed over the night before I flew to Florida. Even though it was December, he insisted on a barbecue. I watched him go back and forth to the grill with foil-wrapped sweet potatoes, mushrooms and onions, and the steaks I had marinated overnight. He never asked for a thing.

Harvey would have had me running back and forth with barbecue utensils—one at a time. *"Where's the long fork? I need a big spatula for these hamburgers. Marcy, we need salt out here. Okay, the food is ready. Hand me a platter."* The suburban man wants to be king of the barbecue—as long as you give him everything he needs to make it. He burns the meat. You mention it and what does he say? "You should have told me to take it off the grill."

Thinking about this made me laugh. Jon asked what I was smiling about. "Nothing," I said. Then I laughed so hard a tear ran down my face.

I set the dining room table with a centerpiece of tapered magenta candles and a gift I had bought him. I added French bread, a butter dish, and Jon's favorite wine. I had searched three liquor stores to find Barton's Super Tuscan.

Jon brought in the potatoes, the vegetables, and then the awesome steaks. His nose was red from the cold, and he shivered.

"Cold out there," he said, rubbing his big hands together, separating his palms, and blowing on them. "I love a barbecue in the dead of winter. But before we eat, I want to take a minute to give you a present."

"Really?"

We were in the dining room. He went to the kitchen and returned with a small gift.

"I brought you something too," I said. I picked up my gift off the table. I held it behind my back.

We exchanged presents.

"Essentials of Japanese," he said, grinning and laughing.

"Essentials of Japanese," I shouted as I tore off the wrapping paper.

We raised the pocket-size paperbacks in the air.

"It's for whenever you come visit," he said.

How was I going to live almost a year without this man?

∽

The following afternoon, my nonstop flight touched down in Florida. Amanda and Jake's wedding was upon us at last. In black pants and a black-and-red shirt, I waited for the kids outside the terminal. I was overcome by heat and humidity. By the time the kids picked me up, I was as melted as a Swiss cheese sandwich.

"Remember the first time we met?" Jake said as he fit my rolling travel bag and suitcase into the trunk of the white rental car. "It was at an airport."

"Well, I'm glad I ran into you," I said.

"You certainly did run into me."

Amanda scooted into the rear, leaving the passenger seat for me. I knew she meant it as an honor, and I thanked her.

At the Seascape, the palm trees lining the property waved hello to me. I thought of the wonderful times we had spent as a family at the resort, our go-to spot on winter breaks. Each morning, the kids dashed to the window to ascertain that it was a sunny day.

"The sun is out," Amanda would say. "Yes, yes, yes."

The Seascape had a welcoming horseshoe front entrance. Young men in pressed uniforms dashed around, parking and retrieving cars. The main building was white and curved. All the rooms featured latticed balconies with wrought iron chairs.

When I stepped from the car, the brightness bothered my eyes. The Florida heat was stifling. Who cared? As the valet drove off, I stopped to kiss Amanda.

"Everything is going to be wonderful," I said. "You chose a perfect place."

Even if it was your father who actually chose it, I thought.

I checked into my room, took a shower, and switched into a knee-length cotton robe I had brought along. My luxurious space was decked out in tropical colors. I stepped onto the terrace that overlooked the rushing high-tide Atlantic, the air fragrant with the smell of the sea. I leaned on the railing. I closed my eyes and became high on the scent of sand and salt.

I heard a knock.

"Open up," Harvey said, loud enough that I could hear it on the terrace, and most people could hear it back in Connecticut.

Talk about ruining a magical moment. I might as well have been in a blizzard that closed all the roads.

I hadn't seen Harvey yet, and I wasn't ready to see him.

"What are you doing here?" I said through the door.

"I need to talk," he said.

"No," I said. "I'm resting. We'll talk later."

"It's important."

"I'll meet you for lunch," I said, trying to keep it friendly on the auspicious occasion.

"It's about Amanda."

"You're just saying that so I will let you in."

"Marcy, let me in."

Grumbling, I opened the door for him and pointed to a checkered chair in the room that was catty-corner to another chair, with an end table in between. "Sit there," I said. "What is it?"

He looked me over.

"You know, we carry silk nightgowns," he said.

"Harvey, I don't need to read your catalog. Just tell me why you are here."

"We can't let her marry him. His mother is a thief."

"I told you that the first night we met her in the steak house." What was it about men? They never noticed anything about anyone. Even after you pointed it out a dozen times or more. Harvey could spend an entire day with someone, and when I asked what he talked about it, he had no idea.

"Besides, isn't there a saying, Harvey? 'Don't visit the sins of the kleptomaniac on her son.' So she takes stupid, little things."

"My mother couldn't find her diamond earrings. So she called me to her room. I looked all over. The older I get, the more I detest looking for things."

"The older you get, the more things there are to look for."

He laughed.

"You know what you don't like more than looking for something you misplaced?" I asked.

"What?"

"Looking for something someone else misplaced."

"That's not true," he said.

"Then how come whenever I lost my phone, you never helped me look for it?"

"That's different. No one wants to look for someone else's cell phone."

"And my keys?" I asked, but he ignored me.

"I passed Jake's mom in the hall. She was wearing Mom's earrings."

"So, did you stop her?"

"Of course. She claimed they were hers, but I know she broke into my mother's room."

"How do you know that?"

"Because she had the guiltiest look on her face and because she has a record. She was in prison for a year."

"What? Did you call the FBI?"

"Better. Feldman looked into it."

"Jake's mother may be a thief, but your daughter is in love with Jake."

"Have you ever heard the saying, 'The apple doesn't fall far from the tree'?"

"Have you ever heard the saying, 'You better stay out of the tree'?"

"So you want to have little thief grandchildren?"

"Look, Harvey, there's nothing we can do. He's your lawyer. He's a good kid. Amanda is in love with him. And he is not the one who stole your mother's earrings."

Harvey insisted we confront Jake about his mother. I said I wanted no part of it. He called Amanda and told her to come to my room. I decided I would act like an audience. I was not saying a word.

"Dad has something to discuss," I said. *Well, so much for not saying a word.*

I listened as Harvey told Amanda that Mrs. Burglar was just that. That she had gone to prison.

"That's ridiculous," she said. "Jake would have told me."

"Maybe Jake is just embarrassed to tell you such a mortifying thing," I offered.

"I'm about to become his wife. If his mother had been in jail, I think he has enough confidence in me to tell me."

I didn't know what to do, so I put my arm around Amanda. I hadn't agreed with Harvey about telling her, but if Jake's mother really had been a criminal and this wasn't some quirk, Amanda should have known. And I had another thought. Maybe Jake had a few more secrets. Maybe he had secrets that were not about his mother but were about him.

I handed her a tissue.

She stood up, wiped her eyes, and shook her head, then straightened herself. There was the Amanda I knew and loved—as strong as they come.

"Where are you going?" Harvey said.

"To get to the bottom of this," Amanda called back as she strutted out the door.

I invited Harvey to leave, which he did, finally, and I changed into my bathing suit. It was black, a maillot. When I wanted to diversify, I wore a similar suit in midnight blue. Dana liked bikinis, and she insisted that I would look fine in a two-piece, so I bought one once. It had narrow wavy stripes to match my stretch marks. Good-bye, bikini.

The pool was the shape of a pregnant egg with a large water slide on one end. The lounging area around the pool was alive with sun lovers, mothers dousing their children in SPF 125 suntan lotion, young couples lying on chaises while holding hands, and teenagers diving in front of the "No Diving" sign.

I had had enough drama. I needed to relax. I went to the hut where the cabana boy, who wore a tangerine Speedo and a navy golf shirt with the hotel's logo, gave out towels and assigned chaise longues for the day.

"Can I help you?" the cabana boy said. He was very handsome. I watched his pectorals moving under his golf shirt. He was tanned to perfection, like a piece of perfect toast. His straight black hair was slicked back. His name was Quest. He was my first Quest.

"May I give you towels and bring you to a chaise?" he asked.

"Yes," I said.

"You are a beautiful woman," Quest said.

I was certain he said that to all the women. The words came free with a chaise.

We walked past chaises with striped towels and books and lotions and beach bags strewn about until we reached one with an umbrella beside it that wasn't being used. I knew that most of the chairs were taken because people came down early in the morning, threw a personal item on a chair, and thereby reserved a spot for later in the day. Chair hogs.

"Yes, you are stunning. From New York, right?" he said as he positioned a towel on the chair and tucked it in.

I always thought "from New York" was incognito for "Jewish."

"Connecticut."

"I hear there is a wedding. Are you the bride?" Quest said.

Okay, so now he has gone overboard.

"The bride's mother," I said.

"No way," he said. "Your daughter must be getting married at fourteen."

"Twelve," I said.

"Oh, you're charming too."

I was about to hand him a tip so we could terminate this endless ooze of bullshit, when I got a much better idea.

"And you must be a movie star," I said.

"An actor," he said. "This is my day job."

"Major movies, I guess."

"I've done some soaps—filmed on location in Florida."

"Did you play a doctor?"

"Yes. For three days last year, I played a surgeon who purposely killed a patient on the operating table, but she came back to life and murdered him."

"Deep," I said. "I used to watch *General Hospital*."

He bent down to whisper something in my ear about Anthony Geary. I got a chill.

"So, beautiful lady, is there anything else I can do for you?"

Then I said it—and yay for me. "I could use some lotion on my back."

"My pleasure," he said.

I lay on the chaise, and he began massaging lotion into my shoulders. He used his fingers and then softly rolled his fists.

"You have magnificent shoulders," he said in an attempt to up the tip. I didn't mind. If he rubbed a little more to the left, I would give him my Volvo.

"Funny about that. My mother always told me that my shoulders were too round. 'Sit straight,' she would say. 'No boy wants a girl with round shoulders.'"

"I want a girl with round shoulders," he whispered into my ear.

I closed my eyes. I imagined he was not alone. In addition to him, Anthony Geary was applying lotion. I added the guy who played Robert Scorpio, the dashing Australian spy.

Suddenly, I heard Harvey's voice. He was in swim trucks—no shirt, no shoes. His toupee was glistening.

"I can take over from here," Harvey said to Quest.

Luke and Scorpio disappeared.

Harvey sat back on the chaise next to me, his elbows clasped above his head. His tummy seemed to wobble. "So I see you have a new type."

"I do. Young and gorgeous."

"And stupid."

"Some things don't take a lot of brains," I said.

Harvey laughed.

"He was on *General Hospital*."

"What did he play, a laboratory rat?"

"That's not nice."

"Can I buy you a drink?" Harvey said.

"No, but you can ask Quest to come back," I said.

"Amanda called me," Harvey said.

"So?"

"Jake said his family had decided never to discuss his mother's problem, that she was getting help, and he was very sorry he hadn't told Amanda about it."

"And?"

"My watch is missing."

Chapter 25

In the morning, almost everyone who had arrived early for the wedding was in the Outrigger restaurant, where there was a buffet breakfast.

The Outrigger was draped with sails. The lighting was polished brass, like you'd find on a cruise ship. There were buoys pinned to the walls. Tablecloths were waves of red, white, and blue. White napkins were folded into the shape of sailor caps. I don't do well on boats. And the Outrigger was enough to make me seasick.

Upon entering the room, I heard Feldman's voice. He was with Harvey, of course, at a table of middle-aged brassiere kings and their queens who had turned the wedding into a vacation in Florida. I could hear Feldman telling the group, "I told Harvey to invite every one of you titans and write the whole wedding off on his taxes. Deduct, deduct, and deduct." So, that was why Harvey had insisted on so many business associates.

Breakfast was included with the hotel rate, so Harvey was joking that he was treating to breakfast. He turned and saw me and suggested I stop to say hello to his cousins from Montreal, so I did. They asked with whom they were seated at the wedding. I replied that Amanda had presided over the seating plan, so I didn't have a clue.

Amanda and Jake were at the center of the room with Amanda's friend Darcy, whom she had known since preschool. Also, there was a man I didn't know in a sweater vest with buttons over a golf shirt. Who wears a vest at a resort in Florida? He was chunky, with a big bottom, like someone who sat all day and stood up only to get a bag of chips and a diet soda. His hair was swept back in a long ponytail. His wire-rimmed glasses were balanced on the tip of his nose.

"Mom!" Amanda waved.

Jake hailed me over as well.

I liked being liked. I approached the oval table to join Jake, Amanda, their friends, and the man.

"Mom, this is Dr. Genesis," Amanda said.

I shook hands with the doctor.

"Dr. Genesis is going to marry us," Jake said.

"Oh, you're the psychiatrist," I said.

"And an ordained Global Life minister," he said. "Are you going up to the buffet, Mrs. Hammer?"

"Marcy. And yes."

We walked over to the sumptuous display of food—a bounty of fruit, yogurt, cereal, a parade of bread that included hard and soft rolls, croissants, bagels, French bread, and English muffins. Brass chafing dishes groaned with scrambled eggs, bacon, sausage, potatoes, French toast, pancakes. There was a waffle iron with warm syrup and a tanker of whipped cream beside it. A man in a tall chef hat was preparing omelets.

I filled my plate with honeydew and cantaloupe, some blueberries and strawberries. I made a waffle. I felt someone behind me as I lifted my waffle onto my plate.

"No lox," Dr. Genesis said, looking down disappointedly at his lonely sesame seed bagel.

"Well, there's so much to choose from," I said. "Maybe they'll have lox at the next bar mitzvah."

"I really need some Nova."

"What a kvetch," I heard my mother say. *"Psychiatrists—they're all crazy."*

"I hate when they cheap out on the lox," he said. "It infuriates me. Does it infuriate you?"

"Not really," I said, thinking, *I can't believe this man is a shrink—my son-in-law's shrink and consulted by my daughter as well.*

"What does infuriate you?" he asked, as though I were opposite him on his couch.

"Are you going to charge me your hourly rate if I answer that question?"

"No. This one is on the house."

"Global Life ministers," I said. Sometimes the truth just comes flowing out.

"Oh, yes, I heard all the parents wanted a rabbi to perform the service."

I knew Harvey and I did. But I didn't know Mug and Max were in agreement.

"Do you cling to the past about everything, Mrs. Hammer?"

I didn't like his questions or his condescending tone. Since when was wanting a rabbi to perform a service clinging to the past?

"No, but I enjoy tradition. You must know what tradition is. See that you are looking for lox for your bagel."

"Jake is an atheist," he said.

"No one is an atheist in a foxhole."

"How do you know? Have you been in a foxhole? Now, was or Mr. Hammer who demanded the pigs in a blanket?"

Jake and Amanda were consulting a shrink to discuss Harv pigs in a blanket? And what happened to patient confidentiality a

Dr. Genesis followed me back to our table. When we go Mug had taken the chair adjacent to her son.

"Thank you for coming. I'm Mug, Jake's mother."

"I've heard so much about you," Jake's shrink replied.

❦

Following a day at the beach and the pool, the immediate family gathered for dinner at the hotel's most popular restaurant. Amanda and Jake had excused themselves in order to have a final evening together as single people.

I arrived first. The restaurant was called the Tropical, and its theme was rain forest. I could hear the sounds of water over rocks, hooting animals in the background, and the occasional rain and thunder. Each table was surrounded by vegetation. A hostess in a camouflage-brimmed hat and boots led me to a six-top with weathered chairs.

As I waited for the others, I slipped out my phone and checked Facebook. I never posted. I left that to Cheyenne. But I was a Peeping Marcy. A sculptor I knew had posted a photo of a cat she'd had to put to sleep. It was a nice tabby, but it looked a bit lethargic. There was also a shot of someone's knee, scarlet, oozing, and swollen. I don't recommend looking at Facebook before dinner.

Elisabeth came to the table in a classic lavender sheath dress and strappy sandals. Her hair was in a French braid.

"Sit here," I said, pointing to the seat next to me.

"Wait. Where's Grandma going to sit?" No one wanted to be next to Harvey's mother in a restaurant. She was haughty enough to bring young waiters and busboys to tears.

"Next to Dad, I guess."

Elisabeth schemed for a moment, attempting to ascertain which seat Florence would pick. She gave up and eased into a chair next to me.

Ben and Jordan joined us. "Where's Grandma sitting?" Ben asked before he sat down.

We ordered drinks, frothy concoctions. Mine was called Blasted at the Beach and filled a beach bucket. Ben and Jordan asked for drinks named after monkeys, Dirty Monkey and Funky Monkey. Elisabeth had Sex with an Alligator. As we traded cocktails, Harvey finally showed up. He wore shorts and a golf shirt. His face was flushed.

"Sorry I'm late," he said, dabbing his forehead.

What else is new? I thought. I figured he had taken a business call.

"Bad news. My mother doesn't feel well."

"Sorry to hear that," we all said, like a Greek chorus.

Harvey sat down in the patriarchal seat, head of the table as always.

"What happened?" Elisabeth said.

"Nothing I can talk about at dinner."

"Dad, just tell us what happened," Elisabeth insisted.

"Her rectum fell out."

"What? Where is it?" Ben said.

Elisabeth shook her head. "It's called rectal prolapse."

"What causes it?" I asked.

"Weakened muscles and ligaments, or maybe severe straining, diarrhea, or constipation."

"I just lost my appetite," Ben said.

"It's painful," Elisabeth told us.

"A real pain in the ass," Ben said.

Harvey buttered a hunk of bread. "It seems that it doesn't bother her as much when she sits on it."

I tried not to laugh. In fact, I sucked my face in. But my eyes met Jordan's, and I lost control.

"She needs a procedure to tack it back up, and she won't go to a hospital here. She says hospitals in Florida are for old people."

"She's ninety," Ben said.

"She won't do it in Florida. She wants to go home."

"I'll see how she is," Elisabeth said as she rose.

"Sit down. She's fine. Albee, the resort manager, found a nurse practitioner. She's with my mother now. She'll fly with her to Arizona. Nice woman. She needs a better bra."

"Who?" Jordan asked.

"The nurse," Harvey said.

"All right. Then I'll visit after dinner," Elisabeth said, reclaiming her seat.

"Better you than your mother," Harvey said.

"What does that mean?" I said, annoyed.

"She's blaming the whole thing on you," Harvey said. "She says she's sick because you are going to divorce me and take the Bosom to the cleaners."

"I might. But what's that got to do with her ass?"

"Does your family always talk like this?" Jordan said to Ben.

"Doesn't yours?" Ben asked.

"We're just warming up," Elisabeth said.

Harvey called the waiter over. We ordered appetizers, mostly salads. Harvey requested the fried platter—beer-batter onion rings, jalapeño slices, and fish nuggets.

I sipped my Blasted at the Beach. Then I switched with Elisabeth for Sex with an Alligator. There was green Midori on the bottom.

"What are you drinking?" Harvey asked me. "It looks really good."

"I'm having Sex with an Alligator," I said. "You should try it."

Harvey pointed to my drink, and the waiter departed.

"We have to talk," Harvey said, as though the family should huddle.

We all listened up. I had no idea what Harvey had on his mind, but he was speaking in his "this is important" tone.

"It's about Mrs. Berger," Harvey said. "She's a thief."

"Amanda already told us. She said Mrs. Berger is in therapy," Ben said.

"Therapy, my mother's ass. I have important business associates coming tomorrow."

Ben started laughing. "Are you saying you don't want her at the wedding, Dad?"

"Why should the mother of the groom be at the wedding?" Elisabeth asked sarcastically.

"No. What I am saying is she has to be watched."

"Well, I'm not watching her," Elisabeth said. "It's my sister's wedding. I plan to dance all night."

Ben shook his head at Harvey as if to say "Not a good idea, Dad."

"Harvey, are you deranged?" I asked.

"I've hired two security guards. They are going to shadow Mrs. Berger. Watch her every move."

"Wow, Dad," Elisabeth said. "You better hope Amanda doesn't get wind of this. I'm pretty sure she feels as strongly about no security guards as she does about no potato latkes."

I was sure he was losing his mind. "Harvey, I think you're getting totally carried away."

"No, the jewelry is what will be carried away," he said, working himself up into a fevered pitch.

I insisted that he not hire the guards, and then I left it alone. One of the positive things about being separated from my husband was that if he wanted to start a nuclear war with Jake and Amanda, the scorched earth was all his.

We savored our appetizers. Everyone tasted something from Harvey's fried suicide platter.

Harvey moaned happily as he polished off the fried appetizers and suggested another order.

"Dad," Elisabeth said, "are you trying to kill yourself?"

"It's not for me. It's for the table."

⌒᪲

After dinner, Ben and Jordan headed out for the night. Harvey and Elisabeth went to check in on Grandma. I said good night and stopped in the ladies' room on my way through the lobby. I was the only one there. As I washed my hands, I stared at myself in the mirror. I thought about Amanda. Tomorrow, her marriage would begin just as mine stumbled to the end. I prayed. I prayed that if for any reason her marriage failed, she would at least be happy for the first thirty-three years.

I wiped the sentimental tears and the smudged mascara from under my eyes. I walked out the door. The corridor was silent. The restaurant had closed for the evening. I turned toward the lobby and went to my room.

I called Jon and told him that Florence wouldn't be at the wedding because her rectum had fallen out of her ass. I said Harvey was hiring US Marshals to tail Mrs. Berger at the wedding.

"I miss you," he said.

"I miss you."

"My brother and his family are coming tomorrow to say good-bye. We're having lunch at Abrielle."

"Abrielle. So good. Please have the fettuccine with basil and brie for me."

"Could be my last cooked food," he said.

"And your last fork for a whole year."

"They have forks in Japan. But if I use one, everyone will know I'm not Japanese."

"I'm glad you will be with your family tomorrow. They'll miss you. I'll miss you. I already miss you."

"You'll be visiting," he said. "We'll take a weekend trip to Kyoto to see the Buddhist temples, the wooden houses, and the gardens. There are a lot of geishas in Kyoto."

"Which is why you better not go there before I arrive."

"No geishas? Well, then, you better be really nice to me when you get there."

"Oh, I will be," I said.

As soon as I arrived, I was going to give Jon a present. I had read that gift giving was an important custom in Japan.

Chapter 26

When I awoke the next morning, the sun was shining. Amanda would have sunshine on the day of her wedding. Now there was something a mere human couldn't plan. I could hear Amanda in my head: *"And this is important—I want a sunny day. Not too hot, about seventy-five degrees. No humidity. Humidity is absolutely out. After all, it's my day."*

I looked at the clock. I had two hours until the hair stylist was scheduled to arrive. I went for a facial. Afterward, in the shower in my room, I thought about some of the things Amanda *had* taken my advice about.

I went down the hall to Elisabeth's room. Just like me, she was wearing a hotel robe. As we pressed the button to take the birdcage elevator to the bridal suite, she said, "I really, really don't want a stranger doing my hair for this wedding."

"Stop complaining. You don't know Jessica either."

"Who's Jessica?"

"Amanda's stylist from Seattle. She wanted us to fly her in and pay for her lodging."

"Well, at least then we would be hiring someone Amanda trusted."

"Does money mean nothing to you?"

"Mom, you cheap out at the weirdest times."

"Well, I told Amanda to ask *you* what you thought."

"Are you kidding? I stopped listening five months ago."

"Oh, please, it will be great. All of us together. We'll remember it forever."

"Oh, no question, Mom," she said glumly.

When Amanda opened her door, Elisabeth hugged her and said, "What fun! I'm so excited about this."

I was relieved that she did not complain to her sister. They hadn't had one argument since arriving—all because Elisabeth bit her tongue so hard and so often that I was sure it was now black and blue.

"Can I go first?" Elisabeth said.

"Mom will go first," Amanda said, bestowing an honor. "Age before beauty."

"Thanks a lot, Amanda."

"You know what I mean, Mom."

"Yes, you mean age before beauty."

The stylist arrived. Her name was Georgia. She was about fifty wasted years old.

Amanda pulled me into a corner. "Do you see what she looks like?"

"The resort recommended her. Albee's staff would never steer us wrong. I'll go first, as you suggested, and if it's a disaster, then you will have to do your own hair."

"On my wedding day? You expect me to do my own hair on my wedding day?"

I didn't know what to say.

Georgia was unpacking combs and brushes. She searched for a wall socket for her blow dryer. I pointed to one under the desk.

"I love to do weddings."

I poked Amanda as though to say "I told you there was nothing to worry about."

"And I do them so infrequently," she said, finishing her thought.

Amanda raised her eyebrows at me, as though to say "See?"

Georgia continued. "Heather was ill and couldn't come today. She asked Dorine to stand in. But Dorine was at a hair show, so she called me. Now, do any of you prefer rollers? I have big rollers and small rollers."

I hadn't seen a roller since before Vidal Sassoon was born.

"Mom, come here." Amanda was standing at the door.

"Excuse me," I said to Elisabeth and the stylist.

"This isn't going to work. You stall, and I'll phone salons until I can find someone else."

"How do you want me to stall her?"

"Mom, I can't do everything."

I returned to the room. "Anyone hungry? How about you, Georgia?"

"Well, if you're ordering . . ."

I rang room service for bagels with cream cheese and a pot of coffee. Georgia said she thought she should start on my hair, but I insisted I needed to wait for a bite.

Amanda reappeared, shaking her head.

"We better begin," I said. "Who knows how long room service could take?"

I had already shampooed my hair in my own room. Georgia wet it in the lavatory sink. I sat at the desk in front of an oval mirror, turning the chair so I could face my daughters instead of the mirror. She started working.

Elisabeth went to the door to let in the bagels. She and Amanda each took a bagel and coffee and went into the second room in the suite.

About fifteen minutes later, Amanda returned for more coffee. "Stop," she said. "Don't tease it anymore."

I swiveled to check the mirror. My helmet of hair belonged on an astronaut's head. I was aghast. But I didn't want to upset Amanda any further.

"What do you think?" Georgia asked me.

"Thank you so much. I haven't looked this way since I was a debutante in Dallas."

"Were you?" Georgia said wistfully.

Amanda interrupted briskly. "Would you like to take the bagels with you?"

"Is something wrong?" Georgia inquired.

I stood and rushed to retrieve my bag from the other room. I scribbled a check for three hairstyles. I handed it to Georgia. She looked at the check, surprised that I had paid her in full. Then she shrugged and waved a bagel at me on her way out the door.

"Do you want to wash it out?" Elisabeth asked me once Georgia was gone.

"I would. But it won't fit in the sink."

"Why are you worrying about Mom?" Amanda said, collapsing on the sofa. "I'm the bride."

We huddled next to her, one of us on either side. We placed our arms around her. Suddenly, Amanda stood up. She faced me, bending over as if she were punishing a toddler.

"Mom, why did you butt in? I was bringing Jessica. Can't you ever just let me do things my way? And Dad, with his pigs in a blanket, and his rabbi, and the brassiere people!"

I sat perfectly still. I didn't want to argue on her wedding day.

"This is your fault, Mom. It's all on you. You don't even care about this wedding. All you worry about is Jon. This whole time, you've acted like you're fifteen and never seen a boy before."

Her angry words stung my face. I held my hand to my cheek to protect it.

"Really, Amanda?" Elisabeth cut in. "Why don't you give Mom a break? You're not married yet, and you don't have a clue what it's about or what Mom went through. Have you ever thought for a moment that what happened to Mom could happen to you? Believe me, I have.

After all, I have been on the other side. I've been the girl who sees a man who is married."

I had to put a stop to the argument immediately. This was no day to argue. I didn't want Amanda remembering this for the rest of her life as a bitter moment that ruined her wedding.

"Cool off right now, this minute," I shouted. "Just stop."

Amanda took a step back, rolling her eyes for effect. Elisabeth lay down on the bed.

I spoke slowly. "Amanda, I'm sorry the stylist didn't work out."

She rubbed her scalp with her fingers. "What about my hair? I have to do my own hair on my wedding day!"

"Oh, Amanda," Elisabeth said. "It's not like you have to give birth in a field."

"Shut up, Elisabeth," Amanda bellowed.

Elisabeth searched the air above her, studying the speckled ceiling.

"I'll go to my room, call the top salons, and have a world-class stylist here by this afternoon," I said. "No matter what it costs."

"I already called other stylists. It's Saturday. They're busy."

"Leave it to me," I said.

"Leave it to you? I'm never leaving it to you again. I thought this would be like everything else I had ever planned," she said sadly. "I'm so good at planning. So organized. You should see me at work. But it turns out a wedding is . . . a wedding is hell."

"I'm eloping," Elisabeth spouted. "When I decide to get married, I'm eloping."

I had reached an all-time low in the history of motherhood. Arguing with my daughter on her wedding day. I wasn't going there. If I couldn't calm her down, the best thing I could do was try to find a stylist.

I left, planning to go to my room and call salons. I had really blown it this time. Literally blown it. After straining to be agreeable for months, I had caused Amanda to go nuclear on her big day. Worst of all, it was aimed at me. Why did she never argue with Harvey? Why was Daddy always perfect? So I had given her incorrect advice about a hair stylist. He had insisted on three tables of brassiere people. By now, he had hired guards. And he was still crowing about his damn pigs in a blanket.

I wondered whether I could flatten my hair so I wouldn't have to wash it out and start over. I felt the top. Rods of steel had more give. I tried to separate a strand, but it was impossible. I was about to literally tear my hair out, when Dana and Candy appeared in the hallway.

"You're here!" I yelled, relieved to see my two friends. Greeting them made me calm, made me feel like everything would be fine, that I would somehow procure the stylist to the stars, that the celebration was about to really start, and that everything that had happened since I'd arrived was just a warm-up for the big event.

Dana, in her trademark stilettos, capris, and shirt tied at her waist, hugged me. Her long blond curls fell on my face. Candy stood beside her in navy camp shorts and a starched, sleeveless white shirt. She wore bangles and an arty necklace made of shells. Her pixie hair was shorter than ever. She looked healthy.

"What happened?" Candy said.

I knew she meant to my hair, but my eyes filled. "I had a fight with Amanda."

"On her wedding day?" Dana said as Candy shook her head as if to say "Clam up, Dana."

"About what?" Candy said.

"The hair stylist," I said.

"The one who did your helmet? I mean hair?" Candy asked.

"Ten, nine, eight, seven, Houston, we have a problem," Dana said.

I wiped a tear from my cheek and laughed. Dana smiled as though to say laughter is the best medicine.

"I know. It's terrible, but I didn't want to make a scene, because I was the one who convinced Amanda that she didn't need to bring a stylist, that the resort would set her up with one. It's a five-star resort.

Who would have thought we'd wind up with a woman who couldn't braid a doll's hair?"

"Well, now you can't say you never gave your children the wrong advice," Dana said.

"Are you saying that the same stylist is now doing Amanda's hair?" Candy asked, aghast.

"No. Amanda fired her. I'm on my way to my room to call salons. Where's everyone else?"

Amanda had relented and invited Dana's entire family. Jeremy and Moxie couldn't make it, because the baby had to nap or something. The twins and Calvin were attending. It was unfortunate that Ellison had a business event in Chicago, so he couldn't accompany Candy.

"They went to the pool," Dana said. "We can help with your hair."

"Maybe—after I find a stylist for Amanda," I said.

"Call if you need us," Candy said.

In my room, I dared to peek in the mirror, wondering how my whole head could be seen in a mirror.

My cell phone rang. I answered.

"Is this Margie Hammer?" a voice said.

Because of the "Margie," as well as the unknown number, I thought the call was from someone selling something. Second mortgages. Life insurance. Financial services. Maybe the Boys and Girls Club or the Vietnam Veterans of America informing me they were picking up gently used clothing and small furniture this week on my street. But I wasn't on my street. I hit "End." Like it wasn't annoying enough that these people called incessantly on my house phone. Now somehow they had gotten hold of my cell phone number.

As I began to type in the number for the salon at the Ritz-Carlton, the phone rang again. It was the same southern voice. This time she said my name correctly. She also said, "This is the police."

Shivers ran through me, and I felt cold head-to-toe as I attempted to recall where everyone I loved was at that very moment, a roll call in my mind. I hadn't seen Ben since the previous evening. Had he gone to the ocean? Had he gotten caught up in a wave? *Oh no,* I thought. *Please don't make this about Ben.*

"This isn't about Ben Hammer, is it?" I said, shuddering.

"Harvey Hammer," she said.

"What?"

"Is your husband Harvey Hammer?"

"Yes."

"Your husband is en route to Roslyn and Martin Gold Memorial Hospital."

Sirens blared in my head. I envisioned the dizzying red light rotating atop an ambulance. I felt as though I would black out. But I couldn't. I had to get the kids.

"Is he all right? Is he okay?"

"En route," she said.

I ended the call, changed into clothes, grabbed my bag, clutched my phone, and raced to Amanda's suite. I tripped in the hall and scrambled to stand. I knocked frantically on Amanda's door.

Elisabeth answered.

"The police just called. Dad is in an ambulance. They're taking him to the hospital."

"Oh no, oh no," Amanda cried out.

"Which hospital?" Elisabeth said. "I have to go there right now. This minute."

"What happened?" Amanda said in a panic before I could answer Elisabeth. The bride was on the edge of the king-size bed, more leaning than sitting, clutching the apricot bedspread.

"I don't know. I think an accident. I was talking to a moron. I just ran here."

"Let's go," Elisabeth said.

"I have to call Jake," Amanda said.

"Call him from the taxi." Elisabeth grabbed T-shirts and shorts from the walk-in closet. She tossed a set at Amanda. When we dashed out of the room, they were both holding sandals.

Outside, there was an awaiting taxi, and we climbed into the back seat as I shouted the name of the hospital.

"I wonder where he was," I said to Elisabeth as Amanda spoke to Jake on her phone.

"I know where he was. He was out buying a gift for you," Elisabeth said.

"What?" I said, confused.

"He told me he wanted to give you a gift on Amanda's wedding day to thank you for agreeing to walk down the aisle with him. He went to a jeweler in town."

I closed my eyes and prayed for Harvey. *Please make him okay. Please make him okay. Please, please, please. My children need their father.*

Chapter 27

When we hit the hospital roundabout, I threw a bill to the driver. Amanda dashed to the reception desk. She pushed past the line of Floridians waiting to ask questions: "Where's the ladies' room?" "Where's the cafeteria?" "Can you tell me what room my aunt is in?"

"Harvey Hammer, tell me where he is!" she shrieked at the receptionist.

"There are others in front of you," the woman said politely.

"Tell me where Harvey Hammer is," Amanda repeated.

The woman shook her head as though to say "In the mental hospital, where you belong."

"Now," Amanda said, gritting her teeth.

I took over. "My daughter is hysterical. Could you please just help us now?"

She typed the name into her computer.

"He's in surgery," the woman said. "So now I guess you will have to wait."

Elisabeth rushed off to find a doctor to talk to. Doctors are always willing to talk to other doctors. It's patients' families they have a problem with. I remembered when my mother had been admitted due to a broken leg. After testing, a doctor informed me that my mom had cancer. He had been so frigid, I could have chipped him into ice. Immediately, my mother knew there was bad news. As soon as the doctor left, she said, "I didn't like his shoes." I wanted to burst into tears, but all I said was "They were way too shiny."

Elisabeth returned. Her face was white. "Dad had a heart attack."

"Oh no," Amanda cried.

My throat went dry. I thought of Harvey. Grasping at his chest. I thought about my children. I couldn't stand the thought of them losing their father. All three needed him. No matter how old they were, they would always need him.

We were told we could wait in the cafeteria. Jake showed up. He pulled Amanda away from the group to the corner where the snack stand was. I watched them hug. I felt so awful, gloomy, and miserable that this had happened on the day of their wedding. I dwelled on the sadness as I worried more and more about Harvey.

They came back. Jake was behind Amanda, rubbing her neck. I moved away, unable to stand the tears streaming down her face. I wanted to hide in the lavatory, to sob, but I was concerned something would occur while I vanished, that a cardiologist would arrive to tell us something. If Harvey died, I did not want my children to be without me, parentless, when a tragedy became news. I did not want to come out of the bathroom to discover them stricken and blank. But Harvey couldn't die. He couldn't. He was full of life. He entered a room like a band. I loved that about him. And in spite of everything, I loved him for these children. I knew for certain that there had been a time he could have convinced me to return to help him through this health crisis. But I also knew that day had passed.

Ben and Jordan arrived. They had been poolside and were in their swim trunks, damp T-shirts, and flip-flops. Their reddened faces glistened with suntan oil.

"Why are you using oil?" I said, reprimanding grown-ups. "You can get cancer from oil. Don't I have enough to worry about?"

"Mom, get a grip," Ben cautioned.

Jake broke in. He said there were enough people at the hospital, and he would tell everyone else to remain at the hotel. We sat over hot coffee, then warm coffee, then cold coffee. Amanda began to pace. I looked at my watch. The wedding was just hours away. I knew some decision had to be made, but I didn't want to get Amanda even more upset by bringing the subject up. Jake made phone calls. Ben and Jordan were silent, fiddling with the empty paper cups. I studied the other civilians in the cafeteria, wondering why they were in the hospital. There was an elderly woman, bent over in a wheelchair, pushed by a woman my age.

I thought about my mother. I wished I still had her with me. I thought how the woman pushing the wheelchair was probably annoyed to have to care for her mother, who was probably driving her crazy. I'd give anything to be driven crazy.

Jake suggested leaving the cafeteria for a change of scenery. We assembled in the family lounge. I took out my phone and started searching relentlessly online for anything about heart, cardiac, stent, bypass. I went as far back as Dr. Christiaan Barnard.

Ben turned on the flat-screen television in the lounge. He saw Wolf Blitzer's face, said he couldn't listen to the news, and switched to a cartoon channel. As we planted ourselves, Bugs Bunny scurried around, holding a carrot with floppy greens.

"What's up, Doc?" Ben said. "That's the question."

We laughed. It felt good.

Just then, a physician, a woman in blue scrubs, a cap, and paper shoes entered the room. Like soldiers, just short of saluting, we approached her. We studied her face for the answers to our questions.

"Mrs. Hammer," the doctor said to me.

I nodded. *Speak, speak. Tell us.* I could feel the kids crowded around me. There were only the five of them, but somehow I felt like there was a crowd, many, many people behind them bending forward, also waiting for the news.

"Your husband is now in the ICU, a standard procedure."

"What a relief," I said. "He's okay?"

"He had a bypass," the doctor said. "He's fine."

"He's okay. He's okay," Ben said as Jordan held him.

I had so many questions, but the cardiologist told us she would see Harvey in the morning. She removed her surgical cap, wiped her thin brow, and departed.

Silently, we gazed at one another through eyes filled with tears. Ben whispered a prayer.

The cardiologist poked her head back into the room. "By the way, he can't fly for two weeks. He'll start therapy while he is here, then continue at home."

"Okay," Elisabeth said, stepping forward to shake her hand.

The doctor turned to me. "And just so you know, one of our physicians knew who your husband was, because she wears Bountiful bras. He's a VIP. So of course, I upgraded him to our luxury level, Mrs. Hammer."

Although Harvey was still my husband, I felt awkward when he was referred to as such.

"Amazing," Ben said. "Even in a hospital, Dad winds up with concierge service."

After the doctor departed, there were deep breaths all around. Ben held Jordan's hand. Jake and Amanda were wrapped in each other's arms.

"What's the wedding plan?" I asked.

Amanda looked at Jake for confirmation. He nodded, and she spoke. "We're not having a wedding that Dad can't be at."

"You're canceling the wedding?" Ben said. "After all this?"

"After all what?" Amanda responded, a squeak in her voice.

"Forget it," Ben said, clearly wanting to drop the conversation.

"What are you saying, Ben?" Amanda insisted.

But it wasn't like Ben to stir the pot.

"All the preparations," Ben said to escape.

"Let's get coffee," Jordan said, and the two guys walked off.

Elisabeth stepped in. "What Ben is saying is that this wedding has been quite the ride."

"Oh?" Amanda said.

"Don't 'oh' me. You know what I'm saying."

"Elisabeth," I said. But it was like trying to stop a train with a feather.

"No, Mom. I think she should know."

"Know what?" Amanda said. "Know that you're jealous? You've always been jealous, because I've always been so close with Dad."

Jake retreated. Only a fool would come between two arguing sisters.

"That's right," Elisabeth said. "My life goal is to be you. Please, someone turn me into Amanda. So kind, always caring for others. So much so, you had to rush to get married in the midst of Mom's separation. You just couldn't wait. Could you?"

Oh no, I thought, feeling my stomach tighten. This argument was about to turn into one about me.

"Mom and Dad and all that had nothing to do with my getting married," Amanda said. "Besides, I've listened to every suggestion anyone made."

"That's why you wanted to get married in Fortuda, where Ben and Jordan could be assaulted for holding hands."

"I didn't know that when I first picked the damn island," Amanda said.

"But it took Dad to change your plan," Elisabeth said in a nasty voice.

"Okay, that's enough," I said, fearing escalation.

"It's true," Elisabeth said. "Ben knows it's true."

I put up my hands like a referee at a boxing match. That didn't stop Amanda.

"Just you wait. We'll all see how things go when you find someone, assuming he's not already married, of course."

Now Amanda had done it. She had gone subterranean, the lowest of low.

Elisabeth's face turned red with anger. "Amanda, say what you want. Go ahead and blast me. You've made us all miserable, so why not continue?"

I could see from Amanda's face that she was about to throw a fireball that would blow up the hospital. Maybe even medical centers throughout the Southeast.

I interrupted. "That's enough. Do we have to go through this now?"

They each took a step back, looking at each other with venom in their eyes. My thoughts went to how my daughters argued as kids. Elisabeth running to me in anger, crying, "She took my doll." Then the two tugging on the bald, naked doll until it was almost headless. All followed by more jerking and yanking as I said, "If you fight any more, I am taking the doll away." Then me grabbing it out of Amanda's small hands and holding it in the air. The inevitable words from Elisabeth would follow. "Now look what you did!"

Jake returned from his disappearing act.

"As soon as Dad is well enough, we are getting married in his hospital room," Amanda announced.

"Amanda, you don't have to decide this right now," I said. "Just wait until the morning."

She burst into tears. "No. The wedding is in the hospital, maybe as soon as tomorrow."

"Are you sure?" I asked.

Jake nodded.

"I am. We are," Amanda said.

There was a lot to do fast if the wedding reception at the hotel was canceled. "Well, as long as you are certain. I'll go back to the hotel now and let everyone know what's going on. I'll handle the hotel and all the vendors."

"I already sent a group text," Jake said. "And I put it on Facebook."

"What did you put on Facebook?" I asked.

"That Harvey had a heart attack, and the reception was canceled."

"How many likes did you get on 'Harvey had a heart attack'?"

I hadn't asked a serious question, but Jake mistook my sarcasm for just that. He took out his phone. "I can't believe it. Over three hundred responses already. I didn't get that many likes when I put my dog Scruffy to sleep. Amanda, look at all of these comments."

Amanda checked his phone. "Who is this person from Zimbabwe?"

"Put that away. We can't cancel a wedding on Facebook. I need to talk to the hotel manager. And I can't leave this hospital knowing that the two of you are arguing," I said to my daughters. "Pull it together. Your father will need you."

Chapter 28

I returned to the hotel and found the manager, Albee Martinez, in his office. He had worked his way up from waiter, and I had known him for many years. He was about my age, muscular, fit, and impeccably dressed. He told me that at his first dinner on his first day as a waiter, Harvey had tipped him generously, even though all gratuities were included in the resort fee. Albee said it wasn't about money. It was that he knew Harvey had caused him to feel as though he was doing a commendable job. Harvey gave him confidence. Lovely story. But knowing Harvey, he gave the tip so that Albee would cater to him throughout our stay.

We talked about Harvey some more. Albee said that Harvey had arrived at the hotel with nightgowns and robes for his three daughters, that he was so excited Harvey was going into menswear. He couldn't wait to wear Harvey's underwear. Albee said he would work with us on the cost of canceling. I said I wasn't canceling. I was postponing. Maybe we'd figure something out. He insisted on ordering me a sandwich and drink and said he had already spoken to the vendors that had been on the premises.

I was exhausted, but I stopped in Candy's room. Dana was there. They were both in shorts. They had been waiting for me to call.

"I don't have a joke about this," I said. "I don't have a joke," I repeated as Dana folded me into her arms.

"It's terrible for Harvey. It's awful for Amanda. Her wedding day," Dana said.

Candy was on the king-size bed. She patted the space next to her. Dana and I lay down, the three of us in a row, propped up on pillows.

I took a deep breath. Another one. Then another.

"How is Amanda?" Candy asked.

"Still at the hospital. They've decided to get married there—whenever Harvey feels one iota better."

"That's unbelievable. When you think how Amanda was about this wedding . . . to just get married in a hospital room," Dana said.

"I am so sad for her," I said, wiping my eyes. "She is being brave. But this has to be devastating."

"Do you want a tissue?" Candy asked.

"No. I want to feel my tears running down my face. I need to feel them. Tell me the truth, do you think this is some kind of bad omen for Amanda?"

"Bad omen? What are you talking about?" Dana said.

"I think she will grow up fast. I think she will realize what is important," Candy said.

Dana stood. "You know what your last comment tells me, Marcy? I need to start pouring Scotch."

"I don't like Scotch."

"What do you think this is, Harry's Bar?" Dana said, making a drink for me.

"Do you want to order dinner?" Candy asked.

"I just want to go to my room and relax. Turn on the TV and stare at it."

"I'll turn the TV on here," she said. "Dana, hand me the remote."

The three of us lay on the bed in silence, watching the Weather Channel because no one really cared what was on.

I finished a second Scotch and I left.

∽

I couldn't wait to get my clothes and shoes off, to remove my bra, which was killing me, because that's what I deserve for wearing anything but a bra from the Bosom. Truth was, no bra I had bought anywhere since I'd donated all the bras Harvey had brought me over the years ever fit as well as one from Bountiful. A minimizer from Harvey's biggest competitor had resulted in raw red streaks where the underwire was. I had to remove my turncoat bra. I needed to collapse, to fall asleep. I waved the card in front of the door to my hotel room. I gazed at the bed longingly, and there was Jon.

I was overjoyed, so shocked, there might as well have been a unicorn on the bed.

"You look awful," Jon said, amazed at my hair, which by now probably looked like a nest.

"Got any birds that need a home?" I said.

"How did that happen?" he asked.

"I deserve it," I said. "Poking my nose into Amanda's wedding plans. How did you get into the room?"

"I had my way with the housekeeper," he said, joking.

I jumped to the bed and lay on top of him. I started to cry, sniffling and whimpering. In no time, I was sobbing. He tried to stroke my hair, but it just wasn't possible.

"How's Harvey?"

"How did you know about Harvey?" I sat up, and he sat up next to me.

"Amanda called."

"My Amanda?" I was incredulous.

"Your Amanda," he said with a grin. "She told me what had happened. She said you might be needing me and asked me if I would call you."

"But you didn't call. You came. You came when I needed you."

"I know you, Marcy. You would return the favor."

"What about your flight to Tokyo?" I said, suddenly remembering that he was supposed to fly to Japan the following day.

He got up and paced the room, then stood at the sliding glass door. He looked out at the turbulent ocean smashing to the shore. "I had to be certain you were okay."

"I am okay," I said. "And I love that you came. You get so many brownie points for coming. You're like a package of Duncan Hines."

"That's sweet."

"Literally."

"I couldn't let you go through this alone," he said, causing a chill in my spine.

He leaned against the glass, facing me. He stuffed his hands in the pockets of his jeans. He looked so great in jeans. And he was in a white shirt.

"He had bypass surgery," I said. "The kids are with him. He's probably advising the nurse."

"About what?"

"What bra she should be wearing. I'm so happy you're here. Did I tell you I'm happy you're here?"

He was beaming. He had come to rescue me, and it was the correct decision.

"But what about your flight?" I repeated. "It must have cost a fortune to change it."

"Worth every penny," he said as he enfolded me in his arms.

Amanda rang later that night. She said that Harvey was asleep. They had returned from the hospital and were all bar-bound for beer and burgers.

"All?" I said, hoping the two sisters had patched up the mess.

"All," she said, reassuring me. "Do you want to join us? It is, after all, my wedding night."

"Amanda, thank you for calling Jon."

"So he reached you?"

"In person," I said.

"He's here?"

"He is, but he is sleeping. And he's leaving for Japan early tomorrow morning."

"Mom . . . Mommy . . . I'm sorry I couldn't—I wouldn't—be happy for you."

I gazed at Jon resting, his blond hair tousled onto his face. "I will see you in the morning."

"Who was it?" Jon asked as he rolled over toward me.

"Amanda. They're back from the hospital."

"I have something I want to discuss," Jon said, adjusting our pillows on the rattan headboard. "Comfortable?" he said.

I moved closer to him. "Now I am."

"I plan to talk to the dean. I will suggest shortening my stay in Japan to six months, and then I will come back to Price, and he can assign someone else. That gives him a whole semester to find the right person. I don't think it will be a problem."

"Why would you do that? What happened?"

"You happened."

My heart jumped at his words. I got out of bed and grabbed my robe. I had to be vertical to think. Jon opened his eyes wide, watching me, waiting for my response. I picked up a water bottle on the nightstand, opened it, took a swallow, then another. I hardly ever drank water.

"No," I responded definitively.

"No what?"

"No way will I allow you to forfeit what you want to do. It just can't be. That's not the relationship I want. I already had that relationship. It means the world to me that you showed up here when I needed you, without being asked, on your own terms, but for the two of us to work out, we have to lead our own lives. Your plan was Japan. You're going to go there as scheduled and create one incredibly fine English program. You stick to the plan. I'll visit. A lot."

I waited for him to respond.

He spoke softly, seriously, with great care in his voice. "Marcy Hammer, I am going to miss you terribly."

"There's something else you should know." I went to my handbag, which was on a chair by the window. I unzipped the inside pocket. "Look, a passport."

He grinned, a smile so big it could have reached the Far East. "Whose passport?" he joked.

I opened the passport and showed him the picture. "Well, it looks like it's mine."

"You're coming straight from Florida?"

"I brought my identification, just in case that was what I decided to do. Don't get a big head. It's not *all* about you. I'm really looking forward to using those famous Japanese toilets."

"Best toilets in the world," Jon said.

"My bottom is sparkling just thinking about it."

He moved toward me on the bed and kissed me. He kissed me everywhere.

∽

We awoke early the next morning, the sun shining through the glass doors to the terrace.

Suddenly, he shot up. "I have to go now, or I'll miss the flight to JFK. I left my baggage there. I have to grab it and catch the flight to Tokyo."

I accompanied him, holding his hand to the deserted lobby, and waited as he got into a cab.

He lowered the window.

"Watashi wa, anata o aishiteimasu."

"Was that Japanese for 'Never buy an American television'?"

"That was Japanese for 'I love you.'"

Chapter 29

I showered and held my head under the faucet for a long time to relieve myself from the feeling of having enough hair spray on my head to kill a live animal. I put my hair in a twist. I pulled on a short, sleeveless dress with a V-neck. I wore matching lime sandals.

I went to the Outrigger for breakfast. One person after another stopped me to explain how dismayed and distraught they were about Harvey, how relieved they were that he was okay, how they understood completely why Amanda had canceled the reception, and that they would have done the same. People were so nice, so understanding. After all, they had all traveled far at great expense for the wedding.

Mrs. Berger was at the buffet, in a Swiss-dot bathing suit cover-up. She told me that Jake had updated her on everything. I looked on as she loaded her beach bag with yogurts, individual cereal packages, granola bars, and packaged jellies, jams, and maple syrups to take to her room. She instructed Bernie to grab more bananas.

"Can you hand me a few of those baby peanut butters?" she said to me.

I gave her two.

"Now don't be stingy."

I passed three more.

She tossed the peanut butter into her canvas bag with rope handles. I peeked into the bag. It was almost full.

"More bananas," she commanded her husband.

Cousin Leona flitted by. She was wearing a maxi dress and holding a platter of food.

I said hello, and she said, "What a shame Harvey gave himself a heart condition. All those big meals."

Was she blaming Harvey's heart attack on Harvey? Or worse, was she blaming me?

"We warned him and warned him. But he kept eating. Practically ate himself into the grave. After you separated, he came to dinner at our house. Don't blame me. Steve invited him. I said you were my cousin, and I couldn't have Harvey over. Steve said I shouldn't bite the hand that feeds me. Anyway, he really piled it away. Can you hand me one of those little chocolate milks?"

So Harvey wasn't the president of Weight Watchers. And I wasn't the chef at Canyon Ranch. Had Leona never heard of genetics? "Harvey did not give himself a heart attack. People become ill for all kinds of reasons."

I couldn't believe I was defending him.

"Overeating being one of them," Leona said.

"Okay, so how do you explain the world-class marathon man who died of a heart attack while running?"

"Did he really?"

I thought back to all the years I had known Leona. Since she was five and I was born. I never had anything in common with her, but she was my mother's sister's only daughter, so I was with her all the time. I decided right there and then, at the buffet, that I was too old to waste time with people I didn't like; that if I lived to be ninety, I had only about thirty more years to my life, that if I lived to be eighty, just twenty years, and that if I died immediately, the last person I would have spoken to on the good earth would have been Leona.

"She's your cousin," I heard my mother say. *"Be the bigger one."*

"Mom, I am being the bigger one."

"How's that?" Mom asked.

"I am about to hand her a little chocolate milk, and I am not going to pour it on her."

I turned from Leona to see my brother, Max. In high school, Max was voted "most likely to be convicted of a white-collar crime." As for me, I could have been voted "most likely to kill the student most likely to be convicted of a white-collar crime."

"Kiss him hello," my mother said.

"Do I have to?"

"Be the bigger one," she said again.

"Mom, you come down here and kiss him."

"You never returned the RSVP card," I said as I looked him over. He was wearing sunglasses and a short-sleeve Hawaiian shirt with a chunky gold Jewish star the size of a synagogue. His chest hairs were on display. I had no idea how I could be related to him.

"Who bothers with those cards?" he asked as he took a plate.

"Clearly not you."

"Listen, Marcy, I was sorry to hear about Harvey. That guy. He always ate like a horse."

Why was everyone blaming the victim, knocking Harvey for his heart attack? If I succumbed, what would people say? *"She only went to the gym when her daughter visited."*

"Don't get angry, Marcy. He's your brother," my mother admonished me.

"You mean the brother I haven't seen or spoken to since the day of your funeral?"

"My girlfriends are in the room, but they'll be down for brunch soon."

Did he say "girlfriends," plural?

Just then, Amanda approached.

"Uncle Max. I didn't know you were coming," she said nicely, even though I knew she liked him about as much as diphtheria and had invited him only to keep me at bay. I had wanted him invited only to keep my mother out of my head. Where was Dr. Genesis when you needed him?

"So, what's going to happen now?"

"Jake and I are planning a ceremony at the hospital."

"I'll be there," my brother said.

"I'm sorry. Immediate family only," Amanda said.

He lowered his sunglasses and glared at me.

"She's very upset," I whispered in a consoling voice as Amanda walked away.

"I'm her uncle. Why didn't you bring up your kids to have a little respect?"

I couldn't stand another moment of him.

"I did bring them up to have respect. They just don't have any for you."

"Marcy!" I heard my mother exclaim.

"Mom, you really have to find a hobby up there. Doesn't anyone play Scrabble?"

I walked off and ran into Feldman. *Don't tread on me,* I thought.

"Tell me the truth. How's Harvey?" he asked. "And don't give me the party line. After all, I'm his best friend."

"I haven't seen him," I said. "He was in ICU when I left the hospital."

"You left him in ICU?" he said accusingly.

"Feldman, Harvey and I are separated."

"Still . . ."

"Where were you when your wife had Claire?" Claire was Feldman's eldest daughter. She was planning to work with him when she finished business school.

"At the office."

"Case closed, Feldman. Case closed."

Chapter 30

I consider myself an artisan at holding a grudge. Still, I couldn't stop worrying about Harvey.

Unfortunately, I had scads of hospital experience. I knew that whenever a member of my family called from a hospital to let me know how our loved one was doing, I imagined the worst scenario. My cousin Leona could say her mom was doing fine. In fact she had just eaten her gluten-free meal and had sex with two orderlies. Still, I would imagine my elderly aunt on a feeding tube, her hollowed eyes rolled back in her shriveled head. I had to see for myself how Harvey was doing. I had to see right away.

Harvey's concierge-level room faced the exquisite park opposite the hospital. His bed was centered on the far side, near the expansive windows, which were open. I could hear birds tweeting. Palm trees swayed in the breeze. Children were playing in the park, and I could hear their voices rising. An old ice cream truck blared a repetitive tune.

At the entrance to the room, there was a small sitting area with two leather recliners. If it weren't for the hospital bed and the medical equipment, it could have been someone's living room.

Harvey was doing fine, or so I thought, until the future in-laws suddenly walked in with big hellos.

"We had to see how you were," Mrs. Berger said. "Even though Jake told us not to come."

"Who listens to Jake?" Bernie said.

Harvey smiled stiffly and politely. He raised his head to get a good look at Mrs. Berger. Was he looking for more stolen jewelry?

"You're bulging," he said to her.

"Excuse me?" she said, lifting her eyebrows at him.

"Your breasts are bulging." He pointed with his index finger, moving it back and forth in a horizontal line.

The man is at death's door, and he is still talking breasts.

"It's the morphine," I said, not knowing the name of any other potent drug that would make a man tell a woman she was bulging.

Mug raised her eyebrow again. Then she raised her bra straps.

Harvey was fixed on her. He probably wished he could hop out of bed and show her exactly what to do to look better.

"Lift and separate," he advised.

Mortified, I slunk behind the visitors and into one of the reclining chairs.

Harvey blinked away sleep. "Here's the thing. You're a D cup. Not a C."

I guess when a man mentions that your boobs are a mess, it's time to go, because they left.

Light filled Harvey's room, but it might as well have been dark, because he was bleak and upset. He said he felt terrible that he had ruined the wedding, that he didn't want the kids to get married in his room. What kind of wedding was that?

"Does the hospital have a chapel?" I asked him.

"I don't know," he said. "I didn't get off the operating table to go and look for one."

I buzzed the nurse and asked over the speaker.

"You want something for chapped skin?" she replied.

"No, is there a chapel?"

"A beautiful one. Praise the Lord. He is surely there."

"Praise the Lord," I replied.

I told Harvey I would check it out. I took the elevator to the first floor. Near the entrance to the hospital, I followed the arrows to the chapel. I opened the double faux-mahogany doors, doors so different from the rest of the hospital they seemed to be a mistake. The chapel was paneled in handsome dark wood. There were four rows of seats separated by an aisle. *An aisle,* I thought. *This chapel has an aisle.* Amanda could still walk down an aisle. I had saved the ship.

I rushed back to Harvey's room with the news. He brightened. But then suddenly and smartly, I wondered if I should have checked with Amanda before speaking up. She might have wanted to get married on a cattle ranch, but maybe a chapel was too old-fashioned.

A nurse came in, so I excused myself. I went to the cafeteria for coffee. I made some calls to the wedding vendors. I spoke to the florist, who had delivered the flowers to the hotel. I asked him to pick up the flowers and deliver them to hospitals in the area. He agreed. Next, I called the seven-piece band. I thought they would require a hefty last-minute cancellation fee, but they wanted full payment. I told the booking agent that my husband had had a heart attack. He said, "Sure he did." I said it was true. He asked if the dog ate my homework. I returned to Harvey's room.

Amanda was there.

"Mom, the chapel is wonderful," she said.

"You have already seen it?"

"Yes, Dad told me about it, and I went to the first floor."

"Great!" I said, beaming.

"But there's a problem," Harvey said.

"What now?" How many more problems could there be? Hadn't we had enough problems in the last couple of days? What were we, a problem factory?

"My doctor won't let me go to the chapel until I have a bowel movement."

Amanda shook her head, then looked at me as though she had given up.

"I can't leave the room until I take a crap," Harvey explained as though I hadn't understood the term "bowel movement."

"So, you will take a crap," I said. "I've known you a long time, Harvey, and you have never had a problem with that."

"But we don't know when," Amanda said.

"We'll wait. We'll just wait until your father goes to the toilet. The only thing that stands between this family and a nice wedding in the chapel is feces."

"Let's just do my ceremony in the room," Amanda said. "I don't want Dad to be under any undue pressure."

"My daughter is not getting married in this room," Harvey announced. And then, like he had used too much energy, he fell asleep.

Amanda started to cry. "This room is fine. All I want to do is get married. I don't give a hoot about any of the accoutrements."

"Give Dad a chance," I said.

⤳

Later, I called Harvey from my hotel room.

"Anything?"

"Not so much as a fart."

"Can they give you something?"

"It has to be natural."

"This is not how I imagined this. I will check back later."

In the afternoon, I went back to the hospital. Elisabeth, Ben, and Jordan were in Harvey's room.

"Anything?" I said.

They shook their heads.

"As long as you are here, we're going to go sit at the beach," Ben said.

"Call if anything . . . you know," Jordan said.

I sat on the edge of Harvey's bed. I really felt bad for him.

"A lot of pressure," I said.

Harvey smiled and straightened himself up. Then he became serious. "Marcy, I could have died."

"But you didn't."

"Please forgive me," he said and reached for my hand.

"I do forgive you. I wouldn't be here if I didn't forgive you."

"Do you want me to call Albee and tell him to hold your room for the two weeks?"

"What?"

"You'll need a place to stay while I am recovering. I can't fly for two weeks."

I was aghast, unable to understand how he could misinterpret our situation. It was a heart attack, not a brain attack. I had read online that people with heart problems often suffered from depression and memory loss. Was it necessary to remind him that we were through, and that Amanda's wedding and her happiness were the only reasons we were pulling together? Did he actually think I would come back to him because he needed a nurse?

"Harvey, I am leaving the morning after the wedding."

"Oh, stop kidding around."

"I'm not kidding."

He looked at me as though I had burned down the bra warehouse. "I need you to take care of me."

"I'm done taking care of you," I said. "What I need now is to take care of me."

"But look how well we have gotten along."

Suddenly, a nasty odor, pungent as a pigsty, poisoned the air. The stink was intense and nauseating, worse than anything I had ever smelled before, like a thousand constipated horses finally taking a shit. I covered my nose with both hands.

"I have to go to the bathroom," Harvey shrieked. "Grab that bedpan, Marcy. And hurry."

The wedding was on.

Chapter 31

The next morning, I knocked on Amanda's door. She opened it a peep, then wider to let me in. Her hair was done in a sleek and sophisticated twist, and her makeup was on too.

"Where's Jake?" I asked.

"Salvaging a tradition. We're not seeing each other until the wedding. He's changing in one of the usher's rooms."

"Are you going to wear your wedding gown?" I asked hesitantly, not certain whether my question would set her off.

"I'm wearing this brand-new white party dress that I bought in Connecticut. I don't see sweeping into a hospital in a wedding gown."

Amanda seemed to have everything in hand, but I worried. She was way too calm for someone who had just given up a wedding reception she had planned for months.

"Are you sure you're okay?" I asked, but she didn't respond.

"So the dress is something new," she said. "And I have something old." She showed me a stunning gold brooch inset with an ivory cameo of a woman's face. It was the pin my mother had worn on her wedding day. Mom had presented the brooch to Amanda years before she'd passed away. "What am I holding on to it for?" she had said. "Am I going to a dance?"

"I can hear Grandma. I hear her all the time," I said.

"What is she saying?" Amanda asked.

"She's saying, 'Amanda, he's a nice boy. Does he have a brother for your sister?'"

"I wish Grandma was here."

"So do I," I said. "So do I."

"Mom, will you hug me?"

I hugged her, and I could feel tears drop on my bare shoulder.

"I'm sorry, Mom."

"Nothing to be sorry for," I said.

"I wanted this wedding to be perfect, and somehow, I lost all perspective. I was afraid to share details, because I didn't want to hear any commentary. I was afraid you would take over, turn it into your wedding. It seems that everyone has an opinion when it comes to a wedding. I worried that Jake and I wouldn't have the ceremony and reception we wanted. That interference would kill the romance. Want to know something? I wouldn't allow Dad to come to the tasting. He wanted to help us decide on the meal. We butted heads for two weeks. I actually told him he didn't know anything about food."

"I'll bet he took that hard," I said.

"Soon I felt like I was protecting myself from my own family—and Jake's mother. She wanted a DJ instead of a band."

"Dad would never have agreed to that."

"I know. He wanted a ten-piece band."

"Isn't that an orchestra?"

"Would you ride to the wedding with me in the limo?" she said.

"Limo?"

"Jake ordered a stretch. He didn't think his bride should call Uber."

"So he's okay with all of this."

"I wouldn't marry a man who wasn't."

I smiled as I thought how much she had grown up so suddenly.

"I'd be honored to ride in your limousine," I said. "By the way, I want you to know that I was ringing the salon at the Ritz when I got the call about Dad."

"Oh, Mom, it doesn't matter."

"Well, I'm sorry anyway."

She leaned forward, toward me. "I've made a decision."

"Let me guess. You're not taking the position at Retail Rebellion."

"True."

"You want to work at Bountiful."

"Well, we knew it would happen one day. And Dad will require help. Not only does he have to heal, but he is planning the new division."

"Bountiful Boxers—for the bountiful man."

She removed her robe, and I helped her slip on her lovely dress. She added strappy white stilettos, then stepped to the mirror.

I stood behind her.

"You look exquisite," I said.

"I'm happy, Mom. I am marrying the man I love."

In the mirror, I could see her eyes filling with tears.

⌒⊙

When Amanda and I arrived at the hospital, we went to the comfortable family room on Harvey's floor and waited.

Soon, Elisabeth and Ben were in the lounge with the bride. They had brought an abundant bouquet of lily of the valley, sweet William, myrtle, and hyacinth.

"So, this is it. The end," Ben joked as he bowed in his poplin suit and handed the bouquet to the bride.

"I love you like a sister," Elisabeth said to Amanda.

"You're wearing my dress," Amanda said.

"I didn't like what I had in my closet, so I went to your room and raided yours."

"I'm surprised you didn't take the bridal gown." Amanda was sniffing back tears. "My makeup is the only thing that has gone as planned, and I am not going to cry and ruin it."

"Dad invited all the bra manufacturers to the hospital for the ceremony," Ben said, joking.

"Okay, I'm crying."

"Group hug, anyone?" Elisabeth said.

We gathered around Amanda and enclosed her.

"I think I'll go get Dad and a nurse and wheel him to the chapel." Elisabeth turned and hugged Amanda again. "Not everyone would have done this."

"Not everyone has Dad for a dad."

I put my hands together over my mouth. I could feel tears coming on.

I stood alone with Amanda as she held the bouquet in both hands and gazed down into the flowers as though she could see between the petals.

"Are you anxious?" I said.

"You mean because I can't stop tapping my foot and my hands are shaking so much the bouquet looks like it's dancing?"

I nodded.

"This is it, Mom. I will be married forever."

I remembered the day I married Harvey. I had thought the same thing. I hoped so much she was right—that today would be the start of forever. After all, what was marriage but a roll of the dice, a naive leap of faith? Something people believed in, even though there was so much evidence to the contrary, evidence that it would not work, but we hoped it would work, because we wanted all the love and comfort of living life with another person. My daughter wanted that. And I knew from my best days with Harvey that it was worth the attempt.

Minutes later, my cell buzzed.

"It's time," I said to Amanda. "Do you want me to walk in first?"

"No, Mom, I want you to walk in with me. I want you to walk me down the aisle."

"Ready?" I said.

We headed to the hospital chapel. When Amanda and I were half-way down the corridor, we heard singing. It was the Beatles song "Love Me Do." I recognized Ben's voice, but there were other voices as well. We stood at the entrance to the chapel. When we appeared, Ben and Jordan and Dr. Genesis changed tunes quickly to "Here Comes the Bride."

Elisabeth and Ben, maid of honor and best man, were standing beside Jake. Harvey was in a wheelchair with a pole and a nurse, who wore white scrubs to the wedding. Jordan, Feldman, Dana, and Candy were in the second row, behind Jake's parents.

Amanda took the first step as she squeezed my hand. Everyone stood as we entered the chapel. We waited a moment, then started down the short aisle. It was all so breathtaking that it hardly seemed real. As if it were something that could happen only in the clouds, in the sky. Sometimes your entire life is punctuated by one magical, amazing, wonderful moment, and you know without a doubt that whatever you did in life, it was the right thing.

I sat down next to Harvey. I was in a chapel in a hospital in Florida, but I might as well have been anywhere in the universe. All I could see was Amanda standing next to Jake. They were hand in hand, their shoulders touching. I was so high in the air I had no idea where the earth was.

Jake nodded to Dr. Genesis. Although he was holding a small book, he referred instead to a slip of paper. He began the short English service by reading a one-sentence blessing in Hebrew, Amanda's homage to her parents.

"Blessed art thou, O Lord, our God, King of the Universe, for allowing us to reach this day."

Chapter 32

The day of my departure, my kids were in the lobby, convening on a vast sectional, facing a white stone fireplace that rose to the ceiling. I needed a fireplace in Florida like I needed to plan another wedding.

"Mom, can I get you a cup of coffee?" Ben asked. I said yes, and he went off.

"Anyone left besides the holdouts in the lobby?" I asked.

"You just missed Dana," Elisabeth said. "She wanted to see you, but she was running late. Jake gave Max and his two girlfriends a ride to the airport. He's on his way back here to take his parents next."

"Jake's mom is hyperventilating about traveling," Amanda said. "She said if they frisk her at security, she's going to slap the agent's hand."

"Well, that should get her on the plane really fast," Elisabeth said.

"The woman is a bit of a nut," Amanda commented.

"A bit?" Elisabeth said.

"A complete basket case. Let's face it. I'm lucky she doesn't like to fly."

"And as I recall," I said, "Mug doesn't like Connecticut."

"She doesn't?" Jordan said.

"She expected more dressage in Stamford," Amanda said.

My motherhood kicked in, and I became serious. "We shouldn't be laughing."

"No, Mom," Amanda said. "We never laugh. We're against laughing."

"You're all terrible," Jordan said.

Ben returned with coffee, one for me and one for him.

"I spoke to Dad's doctor," Elisabeth said. "He'll be released in four days, but he won't allow air travel for two weeks."

I could hear three minds ticking, like bombs about to explode.

"Well, we can't leave Dad in Florida. One of us needs to stay," Elisabeth said.

"So who's staying?" I asked.

Ben looked at me like I had just said something totally insane.

"We thought you were," Elisabeth said.

I studied their faces. I knew their faces were about to change.

"I'm not staying," I said.

"What?" Amanda said.

"What I said."

They were his children, and they needed to step up. Not just now, but forever. Because Harvey and I were apart, Harvey was not my responsibility. We had taken care of our children to the best of our ability, and now in Florida, the day after Amanda's wedding, the tables had turned.

The three of them stared at me.

"Don't look at me," I said.

"Mom, you mean you're just going to leave him here, in Florida, by himself?" Ben said.

Silence filled the room.

I sat down on the edge of the conversation-pit couch. It was low. I wasn't comfortable. I stood back up.

"Am I looking at three adults?" I asked.

Ben glanced at Amanda; Amanda turned to Elisabeth.

I could see from their disappointed, downcast faces that they understood. There was no chance of their parents getting back together. The play was over. The curtain had come down.

Ben spoke first. "Mom's right. Someone has to stay, but I have to be back at law school."

"Elisabeth?" Amanda said. "What could be better than having a doctor at his side?"

Elisabeth climbed out from under the bus Amanda had driven over her. "I can't remain here. I'm scheduled to be in Nairobi as a medical volunteer."

"How long will you be gone?" I asked.

"Two weeks."

"So go another time," Amanda said.

Elisabeth was annoyed. "You can stay, Amanda. You're not going on your honeymoon until next month. And by the way, Ben, so what if you miss a week of school? You'd miss a week of school if you were ill. You'd miss a week of school to go on a trip. You'd . . ."

"I'm not ill. I'm not tripping. And do you have any idea how tough law school is?"

"Not tougher than medical school was."

And just when I thought they couldn't revert any further into their childhood roles, Ben turned to Elisabeth and said, "Want to bet?"

I was waiting for Elisabeth to stick out her tongue when Feldman appeared out of nowhere. He was in resort clothing, but carrying a briefcase.

"Family disagreement? No arguing! By the way, I'm on my way to see Harvey," Feldman said.

"He'll be thrilled to see you," Elisabeth said.

"Everyone is thrilled to see me."

We all smiled.

"When are you leaving?" Ben said. "Do you need a ride to the airport?"

"Leaving?" Feldman snorted. "I'm not going anywhere. Your father is going to need company. I am staying as long as he needs me. I can work from here."

Elisabeth was shocked. Amanda released her shoulders. Ben smiled with relief.

"I'll come back on the weekend," Ben promised Feldman.

"And I can stay with him when he gets back to Connecticut," Elisabeth offered.

"I haven't told Dad yet, but I am going to work at Bountiful," Amanda said.

Feldman turned to me. "That Harvey. You have to give him credit. He brought up three great kids."

I laughed. *"He" brought up,* I thought.

I needed to pack, but instead, I started out the door that led to the pool and the beach.

"Where are you going, Mom?" Amanda said as she caught up with me.

"To the beach. I'm going to dig my toes into sand and breathe in the ocean."

"Do you mind if I come?" she said.

"I would love for you to come."

We cut across the pool area, unhooking the gate that opened to the broad stretch of fine sand and the sea. A few people walked along the more shallow water. I set my sights on the horizon.

As we walked along the shore, Amanda held up her left hand and wiggled her ring finger. Her solid gold wedding band twinkled in the sun. "I'm married," she said.

"I can't believe I'm old enough to have a married daughter. How is that even possible? I have to tell you something. Once, about three years ago, I was in a department store with you. I think it was Nordstrom. I was buying a dress, and we had lost track of each other. After I paid the cashier, I turned to look for you. At the accessories counter, I saw this spectacular young woman trying on dangling gold earrings. But in my head, I was searching for a child, so I didn't realize it was you. I remember you waved to me and called out, 'Mom,' and I was surprised, really surprised. I feel so lucky to have reached this point in my life, to have three wonderful, healthy children I am so proud of. And then there's Jake. The way he acted through this. You know, my mother would have called him a mensch."

Amanda slipped out of her flip-flops, and I took off my sandals. We walked in the water, kicking up little waves, carrying our shoes in one hand. Amanda splashed me, and I returned the favor.

"I'm married!" she shouted, tossing her flip-flops in the air.

"You're married," I shouted.

Water splashed in my eyes, and salt mixed with salt.

Candy came running up to us. "Amanda, everyone is looking for you. Jake is about to take his parents to the airport, and Mrs. Berger wants to say good-bye before she goes."

Amanda excused herself.

"My daughter has in-laws," I said to Candy. "How crazy is that?"

Candy and I linked arms.

"I just spoke to Ellison. He's back from his business trip. He's going to pick us up at the airport."

"Pick *you* up," I said.

"And you?"

"I've decided to go straight from here to Tokyo."

"Well, well. How did you get a ticket on such short notice?"

"That part was easy. I used every one of Harvey's American Express points."

She grinned, and her eyes seemed to sparkle.

"The Guild is closed for the holidays until the second week of January. I have time to talk to Christopher about getting someone in. The plans for Art Explosion are well underway. And there's always Cheyenne."

She stood still and faced me. "How did I ever get by without you as a friend?"

"Ditto, kid," I said.

"Marcy, this wedding is an event I will never forget."

"Tell Ellison that I'm sorry he missed the wedding, but almost everyone missed it."

"Amanda was a very brave girl," Candy said.

"You would have done the same thing," I said. "Your dad would have been there or bust."

"I guess so," Candy said as she looked down at the sand. We were no longer in front of our hotel but a strip of hotels, and the only thing that changed was the colors of the lounges and umbrellas.

"Harvey swears he is throwing a huge party for her once he is well. And you know what? I don't want to know a thing about it. I'm just going to show up with a present."

"And I am going to show up with my fiancé."

"What?" I stopped in my tracks in the sand.

"Ellison asked me to marry him," she said.

"What?" I shook my hands in the air with excitement.

"We're going to a jeweler next week, because he thought I should design the ring and have exactly what I want."

"When did he ask?"

"Last week."

"When were you going to tell me?"

"I'm telling you now."

"Is there a way to have a wedding without actually planning it?" I said.

"Don't worry. I'm keeping it small. No more than one bridesmaid."

"Me?"

She nodded, and my heart was full.

We headed back toward our hotel. My phone was ringing, but I didn't care.

"Your phone," Candy said.

"Are you serious? I'm not picking it up now. I have a million questions to ask."

"Well, at least see who it is."

I shrugged and glanced at my phone. I didn't recognize the number but answered anyway.

"Grace Greene," a businesslike voice said.

I pulled on Candy's arm so she would stop walking. We stood in place, looking out at the sea.

"Hi," I said tentatively, wondering why my attorney would be on the phone. I had told her that I would schedule an appointment after the wedding.

"Marcy, I thought you would want to know that Harvey called my office yesterday."

"Why would he do that?" I had never mentioned a word about Grace Greene to Harvey. I waited for her answer and held the phone with sweaty hands.

"He was seeking representation."

"But he's in the hospital in Florida. He had a heart attack."

"What does that mean? You don't need a heart to call a divorce attorney."

I held out the phone so Candy could hear easily.

"I did not return his call," Grace Greene said.

"What do I do?" I said.

"What do you want to do?"

"I want him to file first."

"Not a problem. My associate mentioned that your husband was clearly in a hurry."

I thanked her for calling. My head was spinning.

"I heard it all, and I know what did it," Candy said.

"Really?"

"He thought you'd stay and take care of him. When he heard you were leaving, he knew it was over. Before he could see the heel of your shoes, he called a lawyer."

It was amazing how right on the nose Candy was. Wasn't that exactly what a really close, intuitive girlfriend could do? Call it exactly right before you even had a chance to figure it out?

I could feel the tears welling up in my eyes. "I'm relieved it happened this way. I needed to divorce him, but I wanted him to initiate the divorce. Who knew he would take his time?"

"I hear Grace Greene is ruthless," Candy said.

"Your cousin told me she is the fiercest divorce attorney in Connecticut. Apparently, she eats stone for breakfast."

"I'll bet she does if Harvey called her."

"I want you to know something," I said.

"So tell me, Marcy."

"I'm taking the high road."

"Really?"

"Harvey can have custody of all three kids."

Candy laughed. "And the son-in-law?"

"One night a week and weekends."

Candy said she was going to the hotel to check out. I took off my shoes and dawdled alone, at the edge of the water. The tide was coming in. Kids were splashing. A couple dunked while holding hands. A father steadied his toddler on an alligator float.

I stared at the water, watching the waves ripple in. I caught a seashell in my hand. In less than twenty-four hours, I would land in Tokyo, and Jon would be at the airport. I imagined him waiting, waving. I loved the image—Jon in his blue jeans and hunter-green polo in a throng of Japanese businessmen clad in black suits and white shirts.

I lingered on the beach, thinking about how much fun we would have. In my beach bag was the Japanese phrase book.

I flipped through the pages, seeking the words I would need upon arrival, my most essential Japanese.

There were so many ways to say "I love you," and so many reasons to say it.

Acknowledgments

Danielle Marshall told me I would be in excellent hands. Then I got lucky. She became my editor and wrapped her hands around mine.

I am indebted to Alicia Clancy for getting on board and getting everything right.

I am forever grateful to Kelli Martin, the wonderful Lake Union editor who gave me my start.

Many thanks to Lindsay Guzzardo for dedicated developmental editing.

What a pleasure to work with Gabriella Dumpit and the entire Lake Union team.

Joelle Delbourgo is my literary agent. This is my second novel published by Lake Union. I'd say Joelle has done an admirable job.

Most Wednesdays, I go to Greenwich Village to acquire some wisdom from *New York Times* bestselling author Jennifer Belle. I am fortunate to have her as my guide.

My beta readers are alpha people. Sharyn Rothstein and Marisa Rothstein are my daughters; Sandra Simon Klein and Debra Simon are the world's best sisters; Lanie Robertson and Colleen Lorenz are cherished friends; Alan Rothstein is my lifelong advisor.

Also, I appreciate the valuable insight of Julie Flaakstad, Fiona Capuano, Desiree Rhine, Katie Sammis, Alison Barto, Nancy Shapanka, and Alexa Goldstein.

I am fortunate to be a member of the Women's Fiction Writers Association.

It is a pleasure and a privilege to know my fellow Lake Union authors.

Thanks to the supportive people at Beth El Temple of West Hartford, Connecticut, *Carolina Woman* magazine, Asset Strategies Inc., and Honest Leo Inc.

Shalom to the Jewish Book Council. I am proud to be a JBC author on tour.

Frieda and Leo Simon of blessed memory. We hear you.

Lucien. Frankie. Sydney. Your names are in a book.

Alan, thank you for forty-one years of service to the Simon Organization. There's a Bombay Sapphire martini—with a blue cheese–stuffed olive—waiting at home for you.

About the Author

Marilyn Simon Rothstein is the author of *Lift and Separate*, winner of the Star Award presented by the Women's Fiction Writers Association for Outstanding Debut. She grew up in New York City, earned a degree in journalism from New York University, began her writing career at *Seventeen* magazine, married a man she met in an elevator, and owned an advertising agency for more than twenty-five years. Marilyn received an MA in liberal studies from Wesleyan University and an MA in Judaic studies from the University of Connecticut.